The
Whispers

ALSO BY HEIDI PERKS

Three Perfect Liars

Her One Mistake

The Whispers

A Novel

Heidi Perks

G

GALLERY BOOKS

NEW YORK LONDON TORONTO SYDNEY NEW DELHI

G

Gallery Books
An Imprint of Simon & Schuster, Inc.
1230 Avenue of the Americas
New York, NY 10020

Copyright © 2021 by Heidi Perks
Originally published in Great Britain in 2021 by Century,
an imprint of Penguin Random House UK

First Gallery Books hardcover edition March 2022

GALLERY BOOKS and colophon are
registered trademarks of Simon & Schuster, Inc.

For information about special discounts for bulk purchases, please contact Simon & Schuster Special Sales at 1-866-506-1949 or business@simonandschuster.com.

The Simon & Schuster Speakers Bureau can bring authors to your live event. For more information or to book an event, contact the Simon & Schuster Speakers Bureau at 1-866-248-3049 or visit our website at www.simonspeakers.com.

Interior design by Michelle Marchese

Manufactured in the United States of America

1   3   5   7   9   10   8   6   4   2

Library of Congress Cataloging-in-Publication Data is available.

ISBN 978-1-9821-5325-0
ISBN 978-1-9821-5327-4 (ebook)

For Bethany and Joseph
Always follow your dreams

Wednesday, 1 January

The body has been found on the beach. At the bottom of Crayne's Cliff, a spot that the people of Clearwater know all too well for the victims it has pulled over its perilous edge through the decades.

The detective stands on the stony coastline, not far from where a scattering of fishermen's huts are wedged into the base of the cliff. They are empty, of course, as is often the case at the height of the winter. He has always found their desolation in the cold months quite haunting, and never more so than today.

He shudders as he pulls himself away, giving the SOCOs space to do their job, and starts to walk back along the beach to where he has parked his car. It is on the other side of the stone wall, built to form a barrier against the waves that can rise high when the sea is rough. Today the sea is a mill pond. In a few hours' time there might be some hardy sailors or even a few crazy paddleboarders out for a New Year's Day jaunt, but right now the beach ahead of him is empty.

He hadn't been called to the scene, but as soon as he heard about it he had to see for himself. His first case, so many years ago, had found him standing on this very stretch of beach. Though that time it had been the body of a young girl that had gone over the edge. Not a woman: not a mother.

He remembers it like it was yesterday, but then, dead bodies are a rare occurrence in Clearwater. Incidents like this are a shock to the community, just like the one all those years ago had been.

As he reaches his car, he pauses and looks back at the cliffs, wondering if anyone else at the station will be asking themselves the question that he is taunting himself with. Could they have known something like this might happen?

Three weeks ago, Grace Goodwin had stood in the station and tried to report a crime, but the officers she spoke with had refused to believe she was right to be worried. And yet his first call this morning hadn't been to wish him a Happy New Year, but to tell him there was a dead body.

part one

September

Four months before

The whispers started on the first day back of the autumn term. As was often the case at drop-off, a group of mothers from across year four had gathered in the playground to chat. Quite often it was the only time they came together, and it had been weeks since they'd last been here at the end of the summer term, so there was plenty to catch up on. They weren't all friends with one another outside of school, but they liked to drop in and out of the gossip, make sure they were kept in the loop of what was happening inside the school gates.

Today they were interested in the fact that there was an unfamiliar face hovering outside their children's new classroom. She had a honey-toned tan, sleek auburn hair pulled back into a ponytail, and wore white cutoff jeans that made her legs look incredibly long and slim. Even in her gold strappy sandals she was at least five foot eight. A little girl with dark pigtails was standing by her side.

It didn't take long for someone to approach her and make an introduction. And when she replied that her name was Grace Goodwin, she'd done so in the very soft twang of an Australian accent. This was enough to draw each of them over to her and, intrigued, they fired off questions at the new mum.

They soon learned she had moved back to England only three weeks ago from Sydney and that she had attended this very school as a child, as some of them had, too. There were a few murmurs that her name sounded familiar. Had she changed it? they asked. To which Grace confirmed she hadn't. But then it wasn't familiar enough that she might have been in their year group and it was too soon to be asking her age just yet.

Grace had lived in Clearwater until she was seventeen, when she and her parents had moved to Australia because of her father's job. Her parents had returned to England five years ago, apparently because of an aunt's ailing health. This was three years after her only child, Matilda, was born, and Grace had decided to stay behind in Sydney until this summer.

Matilda was going to be in 4C, the same class as many of their children. One of the mothers was already talking playdates and snapping out her phone to make sure Grace was included on the class WhatsApp group.

"You need to be on this," the mum was saying. "Anything you need to know about homework, assemblies, anything school-related—just pop on a message and someone will get back to you."

Grace had smiled in return and obligingly given her number, though her gaze kept drifting around the playground as if she were looking for someone else.

She was very pretty, in her midthirties, and looked effortlessly casual yet chic. It was as if she hadn't gone overboard to make an effort for her first school run but managed to come out looking good, nonetheless.

"So do your parents live nearby?" another mum asked her.

Grace told the group that her parents had relocated to Leicester to be close to her father's sister. That after first the aunt and then her father died three years ago, her mum had made the surprising decision to stay put.

Someone suggested that maybe she'd move down to Clearwater now that Grace was back, but Grace replied that she just didn't see it happening, and they moved onto other questions like, "And what does your husband do? Is he local?"

"Actually, Graham works in Singapore," she said. "He's a project manager for a big pharmaceutical company."

"Oh wow, impressive! But that means you moved over here on your own?"

She had, it turned out, and she and Matilda were renting one of the Waterview apartments, the luxury wave-designed complex that took pride of place on the edge of the road to Weymouth, which made it clear that money wasn't a worry for her. Although the apartments tended to attract young couples, with the building's gym and bar, and weren't family-orientated, so surely it wouldn't be a long-term option.

But their attentions quickly returned to Graham and his job abroad, and the knowledge that funnily enough he'd been in Europe until the start of July. Grace told them this with a smile and a shrug, as if it were no big deal that her husband lived and worked so many miles away, but they already understood how hard it must have been for her, being in the throes of moving to England when he had been shipped off in the opposite direction, though it was probably too soon to delve deeper into this particular line of enquiry when they had only known her for five minutes.

Besides, she was professing that it was fine for him to be living abroad, and that Matilda had been very good about the whole thing, and so none of them probed further just yet, though later they would discuss in forensic detail what kind of husband would allow his wife to move across the world all by herself.

"So why have you moved back to Clearwater?" one of them asked. Clearwater was a small headland town that jutted into the sea on the south coast and was connected to nearby Weymouth by a single road. One way in and one way out, unless you went by water. It had a long stretch of shingle beach on one side, and small stony coves cut into the coastline on the other. It was beautiful, they could all give it that, but it was quiet and didn't attract many tourists, who preferred the buzz of Weymouth. It seemed an odd choice for Grace.

"I guess it still feels like home," she said, continuing to scan the playground.

"Are you looking for anyone in particular?" one of the mums asked her.
"Actually, I am," she replied. "Anna Robinson."
"Oh! Ethan's mum? Ethan's in 4C too. Do you know her, then?"
Grace nodded. "We were best friends for years. We met here when we were five." She gestured a hand around the playground.
"Oh wow, that's amazing," another woman exclaimed, although what she suspected they were all thinking was, Well, this is going to put the cat among the pigeons.

In the minutes that followed, they gathered some more basics: Grace and Anna had been inseparable until the day Grace left for Australia. They were both only children—more like sisters than friends—and Anna had spent many nights of those many years at Grace's house.

By that point some of them had already spotted Anna at the gate, huddled, unsurprisingly, with her small circle of friends. They liked Anna. She had always been kind and friendly, and her son Ethan, a popular boy, had never uttered an unkind word to any one of their children.

Anna always turned up to school with a smile, and never bitched about anyone. But she was part of what they all knew to be a very tight clique: four women who had met each other on their children's first day of school and had been inseparable ever since. Most mornings they were huddled together, arms flung around one another, giggling, whispering. Much younger behavior than you would expect for women in their late thirties and early forties.

There was Nancy, a head taller than Anna, tightly squeezing Anna into her side as she rocked with laughter. And Rachel, in too-high heels and a black pencil skirt, dressed for her office job in Weymouth, who was also laughing as she was dragged up the path by her two sons. Beside them, Caitlyn had a hand over her mouth as she giggled behind it.

And now Grace was making her way towards the group, and it took a few moments for Anna to spot her. When she did, her mouth opened wide in surprise. Finally, her face cracked into a smile and she joined Grace in the middle of the playground, the two women hugging each other as the other mums looked on.

Later they would wonder among themselves how Grace's arrival might affect Anna's relationships with her other friends. And as the early autumn term slipped into a biting winter, they would watch with a seesaw of faint amusement and a little pity for Grace.

But it wasn't until the second week of December, when the children had almost broken up for the holidays, that things really got interesting.

1

Wednesday, 11 December

Grace

It's been nineteen years since Grace Goodwin last sat in the Old Vic. Nearly half her lifetime, and yet it still feels like only yesterday. It's different now—less of an old fisherman's pub, with pretensions to be a wine bar—and the crowd it has pulled in on a Wednesday night two weeks before Christmas is mainly young couples.

Scuffed, stained wooden tables have made way for polished oak ones, with purple and gray velvet armchairs tucked beneath them. Chalkboards with menus of cheeses and meats and pairing wines hang on the walls, draped with classy strings of Christmas lights.

Grace has to admit the interior looks much better than it did all those years ago. It is airier and brighter, though the evening feels more claustrophobic than it should.

When Anna had asked her if she wanted to join her and *the girls* for pre-Christmas drinks, she'd been a little surprised. In the three months since Grace had returned to Clearwater, there had been no other invites, and she'd jumped at the chance to come. "We're going to the Old Vic," Anna had told her, "about eight thirty."

Anna and her three friends were already there when she'd arrived bang on the dot of eight thirty, a bottle of wine opened on the table between them. She'd needed to steal a chair from one of the other tables, squeezing herself in between Rachel and Caitlyn.

But Grace is pleased to be back here because the pub holds good memories for her. When they were still at school, she and Anna used to sit in the corner drinking Bacardi and Cokes. Even though they'd been underage, the bar staff had never once waved them away.

"Do you remember the first night we came here?" she asks Anna now, when there is a break in the conversation.

Anna turns to her and smiles, but her lips are drawn into a thin, flat line. Her eyes are dark and seem to look right through Grace, even though only moments before she'd been laughing at something Nancy had said. Nancy is now playing with Anna's hair, tugging it, twisting it into a plait at one side, hanging it over Anna's shoulder and telling her she should wear it like that. Watching them, Grace feels as if she were back in school again.

Only an hour into the evening and she already knows she shouldn't have come, but then, she was keen to spend time with Anna. She has tried over the last three months. At the start there were occasional meet-ups, but even they have waned. The other three are always around, like they have booked Anna up weeks in advance, and it isn't enjoyable being in the presence of these four women, three of whom she still barely knows. Their conversations always veer into in-jokes and shared experiences that she hasn't been a part of. Their mannerisms mirror each other: the way they curl their fingers over each other's arms as they speak, twirl strands of hair as they hang off words. As a group they make no effort to include her; in fact, Grace wonders why Anna bothered to invite her in the first place.

Suddenly Anna stands up and announces she's getting another bottle of wine, though there is at least a third of a bottle still left on the table in front of them. Her legs, tightly squeezed into black jeans, wobble as she makes her way to the bar, her blond hair still loosely knitted into the plait Nancy made. Her bra is showing through her black chiffon top, and she looks glamorous, if a little too thin. There isn't an ounce of the puppy fat she had when they were teenagers.

While Anna leans over the bar and points to a bottle in the fridge, Grace scans the group of women who are sitting at the table with her.

Nancy Simpson always looks immaculately groomed, and tonight is no exception. Her long, slender legs are pressed into jeans uncannily similar to Anna's. She looks to be at least five foot eleven, though clearly her height doesn't stop her from wearing heels. She's slightly older than the rest of them—in her early forties, Grace guesses. There's not a gray hair among the blond curls that hang in perfect waves down her back.

Her daughter, Elodie, is a precocious child. Over the last four years Elodie has apparently taken all the leading roles in the school plays: Mary in the Nativity, and then Guy Fawkes, Oliver Twist, and finally Simba.

In the three months that Grace's daughter has attended the school, she has clocked the way Nancy sits in the front row at every assembly, every parents' meeting, every choir competition. Her coat and bag are always draped across three other seats, for when her comrades arrive. And when they do, she beckons Anna, Rachel, and Caitlyn to join her, while Grace sits in the row behind.

The first time this happened, Grace had hoped Anna would seek her out and sit with her—she'd expected it, even—but then she'd seen her old friend arrive with Rachel, and glance guiltily at the one seat beside Grace before indicating that there wasn't enough room for the two of them to sit there. As if she couldn't possibly part from Rachel. How was it that she couldn't do that, when Rachel clearly had two other friends to sit with, and Grace had no one?

Tonight Rachel has drunk the lion's share of the wine and is getting louder as the evening wears on. She is wearing a gold glitter shift dress:

too dressy for a night at the Old Vic, Grace thinks, but then clearly the woman is up for a party. She has a dark bob of almost black hair that is neatly tucked behind her ears, and she doesn't stop twiddling a finger through it as she chats with Nancy. Rachel is possibly the one Grace knows the least. She catches flashes of her on the school run, often late, and so it's interesting to see her tonight. She is more fun than Grace appreciated at first, as she tells her entertaining stories.

Caitlyn keeps giggling at whatever Rachel is saying. She is by far the quietest of the group, seemingly the most sensible out of them, and yet also the nicest. She doesn't have Rachel's coolness at the school gates or Nancy's control.

Grace can see the appeal of both Caitlyn and Rachel. She could be friends with them, too, she thinks, if she is given the chance. It is one of the reasons she was keen to come tonight: to get to know Anna's friends better. But not Nancy. Their dislike for each other is mutual. Nancy made it clear in the early weeks of term that she had no time for Grace, a hostility that has only flourished as the term progressed.

With Anna at the bar, the other women's voices have dropped a note as they speak between themselves. Grace struggles to hear what is being said and so edges her chair a little closer, if only to remind them she's still here. As she does so Caitlyn turns to her with a pitying smile.

It isn't hard to see which way the evening is heading, with all of them diving into their drinks like they don't have to get up for a school run in the morning. Anna had told her it was "just a few" before school broke up for Christmas, but for all Grace knows, this is the way their nights always end up.

Now the women are discussing a holiday the four of them had been on back in May. A weekend in Majorca without their families. "Do you remember that waiter?" Nancy is laughing. "He couldn't keep his hands off you, Rach." At the bar, Anna turns round as she waits for the wine, laughing too.

Grace smiles, though of course it's one more conversation she can't join in. She leans back in her chair as her thoughts turn briefly to Matilda and the sitter she'd hurriedly found through the babysitting service she'd signed up for at the start of term but had barely used. She wonders if she should call to check on them. Matilda's behavior had been challenging tonight, and Grace thinks some of it is because she hasn't made any noticeable friendships. All Grace wants is for her daughter to have one special friend like she'd had in Anna.

She has so many memories of her own that she wishes she could share tonight with her friend. Grace has tried to remind Anna of them, but in recent weeks Anna has clammed up on her, shut her down. Maybe Grace was also hoping that by joining the group tonight she would have a better chance of talking to her and reliving moments from their past, the way you do when you are out drinking.

She remembers the two of them circling around the monorail at the motor museum when they were young, laughing, refusing to get off it as Grace's parents waited below, calling them down, horrified when the train started again and they were still on it. They must have completed at least six loops, or at least that is how it felt back then. "Can you believe you are eight today?" Anna had kept giggling.

Grace wants to share this happy memory with Anna when she comes back to the table, but as soon as her friend plonks the bottle of wine down, Rachel stands and links an arm through hers.

"Where are they going?" Grace asks when they have walked away.

"Probably for a cigarette." Caitlyn turns up her nose in disgust.

"A cigarette?" Grace breaks off before insisting that Anna doesn't smoke, because clearly she now does, and yet it is something else that Grace didn't know. Anna's father's constant smoking was supposed to have put her off for good. It had been deterrent enough for Grace, and she didn't have to live in the cloud of smoke that clung to the living room ceiling day in and day out.

"You didn't know she smoked?" Nancy says to Grace. She isn't laughing, but her eyes are lit up and dancing like they have been all evening. Like she is goading her.

"I thought she'd given up," Grace lies, and reaches for the old bottle of wine, tipping a generous amount into her glass.

"You may as well finish that," Nancy says, raising her eyes at the near-empty bottle. Grace stares back at her and does as she is told, pouring out the rest of the wine, though she isn't sure how she'll finish it. Already she's beginning to get that sharp tang in her mouth, and she knows that all she really wants is to switch to water soon, even though she'll clearly be on her own. Nancy grins and turns away, and Grace feels the unsettling churn in her stomach. She'd like to say she has no idea what Anna sees in Nancy, but because she knows her friend so well, she can imagine how easily she'd have been drawn into the other woman's web, unable to see what Grace sees: that Nancy is manipulative and has some hold over her. But then this isn't the first time Anna has let herself be taken in by a friend.

"No, she hasn't given up smoking," Caitlyn is saying. "In fact, if anything, I'd say she's doing it even more at the moment, wouldn't you?"

Nancy shrugs.

"What about her husband?" Grace asks. She isn't sure why she is so uptight about the idea of Anna smoking.

"What about him?" Nancy asks.

Grace hesitates. "Does he smoke?"

Nancy laughs. "What is this?" she says. "Why the third degree? You sound worried about it."

"I'm not worried," Grace mutters as Anna and Rachel return to the table. "It doesn't matter." Only for some reason it does, it grates on her. Perhaps it is because she can picture the Anna she used to know so clearly, and this new, grown-up version is nothing like her. When something taints your past memories, it has a nasty habit of knocking everything off-kilter, making you question things.

She wants Nancy to drop the subject of cigarettes, but instead she pulls out a chair for Anna, who obediently sits, and smiles as Nancy says, "Grace doesn't like the thought of you smoking. Maybe she has a point?" She places a hand on Anna's arm and starts rubbing it gently.

"Yes, she probably does," Anna says blankly, and as she takes off her red coat, her cheeks flush with what could be the coldness of the air, or with what Grace suspects could be embarrassment.

Grace draws her gaze away from Nancy's hand on her old friend's arm. Nancy has managed to make her feel like an overbearing parent, and all of a sudden she understands that this is exactly how she always feels when she is with them. Like a motherly figure, hovering over these women who act like children, the way they plait each other's hair and link arms and save seats.

Grace takes another gulp of her wine, ignoring its bitterness as she considers her options. She could leave now and go home, but she wants to spend time with Anna, and if this is the only way she's able to see much of her old friend, then she mustn't let the others spoil it.

Nancy is now regaling them with another story from Majorca. Inwardly Grace sighs, grasping the glass of wine between her fingers, tipping it back and forth, just so she has something to do. "Sounds like fun," Grace says when Nancy finishes the story and the laughter dies down.

"It was." Anna puts her glass down on the table, her smile slipping. "Sorry, Grace, this isn't fair on you when you weren't there."

"Not at all." Grace waves a hand in an attempt to make out she isn't bothered.

"We went there together one year, didn't we?" Anna says suddenly, and Grace's mind shoots back to the year they were fourteen, when her parents had invited Anna on their weeklong holiday to Alcudia in the summer. "Do you remember, Grace?"

"Of course I do." Grace smiles. She remembers how Anna's father had enthusiastically accepted the offer—it was likely the only holiday Anna would have—and how excited Grace was that she wouldn't be alone that year. That she would have Anna with her in the villa and they could spend their days in the pool and the evenings outside restaurants eyeing up Spanish waiters, begging her parents to allow them to go out on their own.

If they were on their own she would ask her friend why she has brought up that particular memory, because the holiday didn't pan out as they'd expected. Anna is holding her gaze, and in turn Grace finds herself holding her breath, and in that moment she is certain that something is troubling Anna, and she desperately wants her friend to confide in her.

But the moment is gone in a flash when Rachel pipes up, "I keep forgetting how far back you two go."

Grace nods. That is probably because it is rarely brought up, in spite of the many, many stories of their childhood that Grace could talk about for hours. "Anna practically lived with my family for twelve years," she says.

"Really?" Rachel looks surprised. "I mean, I knew you were close, but . . ." She trails off.

As close as sisters. Grace's mum cared as much for Anna as she did for Grace. She can picture as clear as day her and Anna sitting on the footstool in the living room when they were about seven, watching intently as Grace's mum showed them how to knit their first scarves. And how one summer, maybe two years later, they'd built a camp in the garden and insisted on sleeping in it for a week. Sometimes, especially in those earlier years, Grace used to forget that Anna even had a home to go back to, a dad who might have been waiting for her.

"But you haven't seen each other since you went to Australia, have you?" Rachel finishes.

"No. We haven't," Grace says. Though not for lack of trying when she was first there, but then lives and careers, husbands and families took over, and in the end they never did meet up again.

"And Anna says you weren't even in touch for a couple of years before you came back?"

Grace shakes her head. This is also true, bar the odd Facebook comment, but she knows that doesn't cut it as proper contact.

Then, as if losing interest, Rachel starts chattering on about something else and, as it always does, the conversation continues to wrap around the four friends' recent past, their plans for the next day, for the weeks ahead.

"I'm going for shots," Anna suddenly announces to whooping from Rachel, and mock groans from Nancy and Caitlyn. Her mood keeps flipping, from somber and withdrawn to playful, verging on a threat of danger, at times like she is trying to assert some control. Grace can't quite fathom what is going on. The Anna she knew was always so constant and easygoing, which makes her behavior seem more worrying than maybe it should.

"I'll help you," Grace says, and follows her friend to the bar so that she can tell Anna she won't join in a round of tequila. "Is everything all right?" Grace asks when they're alone.

"Of course." Anna turns away swiftly as a barman appears. "Four tequilas," she orders. Anna doesn't even try to persuade Grace to join them, which somehow makes her feel even more excluded, and if she didn't hate the taste of tequila so much, she would have changed her mind for the hell of it.

Grace hesitates and then says, "It's just you seem a little . . ." She pauses, because she doesn't really know how her friend seems this evening.

"I seem a little what, Grace?" Anna says as she presses her card against the machine.

Her coldness slaps Grace, and she finds herself recoiling. Anna had been so excited to see her when she'd first arrived back in August, but now there is a creeping distance between them and Grace isn't sure why, or how to stop it. She looks at the woman in front of her, and right now it is like looking at a stranger. Anna Robinson isn't Anna Fallow anymore, the girl she once knew better than anyone. But surely there are some friendships that are worth salvaging? How can Anna walk away from the close bond they'd once shared?

"A little unhappy," Grace says at last. She isn't entirely sure that is the right word for it, but she doesn't know what is.

"You don't have to worry about me anymore, Grace," Anna replies, and as she smiles, her eyebrows peak.

Grace takes in the smile, the way it doesn't quite ring true. As her eyes scan Anna's face, she wonders what is hiding behind the front that her friend seems to be putting on tonight.

Only, of course, she still worries about her. She always will, because years ago, taking care of Anna was intrinsic to their friendship. She can picture the young Anna who sat in a pair of borrowed pajamas on a school night once again, waiting for her dad to finish work and come to pick her up from Grace's parents' house. You don't spend twelve years so closely knitted to someone and stop caring just like that.

Grace changes the subject. "I can't believe we're back here again." She nods at the table in the corner, desperate to open up a conversation about old times and reach the Anna she was once so close to. "How many times did we sit there and drink?" A memory pops into her head. "Do you remember Christopher Smart?"

Anna's face softens. Christopher Smart was an oddball who had some kind of crush on Anna, and they would always end an evening in tears of laughter whenever he had followed Anna around the pub.

Grace waits for her friend to smile and join in the memory, but instead Anna says, "Will you just stop with the reminiscing, Grace? What is it you can't let go of? Why do you think we need to keep living in the past?"

"Let go of?" Grace asks, her mouth agape. "They're memories, our childhood."

"It's our past," Anna replies bluntly. "What matters now is the present. I'm sorry if you're not happy with yours, Grace, but I am with mine." Anna scoops up two glasses of tequila and returns to the table, where she sits down, leaving Grace staring behind her. Her hands feel numb as they hang loosely by her sides. Tears threaten to prick her eyes, but she doesn't know what is causing them. Whether it's that she *isn't* happy with her life or that Anna is pointing it out to her so callously. Or maybe it's that Grace doesn't believe Anna is happy herself right now.

Anna always did go on the defensive when really she was crying out for help inside. Even on the nights when her dad didn't turn up at school she would make excuses for him, refuse to accept that his work at the factory was a priority, but Grace always saw the sadness behind her eyes.

Grace picks up the other two glasses and takes them to the table. There is no point in saying anything in front of the others.

Over the next hour or so, the mood within the group seems to change. Nancy and Anna have scuttled off into a corner, their conversation seemingly heated as Anna gestures animatedly with her arms. When they return to the table Nancy's face is blank, her lips pursed, but soon the chatter is picked up and more wine is drunk and nothing is made of the blip in their evening.

By eleven Grace is ready to go home, but it's apparent that if she leaves now she'll be on her own.

Rachel has created her own makeshift dance floor beside the table, and the pub has emptied save for a group of three in the far corner, who keep looking in Rachel's direction as she waves her arms in the air in time to a beat that seems purely in her head. At one point she meanders around the bar and turns up the volume on the music. The nearest barman, young with a shaved head, looks in her direction but doesn't say anything.

Grace watches Anna retreat further into herself. She sees past Anna's disguise of loudly spoken words and overly exaggerated laugh-

ter, sees the way her eyes flicker towards Grace every so often. There is
something she is holding back for sure.

So when Anna slides off her chair and heads for the ladies' room,
Grace follows her.

Anna is swaying in front of the mirror, a lip gloss in one hand that
she isn't applying. "Nancy has a hold on you," Grace tells her. She
hadn't intended to say as much, but two and a half hours of watching
Nancy dominate Anna's attention have taken its toll. She fears for her
friend; she does, because she knows Anna too well. She knows what
she can be like, and Grace needs to say something.

"What?" Anna splutters, seemingly incredulous. Her reaction leads
Grace to believe that she can't see it.

"Nancy controls you," Grace says a little softer.

"You're kidding me, right?"

Grace bites her lip. She can see the conversation going only one
way, but now she has said something she can't take back. "No. I'm not
kidding. I just see the way she is with you. With *all* of you," she adds,
gesturing back to the bar.

"It's been bloody apparent from the start that you don't like each
other," Anna spits. "Have you ever stopped to think how hard that is
for me? Always trying to keep everyone happy?" She slips to the side
and grabs the sink to steady herself.

Despite knowing Nancy doesn't like her, it still cuts Grace to hear
it said.

"It's been awful," Anna is saying. "I shouldn't have to choose. I
want to be with my friends, Grace," she says, "and yet I always feel like
I have to come and talk to you."

As soon as the words are out, Grace notices the way Anna's eyes
widen, her mouth parting. Grace thinks, and hopes, that it is because
she wants to grab the words back. But they have been said now, and
it is too late. Their punch is almost palpable. She can feel the burn in
her chest.

She can almost see the pictures of twelve years of their childhood breaking in the air, tiny pieces scattering like confetti. Memories that have been so precious to Grace suddenly feel as though they mean nothing to Anna, and this is something she can't get her head around.

Grace should turn away and leave, but she can't bring herself to do that because, despite the words Anna has spoken, she is here. Right now, Grace has her friend all to herself. Besides, Anna has been drinking, and Grace is certain there is something else going on. All these years on, she still can't walk away from her. They might not share the same bloodlines, but they were as good as sisters once.

"I'm worried about you," Grace says. "And you must know why."

Anna shakes her head, eyes staring, watching her carefully, surely knowing what she means but probably willing Grace not to say it.

"Because I've seen it before, haven't I, Anna? This isn't the first time I've picked up the pieces."

After that, the evening turns even more sour. Grace's words have had the opposite of their intended effect on Anna, who sidles up to Nancy, hanging her head on her shoulder as they giggle conspiratorially over something.

But later Grace notices fractures within the group. There are hushed words between two of them about something that happened at Anna's husband Ben's fortieth birthday party a month or so ago, a dinner the three women attended with their husbands. Caitlyn was in tears, though none of them mentioned this in front of her. And then, maybe not long before Grace leaves, Nancy's attitude shifts and Anna no longer paws at any one of her three friends. She is withdrawing from all of them.

Grace speaks to Anna alone only one more time. Another snatched conversation in before she leaves. It is nearly midnight and she has no choice but to go, because she has told the babysitter she will be back before twelve thirty. She calls a taxi, the behavior of the others confirming what she already knows, that they aren't yet ready to leave.

Anna is ordering more drinks. "Come with me," Grace says. She places a hand on her friend's arm but it is shaken off. "Why don't you share my cab?" She wants Anna to come because she doesn't trust the other three to keep an eye out for her. They don't even appear to notice there is anything wrong.

But Anna tells her she isn't going anywhere, and so Grace waits at the table, surveying the night as it continues to break down in front of her. In many ways it is a relief to get out of there when the text alert tells her the cab is waiting outside.

Thursday, 12 December

The news had spread by twenty to nine the following morning: Anna Robinson didn't return home after her night out. She hadn't been seen since some time in the early hours of the morning.

Her husband, Ben, had woken at six to find his wife's side of the bed unslept in, and when he realized she was neither in the house nor answering her phone, he had apparently called Nancy in a panic.

So far the group of year-four parents had gleaned little more than this and they were patching together stories around the playground, making what they could of the basic information at hand.

Every so often their eyes would dart towards the group of three women standing by the railings, and they'd wonder to themselves what they must be saying because their body language seemed all wrong.

Nancy, Caitlyn, and Rachel were spaced apart from each other, their arms wrapped across their padded coats as they tried to keep warm, bobble hats so low you had to strain to see the expression on their faces.

The three friends were usually part of a foursome, but not today. Standing together, immobile, they spoke in urgent whispers.

The school mums wished they had a bit more knowledge about what had happened the previous night. Had Anna left before the others? Had she got a taxi or tried to walk home but never made it? Had she gone home with someone else? Were her three best friends covering up for her? The latter was a less sinister possibility, yet still worthy of their gossip.

There were too many questions. And the three friends, gathered in their tiny fragmented circle, appeared completely unapproachable.

The mums assumed that the Old Vic had locked its doors at one a.m. and the women had stayed inside drinking. The pub was known for this; everyone had done it at some point or other, stumbling home afterwards along the stony coastline if they wanted to sober up, or back through the narrow and dimly lit roads that wound upwards and away from the sea. Past the tightly packed terraced town houses that lay in ranks of colorfully painted soldiers and eventually on to the new estates.

"What do you think happened?" one of the mothers asked. She nodded in the direction of the three friends. Did they only look so misshapen because Anna wasn't with them? "What do you reckon they did?" she whispered. No one knew if this was meant to sound like an accusation, but none of them questioned it.

"Surely one of them must know where Anna went after the pub?" she went on, and they all agreed, because no one could fathom how Anna could have been left behind when the four of them were so inseparable.

Now they watched as Nancy put a hand on Rachel's shoulder. It was the first contact they had seen between the three friends, but it was only a brief moment before she eased away again.

In the distance, on the opposite side of the road, they noticed Grace Goodwin's car pulling up slowly.

"Was Grace with them last night, too?" someone asked, the thought only just forming.

"I don't know," someone else murmured. It was a good question. In the last three months they had been watching the dynamics between Grace and the foursome with growing interest.

In the early days, Anna was often with Grace in the playground, laughing, smiling, seemingly trying to encourage Ethan and Matilda to talk to each other. But then, as weeks passed, the mums had clocked the way Anna gradually pulled away from Grace. Pulled or been pulled, they didn't know which.

Some thought it might have been the latter; it was no secret Nancy didn't like Grace, though they wondered what her reasons could be. Grace was clearly trying to make an effort, and with her husband away she was single-handedly bringing up her child in a place where she knew virtually no one.

Was Nancy jealous of Grace's arrival?

They didn't know Nancy particularly well—she'd kept it that way— but her life had been the subject of gossip and speculation over the years. Like the fact that her charmingly handsome husband had suffered a break- down at the hands of an unrelenting stock market, and they'd had to move back from London to Clearwater to be near her sick mother. That money was tighter now than they'd been used to.

There was no question that Nancy Simpson was something of an enigma.

Grace Goodwin was now slowly opening her car door, and the parents wondered that even if she was with the other women last night, there was a possibility she might not yet know what had happened, because she clearly was in no rush to get her daughter to school.

On the opposite side of the playground, Anna's son Ethan was playing with a boy called Daniel. There had been no sighting of Ben Robinson, and the mums didn't know if he had dropped his son at school early or if, more likely, Nancy had brought him in. There were only a handful of roads between her house and Anna's, after all. Maybe Ben had stayed at home to focus on tracking down his wife.

"What did he say to Nancy when he called her?" someone asked.

"Just what you'd expect. I heard he asked her where Anna was, and what happened to her last night."

"What did she tell him?"

"No one knows."

"Someone must," she said, and in silence they all turned to look again at the three friends.

Rachel was now sitting on the wall with her head between her hands. Was it too much alcohol the night before or the fear of what might have happened that made her rock gently back and forth?

"Anna hasn't been herself lately," one of the mums said. "I've wondered if it was something to do with her dad. He only died a few months ago, and she's been pretty cut up about it."

The others shrugged, murmuring some kind of agreement.

"When was Anna last seen?" someone asked.

"I heard Nancy say it was two o'clock this morning they all left."

"Two a.m.! On a Wednesday night? God, I don't know how they can do it knowing they have to get up for the school run."

"If she walked off on her own in the dark, then anything could have happened. You know there's no fencing along part of Crayne's Cliff at the moment; have you seen? It got taken out by the winds."

The others shuddered at the thought.

"Why would she have gone up that way?" someone asked, though they had all likely done it at least once—stumbled up the cliffs at the end of a night and stood at the top, looking down at the town below. "You think she could have fallen? It gives me chills just thinking about it, but they'll check, won't they? The police will look there first."

"Are the police already involved?"

There was a moment's silence as they all looked at each other.

"Why wouldn't they be?"

There were more shrugs. No one had an answer to that.

"I didn't think you could report anyone missing for twenty-four hours. An adult, I mean. And besides, why has no one suggested the obvious? Maybe Anna didn't go home because she didn't want to go home."

"You mean she's left her husband?"

"And her son?" A choked laugh. "There's no way . . . "

Anna was a besotted mother. They all knew it. She admitted once that she still wrote notes on Post-its that she stuck in Ethan's lunch box. "Every day without fail!" she had joked. "It's a habit I can't stop." Only today,

Ethan would be opening his box to find no note inside. No, there was no way Anna wouldn't have been there for Ethan.

"I can't imagine her walking home alone from the Old Vic," one of them said. "It's so far from her house. She must have called a taxi." Despite the fact she was always up for a party, Anna wasn't careless, she had a sensible head on her shoulders.

"What does that mean?" someone asked. "If she did call a cab, could something have happened to her on the way back?"

The thought was left hanging as each of them considered the horror. On the whole, Clearwater was spared from such incidents, but it didn't mean they never happened.

"Look. Grace is coming up the path." They all turned to the gates, to where Grace Goodwin was walking in with Matilda, who was swinging her hand up and then down. Grace was smiling, though her gaze was fixed straight ahead, as if her attention was only partly on her daughter. It was clear to everyone that she hadn't yet heard the news.

She was almost level with the three friends when one of them called her name. Grace was about to find out that Anna had disappeared, and the other parents barely breathed as they watched with morbid fascination. They saw the expression on Grace's face fall as her hand let go of Matilda. She clearly hadn't wanted to talk to Anna's other friends, so if she was at the pub with them last night, then what had happened between them?

Now Grace's attention was on Nancy, Rachel, and Caitlyn in turn as she shook her head from side to side. Her frown deepened, as if she weren't getting the answers she needed.

Then the bell rang, piercing everyone's thoughts and creating chaos in the playground as children scurried either to their parents or to their class lines. The mums were caught up in saying goodbyes to their children for the day, a few of them lingering a little longer in a hug and reluctantly letting them go, by simple virtue of the fact that something awful had happened, and they wanted to keep their children close for a moment more.

As the parents walked towards the gate, some stopped and asked the trio of Anna's friends if they were okay, explaining that they had heard the news and asking to be filled in as soon as anyone heard more. The three women looked worse for wear close-up. It appeared the amount of alcohol they'd drunk the night before was taking its toll.

Grace, on the other hand, just stood there staring, her mouth agape, her eyes wide with disbelief. Soon she was abandoned, as Nancy, Rachel, and Caitlyn walked down the path together towards the school gates, Nancy now linking her arm through Rachel's, maybe to hold her up, maybe for safety in numbers, and Caitlyn on the other side of her, like they were about to start skipping down the Yellow Brick Road.

And it had never been so apparent how out of the circle she was.

2

Grace

The morning after their night out, Grace wakes to find Matilda already dressed for school and standing at the end of her bed. She is in a spectacularly good mood because there is a traveling theater arriving today whose members are performing some off-the-wall version of *Aladdin*. Christmas is still two weeks away, and in Grace's mind it's far too early to be swapping lessons for making paper chains, but Matilda has been eagerly throwing herself into the week's activities.

It's a far cry from the hot-weather Christmases they've been used to in Sydney, but now that they're back in England, Matilda has been so focused on the fact that it's bound to snow soon that she hasn't shown any signs of missing their old home.

Grace has awakened to a dry mouth, a headache, and a vague sense of nausea coupled with memories from a horrible evening, although her sore mood is mildly tempered by seeing her daughter so happy. It's barely even a hangover, but it's there nonetheless, and at 6:45 a.m. she'd really rather turn over, close her eyes, and drift back to sleep.

But now her thoughts won't let her, as they dance around her brain, patching together pieces of the evening in sharp reminders. Grace recognizes the feeling settling deep inside her as anger. She has known that feeling too well lately. Each time she hangs up the phone after a distant conversation with Graham it is back again, bubbling furiously.

Matilda has skipped out of the room and Grace realizes that without her daughter, she would really have no one in her life right now. It is sobering to acknowledge being so alone. The night before only served to reinforce that feeling.

On her bedside table sits a photo of her and Graham in happier times. Sometimes Grace thinks she should move it so she doesn't have to look at his face every morning, a reminder that he's living a life she has no idea about in Singapore. She wonders what it would be like to have him here full-time. Would they slip back into their marriage, or have too many years of them each living on opposite sides of the world sunk their claws in too deep to repair?

Whenever they speak and he assures her he'll be in Clearwater soon, he always sounds so positive, so happy at first. It's as if he doesn't give much thought to the fact that she is effectively a single parent, despite her pointing it out to him. But by the end of their conversations everything has always dulled, and Grace usually hangs up the phone feeling worse than she did before their call.

Possibly they should have the conversation when he is here this Christmas, discuss whether he can afford to cut this project short and relocate. Whether he would want to.

Grace sighs as she drags herself out of bed and she goes through the motions of getting herself and Matilda ready for the day ahead. It is not the marriage she dreamed of any longer, that's for sure, but now that she is up, her mind drifts to other things, like the fact she has no interest in seeing any of Anna's friends this morning and knows she'll have little chance of prying Anna away from them to talk to her.

It's a surprise when Grace walks through the gates and immediately spots the little group hanging by the wall, with no sign of Anna. She notices Nancy first. And then Rachel, who is bent over double and perching on a low concrete wall as if she's about to be sick, which in Grace's mind is a revolting way to behave in a school playground. Slightly to the right of them, Caitlyn is biting a thumbnail as she watches Rachel, a look of panic on her face.

Grace's first thought is one of hope; that if Anna isn't with them, then she might be able to get her alone and find out what the hell last night was about. She goes to walk past the group, noticing how Caitlyn, shoulders hunched and almost subservient in her manner, looks so petite next to Nancy, who's wearing a long black coat with fur trim around the hood and knee-high black boots. She looks fantastic, even for the school run. Grace has no idea how the woman can drink as much as she did the night before and still look ready to do it again.

But as she goes to pass the trio, even from fifteen meters away, she can sense that something isn't right. Matilda tugs on her hand, but Grace isn't concentrating on her daughter as she reaches the group. She has no desire to stop and talk while memories of the night before flash like sharp knives in and out of her head. It is not only Anna's words that stab at her, but the way all of them made her feel like she is no part of their lives.

She's nearly past them when Rachel stands up and stops her. "Grace!" she calls out, her hands stuffed into the deep pockets of her oversized Puffa coat.

Grace turns. Rachel's face is washed out, and the remains of last night's makeup is smudged under her eyes.

"Something's happened." Rachel's voice breaks and Nancy steps forward, placing a hand on her arm. "You'll hear it sooner or later," she goes on.

"What?" Grace asks, unsettled by the looks on their faces.

"Ben called me this morning," Nancy says, her voice so command-ing that it drags Grace's attention away from Rachel.

Ben? It takes barely a second, but still Grace has to think who she means. Anna's husband, she realizes quickly. Ben Robinson. A man she has met a handful of times in the last three months, but only briefly. She still hopes to get to know him better, as he is such a huge part of Anna's life now.

"Anna didn't go home last night. And so clearly we're all a bit panicked," Nancy goes on. Her eyes bore into Grace's as if she might think that Grace could possibly know more than she does.

"She didn't go home?" Grace repeats, letting go of Matilda's hand. "What do you mean, she didn't go home?"

"When Ben woke this morning she wasn't there. And she hasn't been since last night."

"Well, has he tried calling her?"

"Of course," Nancy replies, as if it's the most stupid suggestion she has ever heard. "We've all tried calling her. Her phone's switched off. I've left a number of messages telling her to ring me as soon as possible, but for some bloody reason she's turned it off." She draws a deep breath before finally looking away. Grace has never seen Nancy drop eye contact before. It jars her.

"I don't get it," Grace says. "What happened after I left? When you went home, I mean. Didn't she get a taxi with you?"

Nancy bites her lip but doesn't answer. The others remain mute. Grace looks from one to the other and waits for what seems like an age for one of them to answer her. "What happened?" she repeats more firmly.

Eventually Nancy shakes her head. "We were all drinking; you know how it was."

"You mean you don't remember?" Grace knows she sounds accusing but she cannot help it.

"No, I do remember," Nancy replies sternly. "Anna suddenly got up and said she was going outside, and then . . ." Her sentence drifts away.

"And then what?" Grace persists, catching Nancy glancing at the other two before Rachel slumps down on the wall again. Rachel's face is even grayer now, and her eyes are wide as she drops them, seemingly unable to look at anyone.

"Well, by the time I went to go home she still hadn't come back," Nancy says simply, waving her hands about her as if to indicate that Anna had just disappeared into a puff of air. Her eyes stare into Grace's now, goading her to be the one to look away first. It's a battle of wills that Grace expects. As if Nancy has composed herself and is now trying to assert some control again. But with Caitlyn beside her, looking on sheepishly, Grace has the distinct impression Nancy is lying.

"So, what are you saying?" Grace says. "That Anna had already left the pub?"

"Yes," Nancy says. "She must have gone without saying anything to us." There is definitely something that resembles fear in her eyes, but fear of what Grace isn't sure.

She wants to ask if this is typical of Anna, but the question would make it clear that Nancy knows Anna better than she does, and even now she finds she can't bring herself to give Nancy that satisfaction. Instead she asks Caitlyn, "Did you see her go?"

"I . . . er . . ." As Caitlyn falters, a splat of red creeps up her neck. Vibrant patches reach her face as she blinks, shrugging, her face masked with panic. "I'm not sure what happened," she says. "I guess, like Nancy says, she must have left before we did."

Peering a little closer, Grace can swear she sees tears forming in the corners of Caitlyn's eyes and wonders, if she keeps watching close enough, whether they will start to fall. What is it that these women aren't telling her?

"Gone where, then?" Grace asks eventually.

"Maybe she just started walking," Caitlyn suggests. "She could have gone the other way? Along the cliffs?"

Grace recoils at the thought. Her eyes widen as she stares at Caitlyn.

"Why would she have done that?" Rachel asks. But it is too late, because the thought is there now and Grace cannot shake it.

The bell starts ringing and Matilda tugs on Grace's hand again, and Grace bends to her daughter to give her a hug. By the time she's returned her attention to Anna's three friends, their body language is different. Nancy has linked her arm through Rachel's and is now doing the same to Caitlyn, standing on her other side, and it feels as if they are forming some kind of wall of protection against Grace. As if the questions that are forming in her head and toppling over each other to get out aren't ones they want to hear.

Of course, their animosity could all *just* be in her head, she thinks as children scurry past. And of course there could be some reasonable explanation for the fact that Anna didn't return home: she could have met someone at the pub and made a bad decision and now feels unable to face the thought that she hasn't gone back to her husband. She is an adult, after all. But is this possible of the thirty-six-year-old Anna that Grace has been trying to get to know?

Whatever she has done, the knowledge that Grace should never have left her last night is all too present. Back when they were seventeen, they'd had rules: never get in a car when someone's been drinking; always look behind the front seats at night in case someone is crouching, hiding behind them; never leave each other on their own. Ever.

And last night Grace had broken one of their rules. She had left Anna behind, and now look what had happened.

In her heart she doesn't believe Anna to be the type not to go home to Ben, but more than that she knows, with certainty, that she is not a mother who'd leave her son. Which means something very bad has happened. And now all sorts of images ripple through Grace's head: Anna lying in a ditch; tied up and gagged in a basement not even that far from here; her body dumped in bushes that would soon be found by a dog walker, or lying at the bottom of Crayne's Cliff. It is amazing how many vivid pictures she is able to conjure up in a moment.

"Has anyone called the police?" she says as she falls behind the three friends, their arms linking them together in a daisy chain. Other parents from the year are still asking if there is any news of Anna. Nancy is carefully batting their questions away and agreeing that of course she'll let them know as soon as they hear from her, and so Grace asks the question again, louder this time.

Caitlyn stops and shakes her head, turning to look over her shoulder. "God, I hope it won't come to that. Calling the police? Surely we'll hear from her soon."

Grace cocks her head. It doesn't pass her by how irrelevant she is in this scenario, that she may as well be one of the other mothers who has no clue what has happened either, asking their questions, being left out of the loop. She wasn't the one to receive the call from Anna's worried husband and it isn't likely she'll be one of the first to hear as soon as there is news. Possibly she'll just be another person on a WhatsApp group who is filled in at the same time as everyone else.

"Of course someone needs to tell the police," she says firmly, striding up to the group of three who have now paused on the roadside. "Ben must have done it already anyway?" she adds, trying to assume some authority. It would be the first thing Grace would do if Graham hadn't returned home when he was supposed to be there, but then again, she can barely remember the last time Graham *was* lying in their bed.

"Well, you can't report an adult as missing for twenty-four hours," Nancy replies. It seems they have found themselves in some kind of standoff, and Grace is conscious of eyes watching her but she won't back down.

"Which is ridiculous," Caitlyn adds nervously. "Don't you think? In twenty-four hours anything could have happened. Twenty-four hours wouldn't be until the early hours of tomorrow morning." Her voice rises as she speaks, her fear almost palpable, and Grace knows she needs to speak to Caitlyn alone. That she may be her only chance of finding out what happened at the end of the night.

"There's absolutely no way we can wait until then," Grace says. "And anyway, I don't believe we can't report it." She risks a glance at Nancy. "It's up to the police what they do with the information, but there's no way we're not allowed to share it with them."

Caitlyn looks up at Nancy as if she's looking for some confirmation about what to do. Rachel's head is hung low and she gazes at her feet, which scuff at the pavement.

"So what are you all doing now, then?" Grace asks, when no one responds.

"We'll keep trying to get hold of Anna," Nancy says, continuing to assume the role of decision-maker.

"That's it?" Grace laughs, incredulous.

Nancy bites down on her lip again as she stares at Grace. "It's barely nine o'clock in the morning. You call the police and tell them a thirty-six-year-old woman hasn't come home, and they're not going to take you seriously. And besides," she pauses, dropping her voice so the eavesdropping mothers nearby can't hear. "Ben doesn't want us calling anyone. Not yet."

"Why not?" Grace demands. "Why wouldn't he want to?" She can feel her insides catch on fire, a flame that leaps up and rides through her. Why the hell would Anna's husband not want to call the police?

"He wants to see if he can find her before he starts involving them. Christ, I don't know," Nancy says. "He's probably scared that she didn't come home for an altogether different reason."

"Anna wouldn't do that," Grace says.

"I'm not being funny," Nancy replies, "but you haven't actually got any idea what Anna would or wouldn't do these days. You haven't known her for almost twenty years, Grace. A lot has happened since you were seventeen."

Grace opens her mouth and then clamps it shut again, staring in disbelief. She can feel her tongue crackling with words she's trying to form into a sentence, unsure which ones to use. Their friend is missing and they shouldn't be arguing over who knows her best right now. Nancy doesn't have the right to score points with her in this moment, as if Grace doesn't give a toss about Anna. She wants to demand that Nancy tell her what has happened to Anna since they were both seventeen, because she is right about something: Anna isn't the same person.

She feels the other two women watching as Nancy hesitates and then says sharply, "I'm sorry. I shouldn't have said that. I'm worried; we all are."

She doesn't look sorry in the slightest, but despite this, Grace nods slowly. Nancy goes on: "I'm going to call Ben now." She pulls away from Caitlyn and reaches into her pocket for her phone, which she clutches in her hand. "And I'll tell you the minute I hear anything."

Grace waits for her to make the call, but instead Nancy turns and starts walking down the road, hauling Rachel along with her. Caitlyn lingers for only a moment, and Grace takes her chance, reaching out to grab her arm.

"What happened?" she asks. "At the end of the night, did Anna leave before you?"

Caitlyn's head gives a glimmer of a shake. "I don't . . . I'm not sure," she says. "I don't remember, but I don't think—"

"Cait!" Nancy calls. "Are you coming?"

"Yes, I'm coming," Caitlyn says, without taking her eyes off Grace. "I'm sorry." She shrugs. "I don't know."

But you do, Grace thinks as she watches the three women disappear around a bend in the road. *I think you do bloody know.*

Her mind whirls with the weirdness of the conversation, the women's reactions to Anna's disappearance. None of it feels right. She needs to speak to Ben. Surely he is more inclined to act than Anna's friends appear to be. She cannot believe he doesn't want to alert the police, like Nancy says. And there is no way Grace will sit back and wait for Anna to call or wait for news from Nancy that may or may not come.

She makes her way to her car. Yes, she will speak to Ben herself. Before she reports Anna missing, she will hear what he has to say; and then if he still hasn't made the call, she will do it herself.

She will talk to Caitlyn, too. Dig deeper into what happened the previous evening.

But before she does either of those things, she needs to go back to where they were last night. And she needs to walk up the path to Crayne's Cliff. Because as much as she hopes her friend didn't go that way, she cannot shake the fear of what might have happened if she did.

September

Three months earlier

Anna

Outside the window there is a pretty street: rows of semidetached houses on either side, all with patches of perfectly manicured lawns. I haven't had any need to visit this area before, and it was one of the reasons I singled the therapist's name out of a Google search. I felt inconspicuous parking outside, less likely to be spotted by someone I know when I'm half an hour from home.

"Maybe you could start by telling me what brought you here today?" Sally asks me. Her voice is gentle and has a slight lilt to it. She wears her hair mostly scraped back from her face with an Alice band, though a thin, wispy fringe escapes beneath it.

I nod but don't answer for a moment. My stomach is turning over the way it always used to when I was waiting for an exam to start. Even up to the point I arrived at Sally's house I wasn't sure I wanted to go ahead. Is therapy really the answer? I could have probably done with it when I was a child, but it had never been offered to me, and so here I am, thirty-six years old, trying to do it for the first time.

I've been balling my hands so tightly together in my lap that I'm beginning to lose circulation. It's the thought of talking, opening up.

I guess it's never really been a thing for me, which makes my being here at all, all the more ironic. I'm worried that once I start speaking it might open up the floodgates, and I hate the thought of breaking down in front of a stranger.

"What made you pick up the phone?" Sally is prompting me. "That's usually a good place to start."

My mind flicks through myriad thoughts so quickly I can barely catch them, each one contributing to my unease. They stop on the notion that I feel myself losing the last vestiges of control and I want to stop the unraveling. Only I have no idea how. But I also have no idea how to explain this to Sally, and so I tell her, more simply, "My dad died six weeks ago."

"I'm sorry to hear that," Sally says.

I want to tell her it's fine, but I can't say that when I've just told her it's the reason I was scouring the internet a week ago looking for a therapist. Again I find myself nodding. "It wasn't really a surprise by the end," I tell her. "He'd been ill for a while, but that doesn't make it any easier."

In truth, Dad's death hadn't been a catalyst, it was the weeks leading up to it, when he decided it was time to tell me some truths that he possibly should have told me many years ago. Or not at all. I'm not certain which is preferable. I think Dad wanted to give me some answers about my mum and my childhood. Only now I find I am left with more questions and I have no one to ask.

"It doesn't make it easier," Sally agrees. "Were you and your dad close?"

"No. Well, I suppose we were in some ways." I stop and give a short laugh. "God, I don't know, that's a tough question. I guess we were close because it was only me and him when I was growing up, but then on the other hand we didn't get on well. We weren't close in that regard. Sorry. It feels weird, talking like this."

"To a stranger, you mean?" she asks.

"To anyone." I turn to look out the window again, thoughts of my dad filling my head. I've never stopped to think about whether we were close or not. It isn't a question I've been asked before. On the one hand, I doubt Dad would have been able to name one job I've had since I left college. But on the other, I wouldn't have been surprised if I'd found a whole scrapbook of my life over the years in his bottom drawer.

I hadn't though. A few weeks earlier I'd gone through all his drawers and cupboards, as well as the boxes that were kept in the loft. There had been some surprises: mementos he'd kept of my childhood such as essays I'd written, books I'd loved. I was relieved that Ben hadn't come with me to help sort through Dad's things, because I'd ended up sitting in the middle of his bedroom and howling.

Anyway, the point is I don't know what he'd be able to recall about me because we didn't have the type of relationship where we ever discussed anything important. I always left his house with a vague sense of disappointment, not knowing if he'd enjoyed my visit or not. There is no easy way to describe our relationship. In some ways even calling it a relationship feels like a stretch.

"Can you tell me how you have been feeling since your dad passed?" Sally asks.

I raise my eyes and focus on a patch on the ceiling as I consider this. It isn't the first time I have tried to make sense of my feelings. Ben has asked me the same thing. I have always told him I feel sad, of course. But then I always knew that wasn't quite the truth. I just didn't want to admit that I also felt relief. How could I even say that? In the end I tell Sally, "I feel guilty," which is also true.

"Guilty about what?" she asks.

"Maybe that I never tried harder." Thoughts of Grace and her family come into my head, and the many hours and days—years even—that I spent with them instead of with my dad. I wonder if I could have had a better relationship with him if I hadn't spent so much time at Grace's house.

"It's very common to feel like this after someone has died," Sally says. "We are left with all the what-ifs, the what-we-could-have-done-betters. It sometimes takes time to acknowledge all the things that were good."

"Maybe," I murmur.

"Can you tell me a bit about your childhood?"

"Like what?"

"You mentioned it was just you and your dad, so your mum wasn't around?"

"No." I shake my head quickly. I don't want to be drawn into a conversation about my mum. That's not why I am here.

Sally is looking at me curiously, but eventually she says, "Okay, so what was your dad like as a father?"

"He did his best, I suppose," I say. They are words I've uttered many times before, like some kind of mantra. Whenever anyone asks me this I've always said, *He did his best*. It doesn't mean it wasn't good enough, or even that I understand how hard it must have been for him, trying to juggle work with looking after a four-year-old daughter who'd inevitably brought with her a plethora of problems, especially as she grew older. Just that it seems the easiest, least judgmental, and the simplest "brush over and move on" answer.

Sally merely nods, and I know she means for me to dig deeper, so I try to draw a picture for her. "When we were teenagers he'd let us watch movies that were inappropriately scary because he didn't really have a clue what girls our age should be watching. We'd sit there with snacks piled up to our necks, and at school I used to swap one of my shop-bought multipack cakes for someone else's raw carrots because he rarely packed me anything healthy. And I would eventually put myself to bed when I was so tired I couldn't stay awake any longer. But then I always had clean clothes and I never went six weeks without a haircut, because he worked hard so I didn't have to. So," I pause and shrug, "he did his best."

"You said *we*. You and a sibling?"

"No. I don't have any siblings. I mean me and my friend Grace. She might as well have been my sister, though, we practically grew up together. She took me under her wing when she found me sitting on my own in the playhouse at school, crying. We were five, and we were best friends until she and her parents left for Australia when we were seventeen. Her parents did a lot for me. Well, her mum, Catherine, in particular."

I pause and take a deep breath that catches in my throat as my guilt comes flooding back in waves. How was it that not that long ago life had felt pleasingly simple. My family, our health, security—does anything else matter?

Nancy is always telling me I'm a simple person. "There's never any drama with you, Anna," she'll tell me, and it's the way I want it. I always aspired to having a family life like Grace had. Back then I thought that her parents' marriage was the closest thing to perfection, but then as a child you see what you want to see. Now I see that my marriage to Ben is better. "We are in the process of adopting," I suddenly tell Sally. "Not many people know about it; I haven't wanted to tempt fate."

"Oh? How lovely," Sally says.

I nod. "Ben and I couldn't have any more children after Ethan. I thought it wouldn't matter for a long time because Ethan is enough for us," I say. "But we talked about it and agreed we wanted more. I want him to have a bond with another child," I say. "A sister. They found us a little girl earlier this summer. She's beautiful; her name's Zadie." My hand automatically feels for my handbag. In it I carry a photo of the two-year-old girl I fell in love with the moment I saw her picture. I am tempted to share it with Sally, but I have this strange idea that if I get too carried away something will happen, and I don't want to take any risks.

"She's currently with a foster family in Hampshire," I go on. "I don't know, the whole process is taking so much longer than I thought it would."

"You look worried," Sally points out.

"I am. I worry something's going to happen to stop us getting her. I couldn't bear it—" I break off and look away. Ben tells me I'm superstitious. He says nothing is going to go wrong just because I talk about it."

"You've suffered a loss, Anna; it's understandable you think that way." I smile thinly.

"Talk to me about when your friend Grace moved away to Australia. It must have been hard losing your best friend at that age, particularly when you spent so much time together."

"Yes, it was." I remember the way we stood at Heathrow Airport. Tears streamed down my face as I watched Grace retreating through the glass doors towards Departures. "They asked me to go with them," I say.

"Really?" It clearly surprises her.

It had surprised my friends, too, when I told them last week. Rachel had said, "Why the hell would they ask you to go with them? Isn't that a bit weird?"

Nancy was screwing her eyes up as she'd turned to glance at Grace, who was on the other side of the playground, talking to the headmaster. I wondered what they were making of her, the things that were going unsaid. None of us had ever wanted to rock our tight friendship by bringing other people into the fold; it was kind of an unspoken agreement. And yet here was Grace, and I had the sense she was a threat. I can tell that Nancy doesn't like her by the way she questions me. She is suspicious of Grace, and I feel the need to keep my friends apart.

Now I can see Sally pressing forward in her seat and I answer her question. "I know it sounds extreme," I say, "but it wasn't. Not if you knew me and Grace back then."

Catherine had treated me like another daughter. She and Grace's dad took me on holidays with them. All through primary school, Grace and I were inseparable. If anything, it was extreme to split us up.

"But anyway, of course my dad said no to going to Australia with them. I can remember the look on his face when Catherine asked him, and later when we were on our own and he asked me if I really wanted to go. I told him I didn't, because I couldn't bear to see the sadness in his eyes."

"Did you want to, though?" Sally asks.

I shrug. "I thought I did at the time. I blamed Dad when Grace left, which was unfair, but he'd inadvertently made my decision for me without me knowing. I'm glad I didn't, though. I would never have met Ben. I would never have had Ethan.

"But Grace is back," I tell her. "Just after I got back from clearing out my dad's house she called me out of the blue and said, 'Come to your front door,' and there she was, standing on the driveway." My eyes suddenly fill with tears at the memory, and I try to laugh them off. How only two weeks later she'd then surprised me again by appearing in the school playground, having enrolled Matilda. "God, what's wrong with me?" I exclaim.

Sally smiles, plucking a tissue out of a box and passing it to me.

"It was just this moment where I suddenly felt all these emotions coming out of me," I go on. "And to see her there . . . I finally had someone to talk to who knew my dad. No one knew as much about him and my life as Grace did. Sorry, I don't know why I keep crying."

"You've no need to apologize." Sally smiles.

"When we were young I felt that Grace and her family looked after me. They were always picking up the pieces that Dad dropped. Like every Christmas Eve Grace's mum Catherine had this tradition of making us both this special package with pajamas and hot chocolate and marshmallows. And then on Easter Sunday I'd go to their house in the morning and hunt for eggs. We'd still be looking by teatime, they were always so well hidden. You know, it's odd, but I never questioned why there weren't any in my own garden.

"But anyway," I say, "I'm a different person now. I don't need looking after anymore. I'm an adult, for God's sake." I try to laugh but it comes out as a snort. "People change, don't they?" I ask. And Sally agrees that yes, people can change.

At the end of the session she says, "I'd just like you to have a think before our next meeting. If there are reasons other than your father's death that have brought you here."

She looks at me carefully. I think she already knows that there are.

3

Grace

It is a fifteen-minute drive to the Old Vic from school, not helped by a one-way system and a build-up of traffic on the road out of Clearwater. It is enough time for Grace to have called Anna's phone, leaving a message when it diverts straight to voice mail, and then for her head to be filled with a myriad of possible scenarios that explain Anna's disappearance.

She is relieved to have gotten away from the goggling eyes of the other mothers, whose stares she'd felt on her back as she retreated down the road. Clearly none of them wanted to go home or to work, not until they'd engaged in a bit more gossip as they hung outside the coffee van at the edge of the park opposite the school. And Grace is certain that she was as much the subject of their whispers as Anna.

There have been many mornings during the last three months when she has stood in the playground and wondered if they've also noticed the way the little group of women keep to themselves. She'd been so proud to tell the mothers, on Matilda's first day at St. Christopher's, that she'd known Anna since they were five and that they'd grown up together, and yet it quickly became embarrassing, the way Grace always ended up lingering on her own while Anna carried on with her clique.

"Surprise!" Grace had said when she'd seen Anna in the playground on that first day in September. Over Anna's shoulder she had seen the three women her friend had been talking to watching her with interest.

Grace's presence lost its novelty as the weeks wore on, Anna slowly peeling herself away to spend more time with Nancy, Rachel, and Caitlyn. That's why it was such a surprise when Anna had finally asked her out for the pre-Christmas drinks last night.

She turns left now at a mini roundabout, driving alongside the coast on her right and towards the Old Vic, which sits at the end of the road. Its car park is empty save for a beaten-up Escort that is parked across the gate to the backyard. She glances out her window at the pub, which is eerily quiet for what could be a crime scene. The thought makes her pulse jump erratically. It is the sight of such emptiness that gets her the most, Grace thinks as she climbs out of the car. Like no one else is worried enough about Anna's absence to want to look into what might have happened to her.

It is 8:59, hours since Anna was last seen, and yet no one is here asking questions of the landlord, combing for evidence or searching for DNA. Is it too early for the police to be involved? Is she worrying over nothing?

But then they say every minute counts in situations like this. It's hard to believe she shouldn't be concerned.

Now that she is here, the conversation she'd had earlier with Anna's friends plays out in her head. It is hard to know what they think has happened to Anna. Are they dissecting the night into tiny pieces as she has started to do? No doubt they are together right now, reliving what happened at the end of the evening. But what she can't stop wondering is whether they know more than they are telling her.

Whatever has happened to her friend, Grace knows that if she herself weren't at home by 8:59 the morning after a night out, she would hope to God that someone would have reported her missing. By now surely something has gone very wrong.

Beyond the car park and behind a wall, the sea laps rhythmically against the stony beach. Grace locks the car and wanders over.

To her right lie the cliffs. The whiteness of their face looks majestic against the dull gray sky today. From its peak it is the best spot to look down on Clearwater, to the maze of pathways that weave through the rows of terraces. She imagines how different it must look now, with the new housing estates a dusty red spot on the far side and the waterfront apartments a gleaming pinnacle on the outer edge.

Grace hasn't been to the cliffs since she returned; she shudders now as she tears her gaze away from them and looks down the stretch of beach. In the distance, a lone dog walker is throwing a stick on the otherwise empty shingle. There is nothing more to see from this point but the vastness of the water. In the summer it was always lit up with bright flashes of windsurfs and sailing boats, but today there is nothing. The sea is a steely blue merging into the grayness of the sky on the horizon. A cold wind is blowing.

Grace sighs as she turns and leans her back against the stone wall and looks at the Old Vic. There is nothing pretty about the waterfront area: a pub at the end of the road with a view of the sea sucked up by the wall barrier. And a café painted bright pink. There is so much that could be done here, she thinks, but no one has either the money or the inclination. It has often felt like Clearwater has been forgotten, the road its only link to Weymouth, predominantly carrying its residents to and from work.

She draws a deep breath and the coldness of the air brings pain to her lungs. Nancy's parting comment to her still stings: *I'm not being funny, but you haven't actually got any idea what Anna would or wouldn't do these days.*

Nancy is jealous of her. Even last night she had laughed as she'd said, "I suppose we'd better watch out, or you may try to zip Anna off to the other side of the world again." As soon as the words were out of her mouth her face had straightened, to make sure Grace knew she wasn't joking.

Grace doesn't like Nancy, either. She finds her overly assertive and controlling, not happy unless she's running the show. She reminds Grace of someone else they once knew, someone who Anna also got sucked into a friendship like this with, and that is what Grace had tried pointing out last night. Maybe she shouldn't have said anything, but it does worry her, seeing it happening again, because this is what Grace thinks *has* been happening. Maybe she should have tried to reach out further to Anna, to grab hold of her and pull her back. What if she has left it too late?

Grace makes her way back across the car park. She can hear noises from the backyard, bottles clanging together, and so she winds around the Escort and tries the catch on the side gate. It is locked, and so she hammers a fist against the rotting wood and calls out, "Hello? Is someone there?"

"Hello?" The voice is deep and gruff as the clanging stops.

"Can I have a quick word with you?" she shouts.

There's no response, but eventually footsteps approach the gate, a heavy bolt clanks aside, and the gate is opened. On the other side stands the barman she recognizes from the night before, wearing a T-shirt and shorts despite the cold. "Yeah?" he says, cocking his head, one hand holding the top of a black trash bag that looks as if it is about to rip under the pressure of its contents. "You left something behind?"

"Sorry?" she says, confused.

"You were here last night," he says. "I thought you must have left something."

"Oh. No." She shakes her head. "I just wondered if I could talk to you. About one of the women I was with."

He raises his eyebrows and lets out a chuckle. The man must be in his late twenties. He has a full beard and hair that is currently sticking up on top of his head. Last night she remembers finding him attractive, but this morning she can smell dry sweat and a tang of bad breath mixed with the rubbish from his bag. Grace has to stop herself from taking a step back. "What am I supposed to have done now?" he jokes.

"Nothing. I hope," she adds. "Because she's missing."

"Oh." His smile vanishes as he straightens himself up. "What do you mean, missing? Who are you talking about?" She can tell he is defensive by the rigidity of his body. His biceps harden as his grip tightens on the trash bag.

"My friend who was here last night with me. She hasn't come home and I'm worried about her. I wondered if you saw her leave or anything . . ." Grace drifts off, suddenly aware that maybe she shouldn't be speaking to him. If something serious has happened, something that isn't an accident, then she should be leaving it to the police to question potential witnesses.

"You were here with a few friends," he says. "Which one are you talking about?"

"Anna. She has blond hair, small, slim. She was ordering rounds of tequilas."

The barman nods but shrugs at the same time. "I don't know what you want me to tell you."

"I left earlier than any of them," Grace says. "And so I just wondered if you saw what happened to her at the end of the night. If you saw her get into a cab, or if she left before the others. I don't know," she says hopelessly, "anything."

"Well, they were here till late. One thirty, something like that, I reckon. Maybe even later. There was some kind of row breaking out between two of them, but I honestly can't tell you who. I'm pretty sure they all left at the same time, though. One of them called a taxi, and I know it turned up because I saw it out of the window. I was upstairs by then," he says, nodding above him. "That's where I live. So I've got no idea what happened when they went outside."

"But you're sure they were all still here?" Grace presses. "All four of them were here when the taxi arrived?"

He rubs his free hand across his face, his thumb and forefinger pressing into each cheek. "Yeah," he says eventually. "Yeah, they were all still here."

Grace takes a breath, holding it for a moment too long until she can feel the pressure. "Would anyone else have seen them?" she asks.

"I don't know; Mike might have," he says. "He was still clearing up when I went up."

"Who's Mike?"

"Young lad. Woking the bar too. Shaved head," he says.

"Okay." Grace nods. "Do you know how I might be able to talk to Mike?"

"He'll be back here later, sometime after three." The man pauses. "Shouldn't the police be doing this?" he says. "If your mate is missing."

"Yes. They probably should. Only I was here and I just wanted to ask around for myself. Thank you for your time."

"No problem." He turns and hauls his trash bag across the small backyard to drop it in the bin, wiping his hands on his pants as he heads back. "Hope she turns up."

"So do I," Grace says, backing away as he closes the gate.

She stands there for a moment, replaying their conversation. If the four of them were still here when the taxi was called, then Anna hadn't already left like Nancy had told her. There's no way they wouldn't have noticed that she wasn't in the taxi with them. And they'd omitted to tell her that there'd been an argument. Which makes her wonder why they are lying.

Her hands shake as she stuffs them into her pockets and returns to her car. She knows she should call the police, and yet the thought of handing the case over and sitting back fills her with impatience. Grace has always felt the need to confront a problem head-on, and so she already knows that she'll be questioning the women herself.

But for now, with the cliffs imposing against the skyline on her left, she cannot leave until she walks over and sees for herself that Anna isn't there.

Grace knows this area like the back of her hand. Even though she hadn't been anywhere near the cliffs until the previous night, she is standing at the foot of them as if she had never left.

There is a path that rises, at points meandering frighteningly close to the edge, where the cliff face lends itself to a steep drop. Halfway up it merges into trees, and what little light there is on a winter's day gets sucked away as soon as you reach them.

Crayne's Cliff is a beautiful spot, with its little sunken footpaths. And yet at the same time there is something sinister about its sheer drops that hide at night.

As a young child Grace walked the paths here many times, at first with her parents, clutching their hands just in case, always being tugged back if her mum thought they were even remotely close to the edge. Her dad would always say, "It's safe as long as you're careful."

She and Anna were barely thirteen when they'd been first dared to go there by themselves late at night. Both had shaken their heads vigorously. They weren't stupid; they knew the risks. Hadn't anyone heard of the boy whose bike had veered over the edge years ago?

It was a story they'd all been told, or so Grace thought, but then she'd looked it up once, much later, and had never been able to find any reference to the boy.

From then on Grace wondered if maybe it wasn't true, just something her mum had told her and Anna to deter them from taking risks. By then she was fifteen, and she no longer needed fairy tales to demonstrate how dangerous the cliffs could be.

She had her own story.

It's one that Anna knows, too. Which is why the thought that Anna could have stumbled along this treacherous path hours earlier, her body soaked with alcohol, with no light except for the moon, felt both ridiculous and very real at the same time. In her right mind, Anna wouldn't have dared come up here, Grace knows. But had she been in her right mind last night?

Grace carries on along the path, another memory from the evening digging sharply into her head. Anna had paused at the bar at one point and turned to Grace. "Why?" she'd asked.

"Why what?" Grace had replied.

"Why are you so desperate to speak to me alone?" Anna had beckoned the barman over and ordered another bottle of wine.

"I just want to check if you're okay," Grace had said. She *had* wanted to do that. Because for some reason she knew something wasn't right. So she'd wanted to check and maybe, more than that, she had just wanted to have Anna to herself for a moment. Without the other three around, answering for her, overtaking their conversation, reminding Grace that they supposedly knew Anna better than she did.

"*Are* you okay?" she'd asked when Anna didn't reply.

Anna had stared straight through her.

"I want to spend time with you, Anna," Grace went on. "Just the two of us, the way it used to be."

"It's been nineteen years, Grace," Anna had said. "I'm a different person now. You don't have any idea—" She had stopped abruptly.

"I don't have any idea about what?" Grace had asked, but Anna had shaken her head and turned back to the barman.

Grace had placed a hand on Anna's arm, to get her attention, to twist her back to face her. "I don't have any idea about what?" she'd repeated, a little firmer this time, because she needed to know what Anna wasn't telling her.

Anna had pulled her arm away and opened her mouth to speak, and Grace had looked closely into her friend's eyes and sworn that she saw tears. But then Caitlyn had appeared at the bar and asked,

"Need a hand?" and out of the corner of her eye Grace had caught Nancy watching them and imagined that Caitlyn had been sent to collect her.

Yes, nineteen years had passed. And of course their lives had changed. But when Grace moved back she'd been hoping to get close to Anna again. Yet now, when she looks back at the last three months, she can see that she'd been kept at arm's length, but whether it was Anna's doing, or the influence of her friends, she isn't so sure.

Now, as the wind picks up, she takes her gloves out of her pocket and slips them on, tugging her coat tighter around her. A knot of anxiety balls inside her. She should never have left the pub when she did, she thinks, as she strides out on the walk. And yet Anna hadn't tried to stop her when she'd called herself a taxi. Grace swore she had even noticed a flash of relief on her friend's face when she said she was going. A look that had made Grace shrivel inside and wish she had never agreed to leave.

She continues to walk, and the air seems tighter with each breath she takes. The slope inclines only gradually, and Grace is fit, but it isn't this that affects her breathing. The closer she gets to the tip of Crayne's Cliff, at its highest point just around the corner, the more she dreads what she might see.

She tells herself again that by now someone would have found Anna if she were splayed on the pebbles at the bottom of the cliff. But it is so quiet.

The wind is biting, still managing to pierce her ears under the rim of her woolly hat. She pulls it down tighter as she approaches the bend, all the time her heart beating rapidly.

Only she can't look. Because Grace knows all too well what the cliffs can do to someone. And if she looks and sees a flash of the red coat Anna was wearing last night, Grace knows her life will be changed forever. And the anticipation, the dread of what she might see, is too overpowering.

At the bend in the path, Grace stops. Her head is so consumed by the idea that Anna is lying beneath her that when she eventually leans forward and opens her eyes, it takes them a moment to adjust. She lets out her breath, scouring the beach one way, then the other, but there is no sign of Anna or her distinctive coat. No flash of color, nothing that shouldn't be down there. A wave of relief washes over Grace as she takes a step back. She holds a hand over her mouth, not realizing just how much she has been dreading seeing Anna below.

Eventually she steers herself away from the edge and turns on the path, her heart still racing as she heads back in the direction of her car. It is a relief not to have found Anna there, but she is still missing. As Grace paces, she makes a decision: she needs to talk to Ben Robinson.

October

Nine weeks earlier

Anna

I unbutton my jacket and slip it off, folding it and resting it on the arm of the sofa, though I keep pressing it down with one hand because there's some comfort in its familiar feel. It's almost like it anchors me, which sounds ridiculously dramatic but I can't explain the tightening I've had over the last few weeks, the spiraling, the sensation of losing little pieces of me.

I have told myself that if I am here I need to trust Sally, but I've never found it easy to trust people, not totally. There are things I don't share with anyone—not Ben, not Nancy or any of the others. I lost my ability to trust a long while ago, and if I am honest right now, there is only person I could talk to and that is Grace.

Would it make me feel better to talk—really talk—with Grace? This I don't know. Once I knew her better than I knew anyone, but it's been too many years, and so for now I find myself holding her at bay.

Sally wants to know how my week has been. It is an open-ended question that I know is intended to encourage me to talk about whatever is at the forefront of my mind. And the first thing that springs into my head is what happened six days ago.

I had been standing in the school hallway, sheets of A4 paper flapping in my hand as I reeled off the list of actions our small committee needed to complete for open school night in three days' time. This was the fourth year I'd been on the committee, so I knew well enough how much we had to get through before lunchtime, and as yet we'd barely gotten started.

Through the window I saw Grace scurrying across the playground. It was ten past nine, which meant she must have been late dropping off Matilda. Her face was creased into a frown and she only looked up at the last minute, catching my eye through the glass.

Everything okay? I mouthed.

Grace stopped, and I watched her release a deep sigh. I slipped away from the group and went out to join her. "Oh, it's just . . ." She flapped a hand in the air. "Graham," she said, "nothing new."

"What's happened?" I asked. Grace had talked about Graham in as much detail as I had about Ben: basics mainly, like where we met our prospective husbands, how long we'd been married.

She'd met him a decade earlier, a year after Ben and I got together. All of us met through work, though that was where the similarities stopped. Ben has nothing of Graham's ambition or success. He wouldn't dream of living most of the year in a different country, away from his wife and son, nor would I let him. The money that comes from a job that demands your life isn't important to either of us. And yet as far as I'd gathered, the setup worked for Grace and Graham.

But as we stood in the playground that morning, Grace was saying, "The man has no concept of doing what's right for his family. He's a selfish prick."

I could see a flash of hatred in her eyes, or something that resembled it.

"He hasn't seen Matilda in weeks," she went on.

"I'm so sorry. It must be hard, him living so far away. Can he not get the time off?"

"He could if he wanted to," Grace admitted flatly.

"Oh. I'm sorry, Grace," I said. "I never realized things were that bad."

Grace shrugged and looked away. "Anyway, what are you doing in here?" She gestured to the hall.

"It's for open school night on Friday. I'm helping out, so we're just getting together to see what needs to be done."

"That's good of you."

"Yeah, well, I like doing it." I smiled.

"Tell you what, why don't you come to my apartment after open school night?" she asked, her face brightening at the idea. "It would be good to chat. I can do some dinner, open a bottle of wine . . ."

My mind raced ahead to the plans I already had for Friday evening. Every year Nancy, Caitlyn, Rachel, and I go to Giovanni's for pizza after open school night. I was certain Nancy had already booked a table, and it was the first chance the four of us had to talk about our various summer holidays over some wine without the kids running about.

Grace was clasping her hands together, a smile broadening on her face. "To be honest, it would just be lovely to have someone to talk to, and we haven't properly had the chance yet," she was saying, and my stomach lurched at the prospect of letting her down. So I said, "Yeah, great. Why not?"

"Oh, I'm so pleased." Grace leaned forward and squeezed my arm. "It'll be like the old days. I can't wait."

I watched her leave the playground, trying to bat away the thought that I already knew I wouldn't go. Ben has told me before I make things harder for myself when I'm not honest up front, when I don't admit I already have other plans.

I should have suggested another night. I could even have asked her to come with us, and yet I'd done neither, and by Thursday I was still committed to being in two different places the following night, torn between what I thought I should do and what I actually wanted to do. And now I was burdened with both a heavy guilt that I was likely to let my oldest friend down and an annoyance that I'd found myself in this position in the first place.

That evening I called Grace and lied. I told her I was so sorry but Ben was going out and I needed to be home and so could we do it some other time? And then as soon as I hung up I tapped out a message to the girls asking them not to mention our pizza plans, and for the first time in a while I felt like I was back in school again.

"I can't imagine her finding out what I did," I say to Sally now. "I mean, I should have just gone to her place. Grace knows no one in Clearwater these days. I should have been there for her, but I chose the others."

"It sounds like you're beating yourself up about this decision, Anna. Maybe instead of doing that, you can focus on trying to understand why you made the decision you did. Why you didn't ask Grace to come with you?"

"I know that sounds a lot easier," I say.

"But it wouldn't be?"

I give my head a mild shake. Grace is always so keen to talk about our pasts, about our holidays as kids, our camping trips, how she often jokes that her mum thought she had two daughters. It only took a week for Nancy to comment that her incessant sharing was grating.

"You don't have anything in common," she said to me. "You must be able to see that."

It is true. I can see that we don't now we are adults, and Nancy is the one who knows me better than anyone now. She knows, and she also wonders why I am clinging to a friendship I had nineteen years ago. "You don't owe her anything," she has said to me.

As if she knows what I am thinking, Sally says, "Your relationship with Grace must be very different now from what it was when you were children. Do you maybe think you're both trying to find your places in each other's lives again?"

"Yes, I suppose we are. It *is* different. *We* are different to what we were."

Grace had everything I had wanted when we were children. I don't just mean *things*, but her home life and family, too. While she wanted for nothing, I was permanently looking for more. I wanted to be her once upon a time.

"I have everything I want now," I say to Sally. "And I don't think Grace does."

"Do you think there's any part of you that doesn't want to be reminded of the past, Anna?" Sally asks. She has put aside the blue-spotted notebook that is always open on her lap and looks as if she is frowning as she takes the Alice band out of her hair and then immediately pushes it back on her head. "And that being with Grace does that to you?"

I drag my jacket off the sofa and ball it in my lap again, running my fingers along its soft cotton. "Yes, I think you're right. I don't want to go back there."

"Is there any reason in particular?" she asks, and then, "I would like to understand more about your family, the lack of a mother figure in your life."

"No, there's nothing," I add, all too quickly, and even though this isn't true, it has nothing to do with my mother.

Sally chews on the corner of her lip and almost shrugs as she says, "How about you tell me a bit more about Ben before we finish today? I don't feel I know much about him yet."

I smile at the mention of my husband's name. "What do you want to know?"

"Anything at all you'd like to tell me."

"Ben's great. We have a good marriage," I say. "It's steady, we don't argue, we don't fight."

Sally doesn't respond, and I feel the need to go on. "Ben had a very different upbringing from me. His parents are still together and he has a sister he gets on with really well. It's like a Stepford family." I laugh. "It's kind of nice, though. It's what I always wanted to be part of: a perfect family unit. I'm comfortable. Maybe it sounds boring but . . ." I shrug.

"Not boring. There's a lot to be said for finding comfort in a relationship. Especially when everything else is unsettled. If Ben offers you stability, that's good. Have you spoken much to him about how you've been feeling, about the loss of your dad?" Sally asks.

I shake my head. "I don't think he'd necessarily understand," I say, and I can practically see her surprise at what might sound like a U-turn in an otherwise picture-perfect marriage. "My friend Nancy says my marriage is so easygoing," I tell her. "That's what Ben and I are like, we just—" I splay a hand and run it along an imaginary horizontal line. "We kind of float through."

"You don't think you could talk to him?"

I straighten awkwardly in the chair. "It's difficult to explain. We just—I just . . . I just haven't spoken to him." I don't add that I don't want to, but yet for reasons I can't explain to Sally right now, this is the case.

"Have you told Ben you're here today?" she asks.

I turn away and study the road beyond Sally's window. "No. He doesn't know," I admit. "No one does." I bite my lip, not wanting to turn back to see her expression. I'm ready to go now, our time is surely up.

"Anna, is there a reason you haven't told him?" she asks me, likely thinking that there is no good reason not to tell my husband when I am here because of my grief. But possibly Sally already knows this isn't true. And yet the truth is way worse than anything she could imagine.

4

Grace

It is 9:40. Just over eight hours since Anna was last seen. All Grace has managed to ascertain is that Anna and all three of her friends were still at the pub at the end of their evening, at the point when they called a taxi. But for some unfathomable reason, three of them left and made it home, while Anna didn't.

Grace climbs into her car, glancing back up at the cliffs and then to the shuttered-up Old Vic, and drives along the road that runs alongside the coast, glancing out the windows to each side as she goes. Hoping for what, she isn't quite sure, perhaps a flash of a red coat. Maybe a part of her thinks she'll see Anna sitting on the shingle beach, for whatever reason not wanting to go home, but safe.

Only there is no sign of her, and now Grace is approaching the mini roundabout and she needs to turn right to avoid the main road to Weymouth. But this isn't the way Anna would have walked if that is what she'd done last night. She would have taken the backstreets—the lanes you don't want to drive through unless you have to because they are so narrow, but are a shortcut if you're walking.

Anna could have taken any one of a number of routes back to her house. But Grace decides to drive the most direct route to the new estate where Anna lives, crawling as slowly as she can, peering out either side of the car until she is on Anna's road, and then pulling up outside the four-bed detached house that looks like every other one on the street.

The road is a perfect little cul-de-sac of houses, replicated across every other road in the near vicinity, save for a variety in the number of bedrooms. Some have three, a few even five, but the fact is it is easy to get lost around the roads because all the buildings look the same.

At first, a glimpse of her friend's car in the driveway startles her into thinking that Anna is home, but of course it means nothing. The curtains in the Robinsons' windows are all still drawn closed, and Grace imagines what Ben might be doing behind them—frantically pacing as he makes numerous phone calls, maybe? She wonders if he has made one to the police yet.

Grace doesn't know Ben well. He looks uncannily similar to the perfect ideal her sixteen-year-old best friend had hoped for in her future husband. She and Anna had once cut out pictures from magazines, their heartthrobs similar: dark hair and boyish Robbie Williams looks. Grace, on the other hand, ended up with a man who couldn't look less similar. With his gray hair receding at the temples from a young age, Graham hadn't reeled her in with his looks. Instead, she'd become more attracted to his caring and attentive maturity as she got to know him, though somehow even that had dwindled over the past few years.

Grace had been taken aback when she'd first seen Ben Robinson in the flesh. He was the epitome of tall, dark, and handsome, dwarfing Anna, who didn't even reach his shoulders. He had smiled broadly at Grace when they met, shaking her hand, a waft of something Hugo Boss–like drifting from him.

But here it is, three months on, and she knows little more about him other than that his family come from Cornwall, he has a job in

The Whispers

engineering that takes him to London once a month, and that while he and Anna couldn't have more children, Ethan is more than enough for him.

It is the little things that are missing, though, the things best friends should share. Grace has no idea what Ben does that annoys Anna, whether he clips his toenails in the bed or if he always falls asleep reading the news and she wakes up to find his iPad facedown on his stomach. And similarly, she has no idea of the good things: how supportive he was through Ethan's birth or whether he's any good at choosing birthday presents.

There are the deeper things, too, like what makes Ben tick, whether he truly makes Anna happy, or if there are things her friend isn't comfortable with that she might not have even shared with anyone.

Grace also knows Ben has just turned forty, because not that long ago he celebrated with a dinner party. Anna had taken her aside in the playground one morning, pretending to have a conversation about something else entirely when she'd dropped it in. "Oh, Ben's forty in two weeks, we're not really celebrating. All he wants is to have some friends over to dinner. God, Grace, I wish I could invite you, too, but it's Ben's thing, you know?"

Of course Grace understood, because she had only met Ben a total of three times, though it still hurt to learn that his only guests were Nancy, Caitlyn, Rachel, and their respective husbands. It bumped the women and their families into the inner depths of Anna's circle and reminded Grace that she now sat on its periphery.

She climbs out of the car and walks up the immaculately paved driveway. As she knocks on the front door she figures Ben must have been close by, because he opens it swiftly.

His eyes flicker over her with a passing confusion and then a release of breath, and Grace can tell two things. Firstly, that he hasn't immediately recognized her, but that when he does there is a flash of mild relief. As if maybe he has been expecting someone else at his door,

- 67 -

possibly the police, possibly with news he doesn't want to hear. And secondly, it means there is every reason to believe from his reaction that Anna is still not home. Ben's look of panic can only be attributed to him having no idea what has happened to his wife.

"Do you know . . . ?" He hesitates, as if he doesn't truly want the answer. "Do you know anything?" he finishes speedily.

Grace quickly shakes her head as he opens the door wider and steps aside.

"I had to come round—" She stops blindly, not knowing what to add. She had to come round and what? Tell him she is here to offer her support, or tell him the truth—that she wants to know whether he has called the police yet to report his wife missing?

The truth feels invasive, made harder by the fact she doesn't know him. But why shouldn't she be here? Grace is a concerned friend, looking for answers that she's sure others are holding back.

As she steps inside, Ben closes the door behind her and she follows him through the hallway, with its cream carpet and olive walls. Everything about their home is so new and finished. What it lacks in character it makes up for in the simple perfection that only new builds seem to pass off. There are photographs everywhere: of Ethan, of the three of them together. She can't escape their eyes watching her as she moves towards the kitchen at the back, passing the living room on her left.

There in the corner, a Christmas tree is haphazardly adorned with homemade decorations, a pile of wrapped presents beneath, and Grace imagines their Christmas mornings, all of them sitting around the tree in pajamas, opening their presents, a large turkey in the oven, preparing for the onslaught of guests. Is it his family or her friends that come?

Grace has a sudden image of this Christmas morning for them. One without Anna. She quickly turns away from the tree and sees Ben waiting for her in the doorway to the kitchen. Grace follows him into the room. In the middle of it an oak table is cluttered with books and felt tips and a Spiderman bowl filled with soggy Shreddies that give off a scent of stale milk. When Grace had been here before, everything had been tidied into the gray crates that sit in the Ikea bookcase, but today it looks like most of their contents have been tipped onto the table.

"I take it you haven't heard from Anna?" she asks as her eyes scan the kitchen. It feels strange that she could draw Anna's old childhood kitchen from memory, and yet this one feels like a stranger's. The photos that have been collaged into large white frames go some way to bringing life to the years Grace has missed, but she doesn't recognize many of the faces in them.

She watches Ben carefully for what his answers might hide.

He shakes his head as he stands awkwardly in front of her, his gaze penetrating hers. It gives her the impression that he doesn't particularly want her here. "No. And I can't get hold of her—her phone is off." His hand is brushing across the counter in frantic strokes. "Were you there?" He snaps his head up to look at her, as if this is the first time he has considered she might have been. "Were you there last night with Anna at the pub?"

Grace nods. "Yes, I was," she tells him, "but I left earlier than the others. I went home before midnight."

Ben rubs a hand across his face, the heel of his palm digging into his eyes. "Shit," he mutters as his gaze turns from her and drifts out to the back garden. He walks over to the glass door that leads out to the back and slams his palms against its pane. The thud makes Grace jump. When he eventually turns back to her his eyes are glassy, his fingers now drumming against his thighs. "I didn't know you were going. I thought it was just the four of them," he says. Taking a seat at the table, he sits down, steepling his hands in front of him and pressing his lips against them, and she wonders what difference this makes to him.

"What was she like last night?" he asks. "My wife? How was she behaving?"

Grace cocks her head. He has made the word "behaving" sound wrong, like whatever has happened to Anna is her fault.

"I just want to know," he says. "I mean, were they drunk? They all like a drink; I've seen it enough times. They manage to get the owners to lock them in after hours."

Grace tries to make sense of his words, his body language. He sounds more annoyed than concerned, she thinks.

"What was it like last night?" he asks her.

"They were all drinking," she admits, unsure what else he wants her to add.

"And Anna? Did she . . . ?" This time he doesn't finish the sentence.

"Did she what?" she asks.

"Did she talk to anyone else? Was there anyone you saw her with?" he asks, his palms slapping together as he spoke.

"You mean a man?"

"I don't know," he cries. "Yes. A man. Anyone. I just want to know what happened to my wife." With this he pushes his chair back again, stands up, but then seems unsure what to do next. He stands rooted to the spot, staring at her.

"No!" Grace shakes her head. "God, no. There was nothing like that." She wonders if he can really believe that another man had something to do with what has happened. "Is this why you haven't spoken to the police yet? Because you think she's with someone else?"

Ben releases a deep breath and ignores her question. She can see how much it is paining him to ask what his wife was up to last night, and for a moment she wonders if he hasn't been able to ask Nancy the same question. And though she shouldn't admit it, Grace feels pleased that he might not expect the same honesty as he seemingly does from her.

"There were no men. I didn't see her speaking to anyone else at all. I promise you."

Eventually Ben nods and lets out another breath, this one even deeper, so that his whole body deflates with it. "Then where the hell is she?" he says. "What's happened to her?"

"I don't know," Grace replies. "That's why we have to call the police."

"You're right," he says, though he makes no move to do so. Instead he says, "Last night, was she . . . ?" He pauses and frowns. "Was there anything about Anna that didn't seem right?"

There were plenty of things, Grace thinks, though she isn't sure what to tell him. Whether it's the fact Anna was off with her all evening and that it felt apparent from the outset she'd regretted inviting her. Or that by the end of the evening her attitude towards her friends had significantly cooled. Or that none of the others made an effort to include her, and Anna did nothing to change it. But she settles on telling him what she knows for a fact doesn't stack up. "I heard there was an argument between them at the end of the night," she says, "and while Nancy tells me Anna had already left, I know that's not true. Apparently they were all still there when the cab arrived."

"So they left her there?"

"It seems that way."

"But that's not what Nancy told me this morning."

"Nor me," Grace says. "But I don't think they're being truthful about what happened at the end of the evening. They were cagey with me at school this morning."

"This makes no sense. Why would Nancy tell me she thought Anna had left without telling any of them?"

Grace shakes her head. "I don't know, but I do know it's not true. I spoke to the barman this morning and he says they were all still there when a cab was called."

"You spoke to the barman?"

"Just now," she admits. "I went back there . . ." Her words fade as Ben continues to stare at her, his brow furrowed, his jaw set hard.

"Why did you do that?"

"Because . . ." She flings her arms up in the air, palms splayed upwards. "Because she hasn't come home, Ben. I'm worried about her. I want to know what happened."

"And you think I don't?" he says, his voice rising.

"No. Of course not. I'm just trying to help. I was trying to do something to find her."

He takes a step back, leaning against the sink as he shakes his head. "So what are you saying? That they all left together, or that Anna's friends left without her?"

"I honestly don't know what happened." She'd assumed the others must have left Anna there, but now that she thinks about it, she doesn't know this for sure. "But Nancy is telling us both a different story. I'm sorry, Ben, I have no idea why."

He turns round and grips the sink edge beside him. She thinks she can hear the beating of his heart, but then realizes it is her own.

Now he is letting go again and turning back to her, his eyes hollow and empty. *Pick up the phone*, she is silently urging him. *Just pick up the bloody phone and call the police before I do.*

"Why haven't you spoken to the police yet, Ben?" she asks. "You need to. They should be looking for Anna right now."

He nods slowly, as if considering the option, but then says, "Why do you think Nancy is lying to me?"

"I have no idea," she says again. She is getting impatient with him now. She'll get her own phone out and call them in front of him if she has to.

"If Nancy's lying, then she could be covering for Anna." He pauses. "Do you think they know where she is?"

"No." She screws her eyes up. "No, I don't actually think that—I don't know why they said what they did. I'm just saying their story doesn't add up."

Ben bites his bottom lip, his eyes narrowing. "*Was* Anna with anyone else last night?" he asks again.

"No," Grace exclaims, "she wasn't!"

He is watching her carefully, like he thinks she might suddenly back down and change her story.

This must account for his reluctance. Ben's so consumed by the thought that his wife is having an affair that he doesn't want to involve the police in his marital problems. Grace doesn't believe for one moment this is the case, but if Ben carries on along this line of thinking, then is he going to take seriously the fact Anna is missing?

She hadn't considered that Anna's friends' aloofness this morning was because they were covering up for her. Grace's theories about why the friends are lying have been far more sinister, she thinks. But what is their reasoning, exactly? That one of them is aware of Anna's fate? That one of them is responsible for it? Is this really what she believes is possible?

It seems far-fetched, but it happens. It is not unheard of.

"I don't know what's gone on," Grace says firmly, "but Anna wasn't with anyone at all. From what I saw of her—and *everything* I know of her—she would never do that," she says.

He gives her a look, as if he is about to iterate Nancy's words, that Grace doesn't know Anna anymore—but in Ben's defense, he doesn't actually utter them.

"You need to call the police," she says more softly now.

"I know, I was about to . . ." He looks up and catches her eye briefly before he rapidly averts his gaze.

"The sooner they know, the quicker they can start looking for her," she presses.

"I know. I'll do it."

But still he doesn't make any move to get his phone, and now

Grace can feel her frustration with him turning into anger. She begins to wonder what their marriage is like behind closed doors.

On the three occasions she has seen them together, they looked blissfully happy. Anna had spoken about how they spend all their weekends together as a family, except for when Ben plays golf once a month. Grace had watched the way her friend ran her hands up and down his arm when she spoke to him—tenderly, it seemed. Anna had certainly made it appear as though their lives were perfect, so far stretched from the life she shares with Graham. But when Grace had commented on their happiness, Anna has shrugged it off like it was nothing, as if she were taking it all for granted, and at the time Grace had left their house feeling an unwanted resentment. She would never utter a word of that to anyone, of course, could never admit to feeling jealous of a friend, because who would do that?

But then what if she'd read Anna wrong? Grace knows that people don't always tell you everything. She only has to look at her own marriage to see that. And now she wonders if there is another side to Ben, too.

"I know what the police will say," he says. His shoulders are hunched and she can see the way the muscles in his arms have tightened through his shirt. "When I tell them my wife hasn't returned home from a night out with her friends. It's not even ten in the morning. They'll tell me it's too early to be looking for her, that she'll come home of her own accord."

"She wouldn't do that," Grace says.

Though really, how would she know? The only boyfriend Grace had ever known Anna to have was Kevin Winter, and just because Anna was distraught when she found out Kevin had snogged some girl called Yasmin from the year above, it didn't mean she'd never do the same. What if this wasn't the first time Anna hadn't gone home?

"Has she done it before?" she asks Ben now.

"No," he says. "Christ, no, of course she hasn't. She's never done anything like this in her life." He stares and shakes his head, rubbing the heel of his hand so roughly against his chin she can hear the scratch of his stubble. Grace tries to work out whether he is holding anything back or not, but it is impossible to know.

"Then why do you think she's capable of doing it now?"

"I don't—" He breaks off, covering his face with his hands so even though she can't see it, she can hear that he's talking through gritted teeth. Eventually his shoulders drop, along with his arms, and she can almost feel him sinking, though the rest of his body doesn't move. There seems to be a myriad of thoughts going through his head as he's trying to deal with the notion that his wife might have been unfaithful. "I don't know," he says, his voice a notch quieter. "I don't know that she's been honest with me lately." He digs into his pocket and takes out a piece of paper, folding it over in his hands as he stares at it intently. Eventually he passes it to Grace.

On it there is an address for a road in Weymouth. "What is this?" she asks. "Who's Sally Parkinson?"

"A therapist. Anna's been seeing her for months. I've only known since last week."

"Why?"

Ben shrugs. "I have no idea."

"Well, what did she tell you?"

"I didn't ask her." He lets out a small laugh. "She never told me about this; I just found out." He takes the piece of paper from Grace and screws it up in his hand.

"How?"

Ben narrows his eyes, looking sheepish. "I found this in her purse. I wasn't looking for it or anything—" He cuts off sharply. Grace thinks that he might not have been looking for that in particular, but he must have been snooping for a reason, and so why was that?

"Why the hell didn't I ask?" he is saying. "If I had, I might know what's been going on with her lately."

"Why didn't you?" she asks quietly.

Ben shrugs. "Because . . . I don't know . . . I just didn't find the right time to bring it up. Maybe I didn't want to know the answer?"

"Listen," Grace says, "whatever you think Anna may or may not be capable of, the fact is she is missing. And you can't not report it. If she *has* gone off with someone else, you'll find out soon enough, but I don't believe she has. And so what if something else has happened?"

"I know."

"Then come on. Let's call the police now." She takes her phone out of her coat pocket. "I'll dial the number, but I still think you need to speak to—"

"No!" Ben swings round and reaches out for her phone.

"What are you doing?" Grace pulls it back.

"I told you I'll call them and I will. Just let me do it," he says, his eyes shining brightly as they fix on hers. "Please. Let me do it when I'm on my own."

Grace nods and reluctantly puts her phone back in her pocket. "Okay."

"Thank you," he says. "I didn't mean to . . . you know. I'm sorry. This morning has just been horrendous."

"It's fine."

"I just don't like the thought of the conversation. They'll suggest it's my fault she hasn't come home. They'll assume we've had some argument."

Grace nods again, slowly. *Have you?* she thinks.

"We haven't," he adds quickly, with a hint of irritation as if reading her thoughts. "But you can see what I mean; it's only what you're thinking."

"No I wasn't," Grace lies. "It'll be fine, Ben. It just needs to be done."

When Ben doesn't answer, she knows she has no choice but to leave him to it, even though a large part of her doubts he is going to do what he says he will.

"Is there anything I can do for you?" Grace asks.

"You can tell me what the hell I say to my son," he says sadly. "If I have to pick him up from school tonight and his mum's still not home, then what do I tell Ethan?"

"I don't know," Grace admits. It's a sickening thought that it might come to that. "If you want, I could pick him up? He can come home with me, have tea with Matilda."

When Ben doesn't answer, Grace goes on, "Let me do that anyway. I'll pick him up and then one way or another you have some time with Anna or . . ." She trails off. Or what? Sit with the police while they try to find his wife? Or worse, they know where she is but he's going to need that time to work out how to tell his son that his mother is dead?

Grace shudders. But of course she knows it's a possibility because she remembers what it is like to get a call from the police when someone is missing. The detectives will want to know what she knows, along with everyone else. The whole town will be mad with panic. She knows, because it happened once before.

Grace remembers her mum tightly clutching both her and Anna, who was at their house as usual. Catherine's fingers gripped into her skin as she held both girls close, while the young policeman with the bushy eyebrows had stood on their doorstep and told them that their friend Heather Kerr hadn't come home.

But Heather was only a child, and the police were doing everything they could as soon as Heather's foster mother had raised the alarm that her fourteen-year-old daughter wasn't in the house. Would they do the same for Anna? Just because she isn't a child doesn't mean she isn't in danger.

Ben agrees to let Grace pick Ethan up from school, and she's pleased to have him. Even though Anna isn't here right now, in some ways it feels like the closest she's been to her friend's family since she returned in September.

"Will you let me know as soon as you hear anything?" she asks, pausing as she leaves the kitchen, her attention drawn to the to-do list pinned up high on a corkboard.

Order E Lego from Amazon.
Make Xmas Eve box—buy pajamas from M&S.

The note jolts Grace. So Anna has followed Grace's mum's Christmas Eve box tradition for Ethan, just as Grace has with Matilda. It is a thought that warms her—her friend is still living their past Christmases through her new family—but the warmth quickly dissipates as she wonders that this isn't the list of someone who has left on purpose.

"I will," Ben is saying to her. "And thank you, you know, for having Ethan. I appreciate it."

"It's the least I can do," Grace says. "We *will* find her," she adds.

October

Seven weeks earlier

Anna

"We've heard from the adoption agency this week," I tell Sally. "There've been some issues with Zadie's maternal grandparents standing in the way, but they're hoping things can start moving again now. There's a chance we might have her by Christmas."

"Anna, that's brilliant news," she says.

I nod. My thumbnail has found its way to my mouth and I start chewing on a loose bit of skin. This time I have an overwhelming need to show Sally Zadie's picture, and so I fish out the photo and pass it to her.

"She's adorable."

"She really is," I say, and I feel the tears welling up in my eyes at the prospect that this might actually be happening soon. Ben and I have been picking out paint colors for what will be her bedroom. My Amazon basket is stuffed with little pink accessories, gifts that I am ready to press the button on ordering for her.

"Nancy says I'm born to be a mother. That I need more children in my life. She's the only one who knows the adoption might be imminent."

"You must be very happy with the news about Zadie?" Sally says.

"Of course," I tell her, though in truth I feel sick at the thought of it not happening. That something could stop us from getting the child that I already think of as my own.

I force myself to let go of the frown I can feel creasing my forehead. Nancy is always telling me to stop frowning, that I'm giving myself lines I don't want. I can almost feel the press of my friend's fingertips as they flatten my skin, then pinch up my lips at the corner to turn them into a smile. By instinct my lips twitch now.

"What is it?" Sally is asking. She is smiling too, no doubt thinking I have some funny story to tell her, but I don't. Recently all I've been doing is worrying over Zadie and what might go wrong. I've been tying myself in knots over it.

"What if it doesn't happen?" I blurt. "What if I don't get her?"

"Why do you think that's a possibility, Anna?"

I sigh and turn to look out of the window. My heart is skipping in little jumps. Its beat is erratic, and in turn that makes me feel more on edge. It's nothing new, this feeling, it's been with me for a while now.

"Everything is unsettled," I say. "It makes me anxious."

Sally is nodding, her palms splayed on the notebook that is open on her lap. She begins to tell me that grief can do this to you, but my mind isn't on my dad. It is on what happened in the playground yesterday when Nancy stood massaging the knot in my shoulders and Grace walked over.

Ethan was tugging on my arm to get my attention, telling me he needed his water bottle, while Nancy was digging the heels of her hands into my back—"releasing a tough spot," she was telling me.

I spotted Grace as soon as she entered the school gates. She held up her hand in an awkward semi-wave, as if she were apprehensive about coming over. I wondered if she were as apprehensive as I was though. It was getting to the point that I no longer liked drop-offs.

Now, whenever Grace wandered over to us, I felt the tension in the air and I knew I was caught in the middle of it.

"I haven't seen you in ages," she said, her eyes drifting to Nancy's hands as they kneaded my back.

"I've been so busy lately," I apologized, flapping a hand in the air, arching forward in the hope Nancy might stop.

Grace's mouth flattened into a small smile and I immediately felt guilty. Always so guilty. Lately I was spending all my time feeling like everything I did was wrong.

"Maybe we could catch up this weekend?" she said. "Could we do something together, with Ethan and Matilda?" Her gaze flicked to Caitlyn and Rachel, who stood beside me. She seemed nervous, like she had no right asking for my time, and now I had to let her down again because it was Ben's birthday.

"I can't, I'm so sorry. It's Ben's fortieth . . ."

"Oh. No worries." Grace smiled again and brushed her hand through the air.

I knew she was waiting for me to tell her what we were doing and so I said, "We haven't planned much, just a small dinner party." It didn't help that my *small dinner party* included the other three women who were standing with us.

I tried catching Rachel's eye—she was the only one who was looking in my direction—willing her not to speak, and was about to change the conversation, when Nancy laughed.

"Haven't planned much? It's all you've both been going on about for the last however many weeks!" She released her hands from my tight muscles. "And it's going to be perfect for him," she said as she came next to me and squeezed me into her side.

I wanted the playground to swallow me up. I knew what Nancy was saying—she understood all too well how panicked I was over cooking a four-course meal; she was trying to make me feel better. Only, after her words, Grace's expression was no longer one of forgiving generosity. Her face was blank and closed off as she turned to look over her shoulder, back to the playground, making a pretense of searching out her daughter.

"Grace, I wish I could have invited you too, but it's Ben birthday—"

"Oh, don't be so silly, of course you can't," Grace said, turning back to me, smiling again. "He doesn't even know me."

Sometimes I wished Grace would just come out and say exactly what she was thinking. In fact, many times I thought it would be better if we could all be more honest instead of dancing around our fears and anxieties and dislikes. Right then, her pretending not to care when she so clearly did, only made me feel worse.

"Tell you what," Grace said, "why don't you come over for dinner one night next week? I'll do macaroni cheese," she said.

"Macaroni cheese?" Rachel asked.

"Anna's favorite when we were teenagers," Grace told her. "She made me make it for her all the time, didn't you?"

"That would be lovely, thank you."

Grace carried on smiling, but I saw the way her eyes lingered on Nancy's arm, which was hung around my shoulder, and I could see the smile fading.

I wanted to shake off Nancy's arm, pry it off me. But I managed only to stand frozen to the spot.

What I really wanted was to walk away from all of them, because even this short exchange was draining me. Everything felt fake. None of it real. None of it right.

At last Grace made an excuse and wandered off to find her daughter. Nancy's arm squeezed me tighter before she eventually took it away and stuffed her hands into her pocket. "What was all that about?" she asked.

"All what about?" I shrugged.

"You made her invite sound anything but lovely."

"No I didn't."

"Yes you did." She paused. "Anna, if you don't want to go, then don't go."

Next to us Rachel was swearing that she didn't realize the time and she was going to be late for work. She quickly raced off across the playground, leaving only Caitlyn lingering, although she had stepped back from Nancy and me.

"Of course I want to go," I said.

Nancy pursed her lips, her eyes widening. "Well, I don't think you do," she told me, and finally I looked away from her, because right then I really didn't want to be having this conversation.

Today the rain splatters against Sally's windowpane in tiny droplets. It means I can't see the road as clearly as usual. Every so often a flash of an umbrella appears, whoever is underneath it scurrying past until they are out of sight.

I like staring out Sally's window and people-watching on the unfamiliar street; today, with my view blurred, even the rhythmic patter of rain is calming.

Sometimes the hour-long sessions with Sally are a tonic in themselves—just to take the time out and sit here with nothing else to focus on but myself. She isn't pushing me, but I often wonder if she thinks I'm wasting my money when I'm only prepared to open up halfway.

"I want it all to go away," I admit.

"For what to go away?"

I give a slight shrug. "I don't feel like myself. I don't want to be standing in the playground feeling anxious. I'm beginning to dread the school run."

I am pushing Grace to the outer edges of my life. She must know I am I doing it, too. I can hear her saying, *Do you not need me anymore, Anna?*

I did once. I needed Grace more than anything when we were young. Even more so when I was a teenager, before she was ripped away from me. But I *don't* need her any longer. I don't need *anyone*.

I pull myself together, inhaling deeply. "Anyway, Nancy says I shouldn't feel guilty about the party. Grace doesn't even know Ben, not like they all do." I look to Sally for a response.

"But you do feel guilty?" she asks.

"All the bloody time."

Sally smiles. "I think you need to stop beating yourself up. You're all adults now, and all you can do is what feels right for you. But Anna"—she presses forward in her chair—"if you're not seeing Grace because Nancy doesn't like her . . ." She lets the suggestion hang.

I feel the itch getting under my fingernails, spreading into my hands until they tingle. This deep need to talk to Sally, to try to explain.

Instead I say, "That's not it at all." And now, as quickly as that, I don't want to talk about Nancy any longer. Or Grace. And so I change the subject completely. "You've asked me about my mother," I say.

"I have." Sally nods encouragingly. "I'd be interested to talk about her with you."

"I have no interest in talking about her," I mutter, which is half-true. I understand the irony when I mentioned her in the first place, but I suppose she's been there in the back of my head since my dad started talking right before he died.

"Could you tell me what happened?"

"There's nothing much to say." I pause and think about my father's words, how he filled in some of the gaps for me. "She walked out when I was four years old and never came back. We didn't see her again. One day she was there, and the next she was gone."

"That must have been an extremely difficult thing to deal with."

I shrug. I remember the time in patches, and wonder what is a true memory and what I have since made up. Like the smell of talcum powder that always triggers a vivid image of my mum in my head, the feel of her hair, her smell.

What I do know for certain is that in the days after my mother walked out, I stood in the front garden and waited by the gate. Always looking up the road, waiting to see a flash of the bright coat she would wear as she turned the corner and came into sight.

And then one day I didn't wait. And after that I never waited again.

"Have you ever tried looking for your mum?" Sally asks.

I shake my head. My dad never spoke to me about her when I was younger. His way of surviving was to almost pretend it never happened, like she was never there in the first place. "Dad tried to erase her from our lives, and I kind of accepted it because I was so young. But I felt her absence in the little things that mums do, like coming to watch my ballet, or the Easter egg hunts and Christmas Eve boxes that Catherine always did for me.

"A month before he died, Dad told me he always expected she would leave one day. Apparently, she was always threatening it when things went wrong and she couldn't cope. He told me it was easier when she finally went because he didn't want her dipping in and out of my life when it suited her. He didn't have to worry about the worst happening, because by then it already had." I suck in a deep breath before adding, "He kept tabs on her sporadically through someone they both knew. She had another child, he believed, another family, but I don't know what became of them.

"She died five years ago," I tell Sally. "So now I never can ask her how she could have left me. Because a mother doesn't do that, does she? After Ethan was born, I knew I'd never be able to forgive her for what she'd done. Nothing excuses it, does it? Not one reason on earth can justify you walking out on your child."

5

Grace

Grace leaves Ben's house and climbs into her car. She can see him watching her through a slit in his curtains. He is pulling them aside and peering through the gap. He won't call the police. She knows this by the way he has ushered her out of his house, how he questioned her about other men and how the thoughts of what questions would be fired at him are as much of a deterrent.

She pulls out her phone and stares at its screen. If this is the case, she needs to call them herself.

When she glances back at the window Ben has vanished and the curtain has been dropped into place. Possibly she should give him a chance to do what he's promised, though she has every desire to take control of the situation, rather than leave it to him and Anna's three friends, who are no doubt together still. She wonders how much they are telling one another their own truths right now, if they all know exactly what the others know, or if they are merely dancing around their own versions of a story.

Her thumb rolls down the screen of her phone, tracing over its contacts as she starts the engine. Grace has Nancy's number, Rachel's and Caitlyn's, too. All of them were added at the start of term when she joined the year-four WhatsApp group.

The thought of them all huddled together, sharing and plotting, knowing more than she does, tugs at her. She hovers over the number for Caitlyn, the one woman out of the group she is most likely to get the truth from, and before thinking about what she is doing, taps the call button. The phone diverts to the car speaker and Grace rests her head back as she listens to the ring tone and then the answer message click on. She hangs up, cradling the phone in her lap before she tries Caitlyn again. But once more it rings out. She imagines the panic on the woman's face as Grace's name flashes up on her phone. Is she too nervous to pick up? Maybe she even has Nancy lingering over her shoulder, telling her to disconnect the call.

But Grace needs answers. Ben has nothing to give her; Caitlyn isn't answering her. With every door that closes she is getting more panicked that the people close to Anna are hiding something.

She scrolls through her phone again and presses on Rachel's number now, but this time it doesn't even ring before going straight to voice mail. Which leaves only one option: Nancy Simpson.

Grace hesitates. Nancy is the last of the three she wants to talk to, and yet if any of those women know more than they are telling her, she needs to get it out of them. She is about to press the number when the phone ringing startles her: Graham's name flashes up on the satnav screen. Grace taps to answer it.

"Hello," she says curtly. Graham hasn't called her in—she counts out the days in her mind—what is it now, four of them?

"Hello, my love," he says, his voice smooth as it fills the line. She had once found it sexy, but now it sounds weak and pathetic, and does nothing more than irritate her. "How are you?"

"Matilda is good," Grace says. How is his daughter not the first thing he asks about?

"Good. That's good. Sorry I didn't manage to call you back the other night," he replies as she shifts on her seat, flicking on the indicator, ready to drive away. "I'm trying to figure out when I can next get back." There's a pause. "It might not be until the twenty-third now."

"Two days before Christmas?" she mutters. She'd laugh out loud if there was anything remotely funny about it.

"Yes. I'm so sorry; you know I want to be there sooner, but there's a major crisis going on here. Everything's hit the fan at the same time, and I can't even rely on half the guys to—"

Grace's mind cuts out his voice as she shakes her head and starts driving, focusing on how to get out of the labyrinth of roads that lie ahead and make her way to the police station. She doesn't believe Ben will call them, and if she cannot get some answers from the women, she will go to the police herself.

As Graham's voice continues to drone through the car stereo, Grace's muscles clench so tightly she can feel them burning.

"You know, I can't believe you would do this to us," she says finally. "Matilda is eight, she's excited to see you, and you can't even be bothered to make an effort at Christmas? I am doing everything for this family, Graham. Everything. Do you have any idea how this is making me feel? Like you don't actually want to be with us." Her voice is rising into a crescendo.

"Grace," he says, and she swears she can hear him sighing. "Don't keep doing this. I'm trying to get back sooner."

"Don't keep doing what, Graham? Asking you to spend time with your family?"

"Don't keep blaming me."

His tone has dropped, it is flat now, the way most of their conversations go, and even though she doesn't think she has gone too far, he always makes her end up feeling like she has.

Her hands are clenched into fists as they wrap around the steering wheel. "I could do with you here for me right now," she says.

"Why, what's going on?" he asks.

"Anna has disappeared," she says sharply.

"What? How do you mean?"

"She's missing, is what I mean. We went out last night with three of her other friends and she hasn't come home this morning."

"Grace, why didn't you tell me?"

She shakes her head, resisting an urge to laugh. And when, exactly, was she supposed to do that? Besides, she already knows she won't get any comfort from telling Graham.

"Grace?" he is asking.

"I'm just trying to deal with it all," she says. "Her husband hasn't rung the police, and her friends are lying about what happened at the end of the night, and so basically I feel like I'm the only one who wants to find her right now." The words tumble out in one long stream.

"Jesus," he says, at least having the presence of mind to sound shocked. "Have *you* spoken to the police?"

"Not yet."

"Woah. Christ, I think you should, Grace. I mean, if he isn't stepping up, then you need to." He is attempting to be assertive, and she assumes this is partly because having something else to focus on gets him off the hook for his latest announcement, gives him a problem to deal with that isn't his fault. "God, how awful," he says. "You must be so worried. And you have no idea what might have happened to her?"

Grace sighs. "No. I have no idea at all." She squints at the name on a road sign and turns right.

"Do you think she's done this of her own accord? That she's, you know, somewhere she shouldn't be?" Graham asks.

"No. I don't think that. She has an eight-year-old son," Grace snaps, half to make the point that decent people don't leave their children for any amount of time. "Anna isn't selfish."

"So maybe she's had an accident?"

"Yes. Maybe." She now regrets telling him because she has opened up a dialogue she doesn't want to have with the man who continues to let her down.

At the end of the road Grace notices she has taken a wrong turn and slams her fist against the steering wheel as she switches the map back on to the screen and squints at the tiny picture of the tangled web of roads. It isn't until she has made another right turn that she recognizes the road as Rachel's; she'd driven here once before when Rachel's son had accidentally put Matilda's sweater in his schoolbag. The house is farther up on the left, somewhere past the post box, and as she drives closer she sees Nancy's ugly gray Land Rover parked up ahead.

"I have to go," she says, pulling up to the curb and turning off the engine. She can feel her pulse racing as she contemplates walking up Rachel's path and ringing the doorbell.

"Of course." Graham sounds relieved. "Will you let me know as soon as you hear anything about Anna? If you can't get hold of me, just drop me a text."

"Drop you a text?" This time she does laugh aloud. "I've just told you my best friend is missing and you can't even be bothered to pick up the phone if there's any news?" She can picture herself having to write out the message—*Anna's been found dead, by the way. Hope your meetings are going well*—and wonders if he'd bother to extract himself from one of those meetings to call her back.

"That's not it," he says, sounding irritated now. "I'm just having this headache of a problem at the moment and I'm in and out of meetings and calls; but of course, ring me, I'll do everything I can—"

Grace hangs up before she can respond. He'll do everything he can—to what, to take her call? Her marriage has become a series of short phone calls, excuses and postponed visits home, and right now she doesn't need to feel any more alone. Finding Anna is more important than saving her marriage. If she has her best friend in her life again, perhaps she can even begin to cope with Graham's absence from it.

She switches off the engine, still furious with her husband. Grace had every intention of driving straight to the police station, but now she is here and she knows Caitlyn is likely in there too, and if she turns up on the doorstep they have no option but to confront her.

Eventually she opens the car door and steps out onto the quiet street. They live so close—Anna, Rachel, and Nancy—that it makes it all the more odd that Anna didn't come home with them last night, and whatever Graces fears about facing the women, she knows she has no choice.

A group of mothers had splintered off after drop-off and had been stand-ing outside the coffee van opposite the school for over an hour. Their con-versations meandered into schoolwork and reading levels, families, and Christmas. They commented that they wished they'd organized a party for the children themselves when they gathered Anna wasn't going to do it this year, for whatever reason. And then they wondered why she hadn't. It was unusual for her not to have even taken an interest as she always had; there had been something a little distant about Anna lately.

Wherever their conversation strayed, they kept coming back to Anna's disappearance and what might have happened to her, and how there was something odd about this town, no matter what anyone said. How it often felt so cut off from the rest of the world with its one road the only way in or out.

"I couldn't believe the way the two of them were at the school gates that time a few weeks ago," one of them commented.

"Anna?" one of the mothers questioned.

"Yes. And Nancy," she said. "Did you not see them?"

"I heard them," someone else confirmed. Never before had she wit-nessed the two women going at each other the way they had; they had

always been so tight. "It all started with Nancy asking her what had happened at Ben's party, whatever it was, demanding Anna tell her. That she
had a right to know."

"That sounds very pushy," one mum said. Nancy was a strong woman,
she had always thought. You only had to look at the way she held herself as
she walked to know she didn't stand for much nonsense, but she had never
heard her talk to anyone like this.

"I know, right? She said Anna wasn't being a good friend to her. Anna
was in a bit of a state, to be honest, talking back at her, but she looked
pretty drained, if you ask me."

"I imagine she was trying to placate her," someone else added. "You
know, I overheard Nancy saying that she couldn't believe Anna was putting someone else before her? I wanted to ask Anna if she was all right, but
by the time they got to the classroom it was like nothing had ever happened
between them."

"Who was Nancy talking about, then?" someone asked.

"I assume she meant Grace Goodwin. I mean, she clearly doesn't like
the woman. She doesn't have any time for her. Not in the playground, at
least."

There was a collective shaking of heads before another asked, "Do you
think she's jealous of Grace?"

"For what?"

"Living in the Waterview apartments, for a start. Don't you remember
we saw Nancy viewing the showroom when they were first built? She was
desperate to move into one, but I don't think she and her husband could
afford it."

"I don't see how anyone can be jealous of Grace when she doesn't have a
husband around. And you know what I think of Eric. Nancy's husband is
drop-dead gorgeous!" one joked. "What I wouldn't do to have him around
the house!"

"I feel for Grace. None of the group has much time for her. Not even
Anna anymore, and you can see how keen Grace is to be friends with her.

She's often standing on her own at pickup while those four are lingering by the gates till the last minute. I always got the impression they didn't want any of us to join in their conversations."

"So what do you reckon happened to make Nancy tell Anna that she was putting Grace before her?"

"I don't know. But Grace and Anna have so much history. Something must have put Nancy's nose out of joint."

6

Grace

Grace had never intended to end up on Rachel's doorstep, but now she is here, then of course she needs to speak to them. She presses her finger on the doorbell for a little longer than normal, and when Rachel opens the door her expression is at first quizzical and then mildly irritated. "Oh, Grace," she declares.

"I was just on my way back from Ben's house," she says, "and so was passing your road." She waves a hand in the direction she'd just come. "I saw the cars here." Grace pauses and waits for Rachel to say something. When she doesn't, she asks, "Is it okay if I come in?"

Rachel hesitates and eventually says, "Yes," but doesn't move. Then she adds, mumbling, "Yes, sorry, of course," and finally pushes the door open farther as she stands to one side.

"I've spoken to Ben," Grace says as she steps into the hallway. "He's contacting the police." She looks at Rachel for a reaction, but the woman's face is completely blank and just as pale as it had been at the school gates earlier.

"Good." Rachel nods. "I'm pleased he is. I mean—" She breaks off and looks at her watch. "It's been hours since anyone saw her. I know we would have heard from her by now if she'd . . . if she was . . ." She can't seem to find the words she wants. "You know what I mean."

"If she'd gone somewhere of her own accord?"

"Exactly." As Grace looks more closely at Rachel, she can see her skin is quite gray. Faint smudges of mascara are smeared under her eyes where she hadn't washed it off properly. "You'll have to excuse me," Rachel says. "I drank too much last night." She holds a hand over her mouth, and Grace wonders again if she's about to be sick. Rachel's eyes widen as she nods towards the door to her kitchen. "The girls are in there. Go on through, I'll be with you in a minute."

Rachel dives into the downstairs bathroom, leaving Grace standing in the middle of the hallway. She hasn't been inside Rachel's house before, only as far as the front door. The walls are decorated with the odd piece of art, which are no more than splashes of color on canvases, something Grace never has been able to see the appeal of. Each of them has a sprig of tinsel draped over the top, but there is no other sign in the house that Christmas is round the corner.

Grace glances around, looking for what, she isn't sure. Maybe something that will tell her what kind of person Rachel is, whether she can trust her. But there is nothing that gives Grace a deeper impression of the woman, and so eventually she heads towards the open door that leads into an immaculate kitchen as bare and clinical as the hallway.

Nancy and Caitlyn are sitting at a table, nursing cups of coffee. They both look up as she walks in, and for a moment neither of them speaks. Already Grace knows she isn't welcome, that her arrival has put them on edge, but however telling that might be, it doesn't override the feeling of awkwardness that soars through her.

Nancy is gathering herself together now. "Grace, come in, have a seat," she says coolly. She stands as she waves to a spare chair. "Would you like a coffee?" She is already sauntering to the cupboard, where she takes out a coffee cup and switches on the kettle as if she were in her own home.

Grace is taken aback by Nancy's sudden show of hospitality and wonders if she is doing this on purpose. She cannot help but question every one of the woman's actions, certain they are a pretense to hide an ulterior motive, and no doubt she is trying to lull Grace into a false sense of security.

In contrast, Caitlyn remains at the table, playing with her coffee cup, her gaze flicking between Grace and Nancy as if she doesn't know where to look.

"Oh good, you're making coffee, Nance," Rachel says, still pale as she comes into the room and allows her friend to carry on shuffling around her kitchen.

Grace has never had friends like this as an adult, ones who make themselves comfortable in each other's kitchens and help themselves to coffee. She wants it, she realizes, this thing she has never had. This closeness she would surely have had with Anna if she'd never moved away. It is another stark reminder of these women's friendships and how she stands little chance of dividing them if she has to, if it comes to the point she needs one of them to tell her some truths.

"So Ben's talking to the police," Rachel says to none of them in particular as she folds her hands around her mug, looking at Grace, then the others. "That means they'll want to speak to us."

"Oh God," Caitlyn exclaims as she looks at Grace too. "I mean, I know it's the right thing, but . . ." she adds quickly. "It's just . . ." Again she doesn't finish her sentence. "How do you know, have you been to see him?" she finally finishes.

Grace nods. "I've just been with him. He was calling them when I left." There is no harm in letting them think she believes this, because either way she's heading straight to the station herself when she leaves.

"What are they going to want to know?" Caitlyn asks. Her face is taut with panic.

Grace glances at Nancy, whose back is to her as she finishes making the coffee, although it's clear she is listening to the conversation. She eventually turns round and carries the cup of coffee over to the table, placing it in front of Grace. "Well, they will want to know *everything* about last night," she says. "Times; the number of drinks; conversations . . ." She speaks calmly and evenly, and as she does so she pauses and looks into Grace's eyes. "They'll want to know everything that was said." Her gaze lingers for a while, until she eventually withdraws and sits back down at the table opposite her.

As Grace sips her coffee, she watches Nancy over the rim. She continues to be so calm and fluid in everything she does, and yet her face tells a different story. Her gaze stares so intently one minute, and flicks nervously around the room the next. Now she is fiddling with her phone, tapping out a message, her attention supposedly distracted from Grace, although again Grace wonders if this is all an act. If she's even texting anyone. *What is it you're trying to gain, Nancy? Do you want me to think you're really as calm as you're trying to make out?*

"Oh my God," Caitlyn is saying again. Her hands steeple in front of her, then splay out on the table. "How the hell can we tell them that when we can't even remember the end of the night?"

Grace snaps her head up at this, and she notices Nancy turning and giving her friend a look. Do they really not remember?

"I just mean . . . well, we don't, do we?" Caitlyn says. "We don't know what happened."

Nancy drops her phone and reaches over the table, taking hold of Caitlyn's arm. "It'll be fine, Cait. We just tell them the truth. That's all we can do."

"You're right," Caitlyn says. "I know. But what *is* the truth?"

Grace cocks her head, holding her breath at what is such an odd thing to say. "What do you mean?" she asks.

"I mean, what happened? What actually happened to Anna?" Caitlyn stops, shaking her head, tears now falling down her cheeks.

Beside her Rachel is shuffling, feet scuffing back and forth on the tiled floor. Whether it's this or Caitlyn's tears that drag Nancy out of her seat, Grace doesn't know, but Nancy is swiftly around the table, hands placed on Caitlyn's shoulders. "We'll find out," she says. "Ben is right to call the police, and now they can find out what happened." Then she takes hold of Rachel's elbow and gestures to a chair, and even though Rachel doesn't sit, she has at least stopped shuffling.

Nancy's tone has changed from earlier. She now thinks Ben is right to call the police, when only an hour earlier she thought it too soon. But what Grace is more taken by is how the others fall under her charm. *Including Anna*, she thinks. Maybe especially Anna.

Grace has wondered how Anna is so clearly drawn to Nancy. She worries, because of what she has seen before and how wrong it went— someone who dragged Anna in until it went too far. It was a cry for attention back then, and she cannot see that this is the same, though she can't rule anything out. And now she knows that Anna has been seeing a counselor, too—what she would give to talk to her friend and find out why. What is going on that no one else seems to see?

Nancy is picking up a coaster now and making a show of sliding Grace's mug onto it. Grace wants to laugh. How the other women seem to be trapped under her spell, lured by her self-assuredness that might make them feel so "safe." Sometimes all people need is to feel safe. Anna has always needed that; Grace knows this by the way she needed her family back then.

But the trouble with women like Nancy is they're often anything but safe.

Grace turns to Caitlyn. "You *need* to try to remember what happened. Because Nancy is right," she adds purposefully, "the police will want to know everything."

"I don't even remember seeing her go." Caitlyn clasps her hands to either side of her face as she shakes her head. "None of us remember, do we?" She looks up. "But she must have done, because there's no way we would have gotten in the taxi without her. Would we?" Her face is white as she looks first at Nancy and then at Rachel. Neither of them answers her. It is like the air has been sucked completely out of the room. "Nancy?" Caitlyn is asking. Her voice wobbles.

"Of course we wouldn't have." Nancy walks back round the table to her seat, sitting down, and her slow movements appear defined and confident. "Of course we wouldn't. We would never have left her."

Grace's muscles are so tight she can feel the ache in her shoulders. She reminds herself to relax, to breathe. But right now she can't. Because she knows this is a lie. It has to be if the barman is right and they were all still together when the taxi arrived.

All of a sudden Rachel cries out, "But we did." Her legs shake beneath her as she rests her hands on the table to steady herself. The rest of them stop what they are doing and look at her with intense apprehension for whatever is coming next. "We did leave her. Because she was still there."

No one moves a muscle, none of them blinks. The noise of Grace's breath sounds too loud to her in this silence.

What does she mean they left her? Are they all *aware of this?* Slowly Grace tears her gaze from Rachel and looks at the other two, but their expressions give nothing away.

When she turns back, Rachel is wiping a hand across her face, gathering tears that are pooling in her eyes. She looks as if she is about to collapse. "She was still there. I saw her when we got in the cab."

"Rachel?" Nancy is now saying, cautiously. Grace watches her straightening her back, her face crumpling into a frown. Her hands are splayed facedown on the table in front of her. "What are you talking about?" Still Grace cannot work out if she knows exactly what Rachel is talking about or not. Nancy plays such a clever game.

Rachel's voice is quieter this time. "I saw her," she says. "She was standing by the wall in the backyard. When the cab drove off, I leaned back and—" She breaks off, shaking her head, furiously rubbing a hand over her face. "She was just standing there," she says, "watching us."

"She can't have been," Caitlyn says. In contrast to Nancy, who is still sitting ramrod straight, Grace can feel how jumpy Caitlyn is by the way her hands are gesturing about, how she is shuffling from side to side on her chair. "She can't have been there. She'd gone." She turns to Nancy, directs the question at her friend, maybe for support or maybe for confirmation. "She'd already gone, hadn't she?"

Grace cannot make out what is going on behind Nancy's eyes. She is so unreadable, so unlike the other two.

"I mean, why didn't she run after us?" Caitlyn is prattling on, her words skittering from her. Now she is holding her hand over her mouth, her eyes wide with the horror that they had left Anna behind. It seems her first thought is not that Rachel knows they did, but that they'd all had some part to play in doing this to their friend.

Unlike Grace, whose immediate thought *is* why did Rachel leave her behind without saying anything?

"I don't know. God. I don't know," Rachel is answering as she shakes her head.

"Why wouldn't she come with us?" Caitlyn is pleading.

"And why didn't you get the cab to stop?" Grace asks. It is clearly the most obvious question, and yet for some reason no one else is asking it. "I mean, if you saw Anna standing there, why didn't you call out to her? Why did you leave her?"

"Don't blame this on me," Rachel cries. "Don't you think I feel bad enough about it already? I didn't think anything like this was going to happen. I didn't think she was going to disappear."

Grace starts to respond that it's irrelevant whether she is to blame or not, the fact is she knew Anna was still there and she didn't say anything, but Nancy is already speaking, holding her hand up as she gestures to the seat for Rachel to sit down. "Okay," she says as Rachel shakes her head and stays where she is. "No one is blaming anyone here."

The blood is warming in Grace's veins, tiny electrodes pricking at her skin. Her breath is tight, pressure building inside her that is sure to push a scream out if she doesn't find some way to release it.

Don't you dare take control of this, she wants to say. *Rachel has to answer for what she has done.* And yet Nancy is nodding at her friend, calmly placing her hands back on the table, trying to instill peace when Grace feels anything but rising within her.

"I'm just trying to figure out what happened," Grace says through gritted teeth. *Remember to breathe,* she tells herself. *Breathe. Stay calm.* She needs to keep these women on her side if she is to learn anything. "Because it is only what the police are going to be asking." She speaks slowly to make her point.

"She's right," Caitlyn says. "If Anna isn't . . . if she doesn't . . ." Her words taper off. "Christ, if she doesn't come back we're going to have to answer questions like this. They're going to make out it's our fault," she finishes with a small cry. Her hands flap around in the air before they slap down on the table. She doesn't know what to do with herself. "Rachel, why didn't you stop the cab?" Caitlyn asks the question a lot more gently than Grace had, because she is desperate for her friend to give an answer she wants to hear, one that will put her mind at ease.

Rachel takes a step backwards, swaying, tipping forward onto her toes and then rocking back. Her face is paler still, and Grace wouldn't be surprised to see her run from the room again. "We'd had an argument." Now the tears are rolling down her cheeks, but she doesn't bother wiping them away. "And in that moment I didn't particularly *want* her in the taxi."

And suddenly there is another piece of last night's jigsaw, and yet it isn't one that Grace expected. Maybe it's also a surprise to Nancy, whose back is arched rigidly. She looks so furious that Grace wonders if it is because she simply didn't know any of this.

"Oh God," Rachel groans. "I can't believe this is happening."

"What was the argument about?" Grace asks.

"We were drunk," Rachel says, as if this is enough.

"But what was it about?" she persists.

"It was stupid," Rachel says. "So stupid. And it meant nothing. I don't even remember what started it."

Oh, but you do, Grace thinks, watching the way Rachel's eyes flick back and forth between the three of them, though mostly they rest on Nancy. *You just don't want to tell us.*

"I just knew I didn't want her getting in the taxi, and besides, she was standing against the wall, staring at me, leaning against it like she was goading me to come back and get her. And you know I would have done it, Nance." She pleads at her friend. "You know I would have if I hadn't been so drunk, but I was. And I didn't. And now this . . ."

"I know you would," Nancy replies calmly. "And so you can't go blaming yourself."

Grace looks from one to the other. "Hold on," she says sternly. "We need to know what the argument was about. It could be important."

"Do you think?" Caitlyn is asking.

"Yes," she snaps. "Of course I do. How can you *not* think that?"

"It wasn't," Rachel cries. "Not important enough for this to happen." She waves her hands in the air. "Whatever this even is."

"You just need to think if there was a reason she didn't want to come home with you then—"

"That's enough," Nancy interrupts Grace as Rachel starts crying harder now, the heels of her palms digging into her eyes. "Turning on each other isn't the way we do this."

"And who put you in charge?" Grace cries before she can stop herself. She is sure Nancy has shut her down on purpose before Rachel can say any more. But now Caitlyn is looking at her curiously. She knows that getting on the wrong side of Nancy is going to shut all three of these women down. And while she might be leaving with one more answer than she arrived with, she still has no idea what happened to Anna.

"Grace, I don't particularly like the way you keep talking to us," Nancy says as she gestures her hand around the room, making it clear that it's Grace against the three of them. "It's as if you think one of us has something to do with Anna's disappearance." When Grace doesn't respond, she says, "Do you?"

"No," Grace replies, though this isn't strictly true. The truth is that she doesn't know who she trusts. All she knows is that someone is holding back. Someone knows more than she is letting on, and there are still many more pieces of the puzzle to be put together.

But she isn't going to get anywhere. Not now. Not when their backs are up. Regardless of the fact Rachel had an argument with Anna last night, the three of them are putting up a united front. Caitlyn has melted into her chair in submission.

"I don't think that at all," Grace says. She must tread carefully, play one of their games if she wants to keep them on her side, if she hasn't already lost them. "You just have to see it from my perspective. I'm worried about Anna, and—" She pauses. She has to add this, however much it grates. "And I don't know you all as well as you know each other. I'm not blaming any of you."

Rachel nods as she wipes a hand across her tear-streaked cheeks.

"That's good," Nancy says, and for a moment no one else moves or speaks.

When the atmosphere becomes too uncomfortable, Grace goes on, "I need to go now."

It is time for her to go to the police. She will drive straight there and make sure Ben has spoken to them, and if he hasn't, she will tell them everything she knows. "But please call me if there's any news."

"Of course," Nancy says, and pushes her seat back to stand, ready to walk Grace to Rachel's door, to ensure she leaves.

While Rachel doesn't move from the kitchen, Nancy follows Grace into the hallway and at the door she presses her hand against it, holding it closed as she lays her other hand on Grace's arm. It is a gesture she's seen Nancy make on so many occasions with her friends, and yet here it doesn't feel one bit friendly.

"We are Anna's friends," she says.

"I know you are. I am too. I've been her friend since we were five years old."

"This isn't a competition."

Grace stifles a laugh, incredulous at her gall. *No, but that's exactly what you've been making it.*

"You can't place too much emphasis on what Rachel said," she tells her. "I know you think it's important, but it's not the first time those two have fallen out when they've been out and it's always blown over by morning. They're both hot-headed."

"Hot-headed" is not remotely a description Grace would use to describe Anna. Anna is the most laid-back person she knows. But what is the point in arguing this with Nancy?

"And I want to know what has happened to Anna as much as anyone," Nancy says pointedly.

There is something in her tone that sounds quite menacing.

"Rachel and Anna weren't the only ones who had words last night, were they, Grace?" she goes on.

"You're trying to blame me for something?" Grace questions. Her mind flicks back to the conversation in the ladies' room, how she had told Anna that Nancy has a hold over her. It must have gotten back to Nancy. But Nancy says nothing more before opening the door and letting Grace out.

Eventually the mums knew they would get little more information from hanging around the school. Shivering as they ditched their coffee cups into bins, they went their separate ways. Some had work, others would fill the day with mundane household chores, keenly awaiting the time to pick up their children back at the school gates. Today there was nothing more important or interesting than finding out what had happened to Anna Robinson.

And even though they hoped she was safe, there was also a part of them that hoped the story wasn't a letdown—that there was more they'd be able to dissect at pickup, though, of course, they wouldn't admit this to anyone else.

But then they would also ask themselves what if, God forbid, something horrendous had happened to her? Because if she were still missing that after-noon, then there was surely no other explanation for her disappearance.

It was past ten thirty that morning when one of the mothers was busy bundling laundry into her washing machine and the home phone rang. With her hands full, she nearly didn't answer it, but at the last minute she picked up the call from her husband.

"*Have you landed?*" *she asked him.*

"*I have,*" *he said.* "*Half an hour ago, I'm on the way to the hotel now, so at least I can get a bit of sleep before tonight. Did I wake you when I left? I tried to be quiet.*"

"*I stirred,*" *she said.* "*But I went off to sleep again. You'll never guess what?*" *she added, shutting the washing machine door and leaning against it.* "*Anna Robinson, Ethan's mum, hasn't been seen since last night. She's missing.*"

"*What do you mean she's missing?*" *he asked.*

"*I mean, no one knows where she is. Nancy says Anna's husband is worried sick. No one can get hold of her. She went to the Old Vic last night with that usual gang of hers but then never went home.*"

There was a pause on the other end of the line. "*Did you hear me?*" *she asked her husband.*

"*Yes. Yes, I heard you,*" *he said eventually.* "*It's just that I'm pretty sure I saw her . . .*" *He paused before going on, as if he were thinking through what he had actually seen last night.* "*On my way to the airport this morning. I drove along the coast road because they'd closed the one-way system overnight.*"

"*Oh my God, you really think you saw her?*"

"*Yes.*" *He stopped again.* "*Yes, I'm sure of it. I mean, she was in the distance, but at the time I knew she looked familiar, and now after what you've told me, I know it was her. She was wearing that red coat you always told me you wanted.*"

"*Then it has to be her. What time?*" *the mum asked.* "*When did you leave home?*"

"*It must have been about two-fifteen; maybe a bit later, I suppose. I left home at five past.*"

"*What was she doing?*" *she asked. Her questions tumbled out as she stood pressed against the washing machine, which was now burring into action behind her.* "*Where was she? Was she on her own?*"

"*Yes, she was on her own, but I don't know what she was doing; she was just . . . there. I thought she was walking along, but I'm not sure. She might have just been standing there looking up at the cliffs."*

"And she was definitely on her own?"

"Yep."

"What was she doing looking up at the cliffs on her own at that time of night?"

If her husband was right, Anna wouldn't have even been heading in the right direction from the Old Vic. It made no sense.

"How would I know? I've got no idea. Now I wish I'd stopped, but I didn't at the time because I was running late, you know, and I didn't think . . ." He trailed off.

"It's not your fault," she said immediately, though when their conversation ended, she would wonder at this—whether she believed her husband should have stopped if he thought he knew it was Anna.

"But you're going to have to speak to the police," she said. *"You know that, don't you? If she's still not back. You're going to have to tell them what you saw."*

7

Grace

Grace stands outside the two-story 1950s redbrick building just off the coastal road. She had visited this small-town police station a handful of times in the past, and she has no doubt the inside looks exactly as it did in the nineties.

She is proved right as soon as she opens the heavy door and walks into the reception area. In a moment she's taken back to her teenage years, walking in with her mum, hovering on the ripped red-leather seats in the corner of the room as they waited for a detective to come out to speak to them.

The seat covers have been replaced, but they still sit in the same spot, curving around the corner of the room, the desk with the open hatch, the corkboards filling one wall. She even recognizes the smell: a mustiness coated with a faint tang of something like tobacco.

Behind the desk a man is speaking into the phone. He holds up one finger to let her know he will only be a minute. He is smiling at her behind a full beard and thick eyebrows that knit together in the middle. One arm is resting on the counter in front of him. She places him in his mid- to late-forties, a good ten years older than she is, and yet she also notices how toned he is beneath his thin white shirt, its sleeves rolled up a few inches above his wrists. A tail of some tattooed animal snakes out from one arm.

He doesn't fit the setting, she thinks. He would be much better suited to a surfboard than behind the desk of a police station, and yet at the same time his smile makes her feel comfortable. Like she has made the right choice coming here in person, rather than phoning.

As soon as he hangs up the call she steps forward. The creases carved into his skin only serve to make him look more attractive, more weathered. The lines around his eyes betray the fact they've seen too much.

Grace clears her throat. "I'm here to report a missing person," she tells him. She is nervous, though she doesn't know why exactly. Maybe it's being in a police station: the authority; the seriousness of the situation. Maybe it's that she doesn't know where her inquiries are going to lead. Whatever it is, she has left Rachel's house more on edge than she has been all morning, and now she is standing here with the man behind the desk smiling kindly at her, and all of a sudden she has an urge to turn round and run out of the building.

"Okay, can you give me some details?" he asks her.

"Her name is Anna Robinson." She speaks as clearly as she can, despite her nerves. "She's thirty-six years old. Nearly thirty-seven. Her birthday is in January. Sorry, I don't know what details you want me to start with."

"That's fine." His smile widens. She can see the twinkle of his bright blue eyes and finds herself thinking again that he is very attractive. And weirdly this makes her feel calmer, makes her believe she has nothing to worry about. She is here to report a crime, not even one she's a victim of, and certainly not one she is guilty of.

And yet she realizes that is exactly how she has been feeling. The nerves have come from a place of worry that she had some part in what has happened. She has been feeling this way since Nancy's parting comment, her overt suggestion that there was more to Grace's conversation with Anna late into the night than Grace had walked away believing.

She has been turning their conversation over and over in her mind. What more was said after she had accused Nancy of controlling Anna? But they hadn't argued, not like Rachel had. And yet, what version of the story had Anna relayed to Nancy later that evening? Or is Nancy just twisting it?

Grace had left Rachel's house, trying to piece together the women's actions. She'd been so focused on Nancy that she had almost dismissed the other two's presence last night, and yet it was Rachel who'd surprisingly given her the most information. Rachel, whom she still doesn't know anything about, who was fun and lively last night but has crashed this morning. And Caitlyn, who Grace is certain knows nothing more, except that Caitlyn's jumpiness made Grace feel even more nervous.

She'd been wondering what Rachel's argument with Anna had been about, and whether it had anything to do with something that had happened at Ben's party, as she'd overheard earlier in the evening. Is that why Nancy had been so keen to cut Grace's questions short earlier? Is there something about that night they don't want anyone finding out?

"Her date of birth is a great place to start," the man is saying, "but maybe you could give me some broader details—her relatiohship to you, when you last saw her. When Anna was last seen by anyone."

"She's my oldest friend and it was last night that she disappeared," Grace tells him. "We had a night out at the Old Vic on the coast road." She points in its direction, just around the corner. "Anna hasn't come home."

"Do you live with her?"

"No. I mean, she didn't *go* home. She lives with her husband and her son, Ethan. He's eight years old. I know she wouldn't have done this on purpose," she adds. "She wouldn't leave her son."

The man nods. "And you were out with your friend, Anna, last night?"

"I was," Grace says. "But I left early—or earlier than Anna. She was still there with three friends of hers. This should have been reported already. Her husband, Ben, told me he was going to, but I just . . . I didn't get the impression . . ."

"That he has? Okay, well, I'll have to check that for you, but as far as I know, nothing's come into the station yet."

Just as she feared. Ben still hadn't made the call. "It's not the kind of thing Anna would do," she goes on. "Not going home. I'm aware adults can't be reported missing for twenty-four hours, but it's not right. I know something's happened to her," she says. She is already worrying that he might not be taking her seriously.

"Okay," he says. "Not to worry. What I'm going to do is get a station officer to come out and take some more details from you. Is that okay with you?"

Grace nods. "Of course."

He nods in return. "Good. Could you give me your name?"

"Grace Goodwin," she says.

"Grace Goodwin?" The policeman cocks his head as his eyes roam her face intently, an action that unsettles her. Eventually she has to look away, dipping her own gaze down to his ruddy cheeks with their last flush of a summer tan.

She feels a fizz tingle through her body at the way he is looking at her. No one has looked at her like this for a long time. Not even her husband. Especially not her husband. "Yes," she replies finally. But when she returns his gaze, she sees something else in it, and in that moment she is trapped in a bubble of embarrassment. Because she isn't so sure he is looking at her with desire. It is as if he is trying to place her, like he knows her name.

There is every chance he might, too. Grace never took Graham's surname, always wanting to keep her own as the last and only Goodwin in their branch of the family tree. She has been so glad of her choice ever since her father died, pleased she argued it out with Graham, who'd wanted her to become a Parson.

"Have you always lived in town?" the officer asks her.

"I moved back to Clearwater in August," she says. "I lived here when I was a child. My parents moved to Australia when I was seventeen."

He is definitely at least in his midforties, which means they can't have been at school together, and yet there is something familiar about him also, now that she thinks about it.

Eventually he shakes his head. "I thought I recognized you, but I don't think I do," he says. "So you moved back here from Australia?" His face breaks into a smile. "I don't know why you'd want to come back to this old town from there." He laughs, then gestures for her to wait on the corner seat.

Grace goes to say *my husband*, but something stops her, and now her mind has drifted to her dad. He used to say the same of Clearwater. "There's a lot more to the world than this old town, Grace," he'd said to her when he'd stood in her bedroom doorway, watching her pack a suitcase for Australia, tears rolling down her cheeks after a conversation with Anna, both of them heartbroken at her imminent departure. "That's why we're leaving."

She had always known her dad was destined for bigger things. In later years she'd wondered why it took him so long to get out. She was never surprised that when they came back to England, he'd decided they'd live near his sister.

"There certainly is," her mum had echoed, her voice eerily quiet. Catherine, in contrast, was just happy to follow Henry wherever he wanted to go. She was much better suited to a small town like Clearwater but at the same time always believed there was something about it, like she knew something bad would one day happen here. She'd always been able to *feel it in her bones*. It used to give Grace chills to hear her mum talk that way, watching her fiddle with the wooden necklace that hung around her neck like worry beads.

Years before they left, Catherine would often say, "There's something not right about the town, Henry. I know it. I know it deep inside me." To which Grace was sure her father would have rolled his eyes.

Of course, that was when the community of Clearwater was in the midst of the search for a missing teenager, and surely any one of its residents might have been saying the same thing, but it wasn't what Grace wanted to hear. As she and Anna had hovered at the top of the stairs, crouching on the carpet, fingers curling around the banister, they'd listened to Grace's parents talking, their eyes wide with fear.

"I knew it. I always said it before it had happened," Catherine had admitted to her husband in hushed tones that Grace and Anna had had to strain to hear, though they'd still managed to catch every word. "Before Heather—" But Grace's mother had broken off because she didn't like to utter Heather Kerr's name in the house, in case it brought them bad luck. It was one of her many superstitions. As if talking about Heather might mean she would one day find herself in the same situation as poor Heather's foster mother.

Luckily, her dad would never listen to such nonsense. He didn't have time for superstitions and worry beads; he was much more practical.

Grace could imagine her mum's response if she told her that Anna is missing now. Her mum would say this is exactly what she'd always feared. Another missing girl. Never mind that Anna is almost thirty-seven.

She would probably get behind the wheel of the Fiesta she hasn't driven for over a year and drive down in a panic. It would be the first time she'd have visited Grace in the three months she's been back, her excuses meaning Grace and Matilda have driven the four-and-a-half-hour journey to Leicester to see her on two occasions instead. Yes, her mum is seventy-nine now, and Grace doesn't expect it of her, but there was a time when her mother did anything for her and so sometimes she finds it hard to accept that her mum is getting older, that she is more set in her ways.

But she would come for this, Grace is certain. She would risk her safety on a motorway if need be, and so there is no way Grace will consider telling her yet.

Catherine's voice is now playing out in her head. "I've always told you about Clearwater and those damned cliffs . . . I never wanted you moving back. You know I didn't, Gracie."

She would have called her dad if he were still alive, though. Told him about Anna and got sensible, straight-talking advice in return. He would have been there for her. If she needed him, he would have listened.

Grace misses her dad. The day he was taken away from the world, a piece of her went with him. Her mum was always telling her how similar they were. And she loved hearing it. She wanted to be just like him. All her life she wanted to show Henry how alike they were, because she certainly didn't want to become her mum, worrying over every little thing, unable to cope. Her dad would be proud of her, the way she has moved back to England without her husband, how she copes with the fact that Graham isn't there for her. Not like her mum, who constantly frets that the two of them live in different countries, that it isn't right for Matilda. Grace just wishes she'd found a husband more like her dad.

The police officer's voice brings Grace back to the present as he tells her that a station officer, Peter Samson, will take some more information from her. He is still staring at her like he knows her, and the more she looks back at him, she is thinking the same and yet she cannot place him. It is beginning to unnerve Grace now that his smile has faded, as he gestures her through to a room in the back.

October

Six weeks earlier

Anna

Sally's spotted notebook is open on her lap. Her gold pen with its bright pink gem dangles from the end of it as she clutches it in her hand. Every week I need to resist the urge to lean forward and peer onto its pages to see what is written, but Sally carefully presses her palms against a fresh page, smoothing it flat before she begins again, and so I never get the chance.

In the corner stands a metal filing cabinet, and today one of the drawers is half-open. I can see the folders inside stuffed with documents. I wonder if Sally spends her evenings writing out her notes in full, drawing conclusions on her patients that are then filed away— and for what? What happens to all the people whose notes she's compiled in her cabinet when their sessions come to an end? Do they all have happy outcomes?

"How have you been?" Sally starts, as she always does.

"It was Ben's birthday dinner party on Saturday," I tell her. I release my lip, which I've caught between my teeth. There's a slight tang of blood, and when I reach up my finger to touch it I find a bright red spot on the end.

"Of course," Sally says. "How did it go?" She presumably knows it didn't go well by the way she is looking at me quizzically.

"My pavlova was a disaster." I give a short laugh, trying to make a joke of the night, but in reality it had been anything but funny.

The dinner was over, the food eaten, though we were still sitting at the table, nursing glasses of wine. Caitlyn had helped me clear most of the dishes into the kitchen, but the table still looked a mess, with all of our glasses, a clutch of empty wine bottles, and a dull red stain that had bled through the white linen tablecloth.

Not that either Ben or I were the type to fuss over that kind of thing, and it was currently covered in salt and plumped up with a tea towel, which produced an unattractive bump in the table. We were all too full of food and wine to care, and by then Rachel's husband, Mark, had turned up the volume of the music.

Mark had been fiddling with his iPhone for the last fifteen minutes, trying out playlists on the group, asking them to name the tunes, which only Nancy and Ben had shown any interest in doing, the three of them huddled at one end of the table. Mark would have been in his element if I'd suggested a game of Risk. Everything revolves around games and winning with him, a contrast to Rachel, who'd prefer to be on her feet, dancing.

I'd noticed some oddities in our group when I deliberated over a seating plan. We all get on well and yet there are many differences among us. "Don't sit me next to Alan," Ben had said, referring to Caitlyn's husband. He'd grinned to show he didn't really mind, but as lovely as Alan is, we all silently migrate from him on a night out. The others are much more fun.

Like Nancy's Eric, with his plethora of stories that I'm not sure are strictly factual but that often have us laughing until tears roll down our faces. And yet when Nancy and Eric are both drinking, the night doesn't always end well between them. Many's the time they have left not speaking to each other.

I put Nancy and Eric at opposite sides of the table, placing him between Rachel and me. Rachel always made us laugh with her outwardly base comments about how gorgeous he was, but Mark never batted an eye. Deep down he likely knows, as well as Ben, that neither of us would want to be married to Eric, who is more interested in himself than Nancy.

When Mark's iPhone screamed out a Beyoncé track, I glanced up at the ceiling where Ethan was above, fast asleep in his bed. I'd already been up to check on him twice since the others arrived, and both times marveled at how he lay splayed on his bed, the duvet tangled around his limbs, so peacefully oblivious to the noise below. But with the music level rising, and Rachel's intermittent shrieks of laughter, I couldn't imagine that he wouldn't wake.

Given the cooking of four courses, scurrying back and forth between the fridge and the table and preparing a cheese board for which everyone protested they had no room, I found I hadn't been drinking as much as the others.

It was only ten thirty, and I knew it would be at least another three hours until any of them left, so the only way I could stop myself from falling asleep at the table was to pour myself a large glass of the expensive Chablis Nancy and Eric had produced.

An hour later, the music and voices had risen again. Rachel had dragged Ben through to the living room by now. And Caitlyn, Nancy, and I followed, laughing at Ben's horrified glances. Then the men came too, until all eight of us were dancing, laughing, and singing at the tops of our tuneless voices.

We dipped in and out between what was now a dance floor in the living room and the kitchen, topping up glasses, carrying on drinking. We had to speak into each other's ears to be heard. Nancy had her mouth pressed against my ear as she whispered that she loved me and I was the best friend in the world.

I had lost track of time when I thought I'd heard a cry from upstairs. Stumbling up to the floor above, I crept in to check on Ethan. Leaning over my son, I breathed in his sleepy smell, straightened the duvet, and resisted the urge to kiss him in case he woke, but he was fast asleep.

I was making my way out of his room when a noise rang out again. It wasn't loud, and I didn't think anyone else would have heard it. I couldn't quite make out where it was coming from.

The bathroom door was slightly ajar at the other end of the landing, a shard of light streaming out from a thin gap in a long line across the carpet.

There was a yelp now, a hiss of "stop it." It sounded wrong. Wrong enough that I froze outside Ethan's room.

My mind scurried through the people downstairs. The moment I'd walked out to check on Ethan, who was still in there? Caitlyn? Rachel? Ben? I couldn't remember who I last saw. All I knew was that I was talking to Alan in the corner of the room, pointing out our neighbors opposite and telling him how the woman had run over her husband's foot with her new Alfa Romeo before hitting the gate posts on her way out. When I'd heard the cry, I immediately told Alan I'd be back to finish the story and scarpered out of the room.

Now I stood frozen as the bathroom door flew open and a woman's voice cried, "Will you just stop it."

"Isn't it too late to decide you don't want it?" a man's voice replied.

I didn't have time to slip back into Ethan's room, out of sight, when my friend came out of the bathroom, mascara smudged under eyes that were filled with fear, adjusting her skirt as she turned and caught me staring.

I know that everything is different now. Even though not everyone realizes it yet; two of us do, and that is enough to send splinters between us, secrets, lies.

Sometimes all it takes is one occasion, one night, and friendships change forever. I know this only too well because I've been through it before under very different circumstances, many years ago.

As she always did, Grace had taken care of it for me then. She had looked after me, trusted me, done things a friend should never have to do, but when she's your best friend, she does that for you. That's what she kept telling me. "I'm your best friend, for God's sake, Anna. Of course I'm going to lie for you."

"Can you tell me what happened?" Sally is asking.

"I can't." I shake my head. I'm not sure if I am talking about the night of Ben's party now or what happened all those years ago. They are shuffling for space in my head, and I don't want to think of either.

Sally's head is tilted to one side and she edges forward on her seat. "Anna," she says, "what is it you're afraid of?"

"Afraid?" I reply. *What makes you think I'm afraid?* I want to say. *Of course I'm not!* But the truth is I am. I have been—increasingly so lately. Afraid that it is only a matter of time before my world comes crashing down around me.

"You look like you are, Anna," she says gently.

I am so close to telling Sally everything. Then she will know why I am really here. That I fear losing everything in my life that's important to me: Ben, Ethan, little Zadie whom I haven't even been given the chance to love yet. My fingers itch to get at the photo again—just to see her face, to remind myself she is real. But I know even when I see her it won't stop the dread from rising. *I have a secret,* I imagine myself finally telling Sally. *One I fear will change everything.*

8

Grace

Peter Samson, the station officer, is waiting behind a desk in a room at the back. He is thin and balding on the top of his almost-shaved, gray head and wears round, black-framed glasses that he squints through to peer at Grace. He confirms that no one has reported Anna missing as he ushers her into a seat.

"So her husband hasn't called? Only, he told me he was going to."

"No," Samson says. "Not as yet. Maybe your friend has already returned home?"

"I only saw him about forty minutes ago," she answers. "So I don't think so. He would have called if she had," Grace adds, though she isn't sure this is true. If Anna is back, then they'd likely be in the middle of a blazing row right now, Ben demanding answers to why she's only just returned.

But she doesn't believe anything is that simple; and regardless, she is here now to make sure the police handle Anna's disappearance with the urgency that Ben and all of Anna's other friends should be pushing for.

Peter Samson is a sharp contrast to the officer at the front desk, whose name, Grace didn't catch. She wishes he emitted some of the other man's warmth as he chews the corner of his lip and opens a notepad. He is easily in his late sixties, close to retirement if he isn't already there, and looks almost too relaxed and comfortable in his thick cable sweater and corduroy trousers. Grace is beginning to wonder if she has been passed off to Peter on purpose, if the officer at the front desk thought she'd be wasting anyone else's time.

"Why don't you tell me about your evening?" he says. "Who you were out with, where you went . . ."

Grace gives him the names of the other three women, tells him she arrived at the Old Vic at 8:30 p.m., when all four of them were already there, and that she left at midnight. That they went nowhere else all night.

"Was everyone drinking?" he asks.

"Yes. They all drank a lot."

"Roughly how much?"

"I don't know, Anna and the others were drinking tequila, plus they had near enough two bottles of wine each before I left."

"Is this common? Does Anna drink a lot?"

"I don't think so," Grace says. "It was a night out, a pre-Christmas celebration."

"Drugs?"

"No."

She shakes her head adamantly, but he must see something in her eyes because he says, "Are you certain?"

She isn't certain. There were enough trips to the restroom, times when the others had swept each other off, giggling, linking arms, but she cannot imagine Anna taking drugs. Nor any of them, if she were honest. "As far as I know, Anna wouldn't do that," she says.

He continues to probe for details about the evening. "What was she wearing?" he asks.

Grace describes Anna's skinny jeans; her chiffon top that showed her bra; the distinctive long red coat that reaches her mid-calves, which she would have been wearing when she left.

"Was she speaking to anyone you didn't recognize?"

Grace tells him she hadn't been, that it had only been the five of them clustered around the table all night.

"And did she suggest going anywhere else after the pub?"

"Not before I left," she tells him.

"Okay." He pauses, scribbling notes furiously into his pad. "How would you describe Anna's mood last night?"

"It's difficult to describe," she answers. "But there was something not right. The whole evening, its atmosphere—it all felt a little off to me." She hesitates, not knowing what to give him. All of this is her gut feeling based on the fact that Anna wasn't the woman she had imagined her to be. Based on a girl she knew nineteen years ago. "There's nothing in particular."

"But you say something wasn't right, that it felt off to you. Can you try to give me a bit more?" he persists.

Grace's gaze drifts from him to the far corner of the room, where a video camera hangs from a bracket. She wonders if he has been recording her, though he hasn't mentioned as much.

She thinks back to the previous night. She needs to relive it in as much detail as she possibly can: the way the women were from the outset, the drinking, Anna's mood, Nancy's pawing at her, the lies this morning.

"Things were tense," she starts. "Anna was uptight from the beginning of the evening."

"What makes you say that?" he asks bluntly.

"She didn't look happy. I could tell there was something on her mind, but she didn't say what it was."

"Not at all?"

Grace pauses before shaking her head. "No."

"Okay, go on."

"Like I've said, they were all drinking, buying rounds of shots and bottles of wine."

"But you weren't?"

She shakes her head again. "I was drinking, but nowhere near to the same level."

He continues to write, and so she carries on. "At one point Caitlyn was in tears. I have no idea what about. She was at the bar with Nancy and Anna, too, but . . ." She pauses. "When she came back to the table it was all hushed up. They didn't talk about why she'd been crying, just acted like it hadn't happened, as if they didn't even think I'd seen her, though of course they must have known I did." She is trying not to say this with contempt, trying to sound impartial as she reels off the facts, regardless of how much it had pissed her off at the time.

"Rachel was drinking the quickest, she was quite frantic in the way she knocked back her shots, but then, I don't know, maybe that's just her. She admitted this morning that she and Anna had had an argument." Grace tells Samson what she has learned, and how Rachel knew she had left Anna behind.

"But the odd thing is, Nancy and Caitlyn had both been adamant that Anna had already left before them."

He peers at her through his glasses.

They are lying. The words are on the tip of her tongue, but she is trying to infer them rather than be too explicit. If he draws his own conclusions, then surely that will carry more weight.

After a moment Grace adds, "But if anyone knows what Anna's state of mind was in by the end of the night, then it's Nancy. She wouldn't leave her alone all evening." She pauses. "It's her you need to be speaking to right now."

Samson nods slowly, eyeing her all the time. "Anything more you can add?" he asks eventually.

Grace's mind flicks back to what Nancy had said about Rachel and Anna. *They weren't the only ones who'd had words last night, were they?* She wonders what Nancy was trying to imply.

She and Anna didn't have words. Not like that, anyway. And certainly not anything she is going to mention to Samson, because doing so would only make things worse for Anna in the long run.

"You need to talk to Nancy," she says again, urgently.

"Ms. Goodwin, what has brought you here?" he asks.

"What do you mean?" Grace is taken aback by his question.

"I mean, why have you felt the need to report Mrs. Robinson's disappearance when her husband hasn't? I'm just interested," he continues, "to hear why you think this is so worrying."

"You don't think it is?"

"I hope it isn't," he tells her straight. "And I'll level with you—plenty of people disappear every day of their own free will and it isn't a crime. But," he adds more softly, "I can see you are worried about your friend. So I just want to know why you have come here when Mr. Robinson hasn't."

"Because . . ." She looks at him blankly before leaning forward. "Because there is no way Anna would leave her son," Grace tells him. She may not know Anna as a mother that well—she wasn't there for the stories of labor, the tears through the night feeds, or the celebrations of first steps—but Grace *was* there when Anna was growing up, and she can hand-on-heart tell anyone that Anna would never leave Ethan like her mother had left her. "I know that beyond a doubt. There is no way she would ever leave her child."

November

Five weeks earlier

Anna

Sally has become a constant in my life over the last two months. Her face and mannerisms are familiar to me, like the way she always crosses one leg over the other as she settles into her chair, rests her notebook on her lap, smoothing out a page with one hand as the other grips her gold pen. The gem on the end of it continues to wiggle furiously as she writes.

They are all soothing, these little things.

She is shuffling into her armchair today, taking off her cardigan and draping it over the back of the chair. The window is ajar because the room gets so stuffy. For a moment she forgets to turn to a fresh page and I see scrawls of handwriting filling her book.

How desperately I want to know what they say. For the most part, I don't see how we are getting anywhere when we've only been scratching the surface.

I think of my life in layers that I can peel away at. We have only been stripping back the outer skins, but maybe Sally knows this. Perhaps she doesn't care; she knows we will get there eventually. There's a chance she's already garnered more from our conversations than I give her credit for.

I let out a deep sigh by accident.

"You seem unsettled today, Anna," she says.

"More than usual?" I joke, before frowning. "I just want everything to go back to normal."

"What does normal look like?"

"Like everything is under control. It doesn't feel like it is. Nancy's always saying I'm the calmest person she knows, and yet right now I feel like . . . it feels like it did all those years ago." I know I need to start telling her more.

I had just turned fourteen when the new girl arrived at school late one January. Her name was Heather Kerr and her hair was streaked purple at its ends and she wore her socks rolled down under her feet so they barely showed above her scuffed black shoes. She would sit in the back of class in lessons painting Tipp-Ex onto her fingernails and punching holes through the end of them so that she could push her stud earrings through like some kind of fingernail jewelry.

She was the coolest girl I'd ever met. Often I'd sit at the back of the class watching her, wondering how it must feel to have that kind of irreverence. To not have to worry about what anyone else thinks.

One night I stopped off at the chemist on the way home from school for a packet of sanitary towels and my attention was caught by the purple hair dye for sale on the end of the rack. If it hadn't been reduced to £2.99 I might not have bought it.

Later that evening I stood in front of the bathroom mirror and stared at the box for fifty minutes before finally opening the seal and reading the instructions. I was still deliberating over doing it, thinking of my dad and what he would say to me if he saw me with purple hair.

Our relationship had increasingly deteriorated by then; we came and went like flatmates, polite and kind but with little of much importance to share.

Often I blamed him for this, as teenage girls do, but sometimes I would also blame myself. For spending too much time with Grace's family, for believing my need for a supposedly perfect family unit was more important than making the best of what I had. He loved me, I knew he did, and yet sometimes I believed different. But might we have had a better relationship if I hadn't been searching for a different family at Grace's?

Eventually I ran the color through my hair and found myself wishing he might even get angry with me. But at dinner that night he looked up, his forehead creased in confusion, and he didn't utter one word. I was sure he'd noticed, but for some reason he didn't comment.

And yet Grace's mum, Catherine, did. The following day she ran her hands through my once-blond locks and said, "What's this? Oh, Anna, what have you done to your beautiful hair?"

There was no malice in Catherine's voice, no anger, but disappointment flooded out in her words, and in an instant I felt a sickening regret. I had let her down. And that was so much worse.

Grace had been watching from the doorway, her face also dropped into a frown. "What have you done that for?" she asked.

What had I done it for? It now seemed a very good question, because when I'd looked at the finished job, I didn't like it one bit. "I just wanted to," I replied, because that was all it was. Just for once I wanted to do something that wasn't expected of me.

Three washes later and my hair was "back to normal," as Catherine put it with a smile. Her disappointment had faded along with the purple dye, and I was only left with my own. I was left feeling hollow. Heather Kerr was continuing to pierce body parts and sketch ink drawings onto her own skin, and I continued to watch in awe.

I wondered why I'd been so rash in doing what Catherine had expected of me, and whether I might have felt better in the end if I'd just stood up for myself.

Two weeks later I bunked off class with Heather for the very first time. Another three and I snuck out with her in the middle of the night. We'd become friends, doling out and accepting dares as if we were invincible, and all of a sudden I felt free to be whoever I wanted to be.

One evening Catherine took me to one side. "Anna, we don't see much of you these days. Is everything all right?" Her face was creased with worry. She and Grace's dad were at least ten years older than my father, and that evening she was looking her age.

"What's Grace said?"

"Well, actually, Grace hasn't told me anything," Catherine answered, pulling back, hurt. *She's not your mother,* Heather had said once of Catherine. *I don't know why you're bothered about what she thinks.*

I was sure Grace must have told her mum everything I'd been up to, and even more certain that Catherine would always take her daughter's side, and as such might even tell Grace not to hang around with me anymore. Maybe I was afraid of this, but I was also sucked into my new friendship with Heather. I started pulling away from Catherine and the rest of the family for a short time while taking this very different path. Heather didn't offer me the comfort I'd once craved from Grace's family, but she offered me something else: excitement.

It was only a few weeks later, after things had taken a turn for the worse, when I found out for sure that Grace hadn't uttered one word against me to her mum. She was gutted at what I'd been doing, but I was still her best friend, she'd told me. Grace had stood by me, had waited for me to come back to her. How many friends would have done that?

"I feel guilty," I tell Sally.

"Because of Grace?" she asks. When I don't respond, she presses on. "Do you feel like you owe her for being there for you when you were younger?"

"Yes. That's exactly it."

"You think she provided a family you didn't have?"

"I've always thought that. You know, a few months back, when Dad and I were properly talking, I asked him if he remembered me dying my hair purple. He did," I say sadly. "He didn't say anything because he never knew if he was saying the right thing. He told me, 'I didn't want to hurt you. You were a teenage girl; I had no idea if everyone was dying their hair purple or not.' It made me feel sad that we never had a better relationship," I say to Sally.

Sally nods and waits for me to go on, but when I don't, she asks, "Why do you feel like you can't have a friendship with Grace? Because I wonder if there's a bigger reason here, something else."

I close my eyes and turn away from her. The intricacies of friendships are too difficult to explain, sometimes even more so than a relationship with a partner or a spouse.

"Anna, Grace might have been there for you once; don't you think she'd be there for you again if you needed her?"

"Yes," I say. "Actually, I think she would stop at nothing to be there for me."

9

Grace

Grace leaves the police station and heads back to the apartment she has rented for twelve months from the woman who professed to have a plethora of rentals scattered across the town. She knows she is paying much more than she needs to in Clearwater, but there was something very appealing about the ease of moving into the Waterview apartments, so new and clean and furnished. Plus, she and Matilda have panoramic views of the coast and a swimming pool at their disposal, which she hates to admit they haven't used anywhere near as much as she'd intended.

Back at the apartment, with the wind whipping against the panes, it is hard to concentrate on much other than what might be unfolding right now. Since leaving the police station she's been thinking about how she told Peter Samson to speak to Nancy and what he took from their conversation. Grace hopes she is his first port of call.

But past one p.m., she's still heard nothing from the police, or Ben, or any of the women who should have been contacted by Samson and his team. Her mobile has been uneasily silent, although she has checked it every five minutes, picking it up and pressing on the screen. Each time, a photo of her and Matilda appears, but there are no missed calls or even messages from the class WhatsApp group.

Instead she can only imagine what is unraveling. Surely the police have questioned Ben and Nancy and the others.

Before she left, Samson said to her, "Please don't worry. We will be following up on what you've told us."

Don't worry? Of course she is still going to worry. Anna is missing. And what makes it worse is the sense that she is the only person who *is* worrying.

But at least Grace has Ethan coming over tonight, she thinks. It might sadden her that this is the first time she's had him for tea when it is something she'd thought she'd be doing more often, but in Anna's absence it is almost comforting to think she'll have him here.

Earlier she had asked Samson what was going to happen after she left the station.

"I'm going to be passing this on to our team, who will speak to Mr. Robinson and the friends who were with you last night," he assured her.

Grace stands by the window and watches the rain as it starts tapping against it, and presumes they have to have done this by now. The waiting is interminable; the only thing she can think of to take her mind off it is the small task of deciding what to feed Matilda and Ethan tonight.

She opens the fridge door and stares inside, no clue what to give the boy for tea when she has no idea what he eats. There is leftover roast chicken that is two days old and a shop-bought, fresh pasta sauce that she knows Matilda will turn her nose up at. Closing the door, Grace opens the freezer instead. At least there are plenty of fish fingers— surely every eight-year-old is happy with those.

Grace checks she has enough frozen chips and peas too: an easy meal, but no one will be judging her culinary skills today.

Nancy's voice rings through her ears regardless, goading her for packing the kids full of frozen foods: a meal that anyone could make. Nancy no doubt makes a fuss of home cooking every night for her family of four while they all sit around the table and chat about their days. Her seemingly perfect life is a pretense, Grace is sure. There is something amiss about it, and she hates to admit that over the weeks of knowing her, Grace has taken to deconstructing what she knows about Nancy and her husband, Eric.

She has learned that they once lived in London and Eric had a very demanding job on the stock market. And yet she has no clue where he works now, though she assumes it's a job that still pays well, the way Nancy talks about his career like he is the only person in Clearwater to do anything that doesn't involves boats.

Grace has seen Eric a handful of times at the school gates and spoken to him at the science fair. He is at least six foot tall and incredibly charming, but there is something aloof about the pair of them as a couple. On paper they're a perfect match, but they don't interact as other married couples do. Nancy's arms are never flung around his shoulders like they are when she paws at her friends. She doesn't touch his arm when she speaks to him, as she always does when she is with Anna. Nancy, by all accounts, doesn't want ownership over Eric like she does with her friends.

Grace dismisses the idea that her own marriage is probably a source of suspicion for the mums at school given that none of them have met Graham. To her it is blatantly clear—she is married to a man who has no interest in his family. But there's nothing to be gained from broadcasting this.

It is a surprise when Grace looks at the clock and sees that it's a quarter to three. It's nearly time to leave for pickup, and her phone has remained deathly silent. It means that the short drive to school, finding a place to park, and getting out of the car increasingly fill her with sickness and trepidation. She hates not knowing what she is walking into. Surely the other women have been contacted by the police by now. Possibly they all know it was she who reported Anna missing and not Ben. Maybe Nancy has even gathered she sent them in her direction.

Underpinning the apprehension of seeing them is the fact that she feels so alone. There is no one close to look out for and walk through the school gates with. No one to give her any moral support. She has felt this way since she first set foot back in Clearwater four months ago.

After arriving, she takes a deep breath and strides across the road, attempting an air of purpose. She has Anna's son to pick up today, as well as Matilda, and she wouldn't be doing that if there had been any news, she reminds herself. It is this thought that encourages her to walk through the gates and up the short path to the main playground, past groups of parents gathered outside their respective classroom doors.

At the far side is Matilda's class, a single-unit mobile room that sent the parents into a flurry of complaints in the first week of term. Grace couldn't see what all the fuss was about. It is heated, large, and has enough pegs and cubby holes for every child.

The group of parents feels bigger than it would usually be at this time, as if they have all turned up earlier on purpose, desperate to know if there is any news. She scans the crowd for Anna's friends and spots only Caitlyn on the farthest side of the group with mothers flocking around her, no doubt asking for an update.

The teacher is already standing outside the classroom, handing over children, many of whom are out of class and running around their parents' legs. Grace cranes to peer through the window as she approaches and sees Matilda standing in the short line behind the teacher. By the time she reaches the door, Matilda has pushed her way to the front and is stepping out, now by her side.

She wraps an arm around her daughter and says to the teacher, "I'm collecting Ethan, too." Grace peers through the window to see where he is.

"Oh!" Miss Williams exclaims, and when Grace looks back at her, her face is etched with confusion. "But Ethan's already been picked up." Her expression is now melting into momentary panic as she glances around the playground and then back at Grace.

"But I'm supposed to be having him for tea," she says. "His dad was going to call the school and let you know."

The teacher shakes her head. "He did the call the school, but . . ." Her mouth hangs open, her brain no doubt furiously trying to catch up. "Oh, I'm sorry; look, you're going to have to wait here and let me find out what's happened."

"You mean it wasn't him who picked Ethan up?" Grace goes on.

Miss Williams shakes her head, noncommittal as she apologizes again, and adds, "Please just wait here a moment and once all the children have been collected, I'll find out what's happened."

Reluctantly Grace stands to one side as Miss Williams holds on to the five remaining children. She bends down and asks one of them if his mummy is working and likely to be late again, and does he want to go straight to the late room now? The little boy tells her in a too-serious voice that Mummy has a meeting this afternoon and that he probably should, and all the time Grace notices the look of anxiety on the teacher's face, as if she is worried she's done something wrong.

"Why are we waiting?" Beside her, Matilda is fumbling in her book bag as she finds a drawing that she thrusts into Grace's hands. "I did this today, do you like it?"

"Oh wow, yes, it's brilliant," Grace replies.

"You're not even looking at it, Mummy. Why are we still here? I want to go. And what snack have you brought me?"

"What? Oh, I haven't brought one today, sorry, honey. Mummy's been busy." Snacks had seriously been the last thing on her mind.

"But I'm starving!" Matilda cries, stamping her foot.

"Matilda, will you stop that," she hisses. "Don't behave like that in the playground; you are eight years old, and you'll survive without food until we get home. Didn't they give you any lunch today?"

"Yes, but it was horrible. It was covered in orange and I didn't eat it."

Grace rolls her eyes and glances back at Miss Williams, who now only has two children waiting. The boy she had spoken to remains by her side along with a little girl who is staring at the ground, kicking her leg back and forth.

"I'm sorry, I'm just going to take them both to the late room and then I'll be right back," she tells Grace.

"Mummy, why are we still here?" Matilda whines, stretching out the word "here." "I said I want to go home."

"Because I'm waiting to find out what's happened to Ethan, darling," she tells her. "I'm supposed to be picking him up today."

"Why are you picking Ethan up?"

"Because he is supposed to come to ours for tea."

"Why is he coming to ours for tea?" she asks, surprised.

"He isn't, by the look of it," Grace mutters, watching the teacher deliver the children through a door and then turn back and head towards the school office.

"I want him to come," Matilda says. "Can he still come?"

Grace looks down at her. "Do you like Ethan?" she asks. "Do you play together?"

Matilda shakes her head. It crosses Grace's mind that she hasn't invested in teas and playdates as much as she should have done over the last term. "Who do you play with? Is it still Sophia?"

Matilda shrugs and looks away.

"Is she still your best friend?"

"No," Matilda says defiantly.

Grace studies her daughter. "Has something happened?"

"No. I just don't like her anymore."

"Oh, Matilda," she sighs. "Okay, I promise as soon as I find out what's happened to Ethan I'll make sure he comes to tea soon, okay?"

Matilda doesn't bother answering as Miss Williams reappears from the office and heads over to them. "We did have a call from Ethan's father, but he told us Ethan was going home with Elodie's mother."

Nancy. Grace could have guessed. "Right," she says. "Thanks. I must have gotten my wires crossed, then," she adds through gritted teeth, and turning to Matilda says, "Come on, let's get you home."

As she holds on to Matilda's hand and walks her out of the playground, Grace can't shake the thought that this has all been meticulously planned by Nancy. She must have found out from Ben that Grace was supposed to be picking Ethan up and made damned sure that didn't happen. And for whatever reason, Ben hasn't bothered calling her to let her know.

She is fuming as she reaches the car and opens the back door for Matilda to climb in, slamming it shut and getting into the front, tossing her handbag onto the passenger seat.

"Why are you so cross?" Matilda asks from the back.

"I'm not," she snaps, picking up the phone and dialing Ben's number, which rings and rings before eventually clicking into voice mail.

"Why aren't you driving?" her daughter now pipes up, kicking a foot against the back of her seat.

"Don't do that," Grace says, reaching round and taking hold of her daughter's foot, her fingers loosely gripping Matilda's shoe. "I've told you not to kick like that."

"Why aren't you driving?" she asks again, as a loud thump on the window makes Grace jump. She turns to find one of the parents, who she thinks is called Samantha, rapping her fist on the window, crouched over and peering in.

Grace opens the window and the woman takes a step back. "Sorry, I didn't mean to surprise you," she says.

Grace shakes her head. "No worries. You didn't."

"I can't stop long, I haven't collected Holly yet." She nods towards the school, presumably referring to the girl who was taken to the late room. "It's just that my husband called me earlier and said he saw something this morning. And I haven't really known what to do about it all day, only I told myself that if I saw any of you here I'd mention it, but I know I've probably missed the others now and . . ."

Grace stares back at the woman, who has trailed off. Her first thought is not what this woman might have to say, but that she was clearly looking for one of Anna's other friends. "Yes?" she asks eventually.

"Well, he thinks he saw Anna this morning, at about two-fifteen."

"Really?" Grace shifts forward in her seat. "Where?"

"On the coast road. He said she was staring up at Crayne's Cliff."

"Crayne's Cliff?" Grace repeats.

Samantha nods.

"What do you mean?" She shakes her head. "What was she doing?"

"That was it. He says she was just looking up at them, or out to sea or something."

Grace feels her blood run cold. "What happened?" she asks, so quietly, as if she doesn't really think she wants the answer.

"Nothing. He was running late for his flight." Samantha has a look of unease. "Now he wishes he'd stopped, of course, but then he had to get to Bristol and he didn't really think anything of it at the time."

"And he didn't see Anna doing anything?" she asks again.

"No."

"Has he spoken to the police?" Grace asks.

"Not yet. That's why I wanted to speak to one of you first. I thought I'd be able to grab Nancy but then, like I said, I was running so late and I knew she'd already be gone, so when I saw you . . ."

You thought I'd do, Grace finishes in her head. "He needs to speak to the police and tell them what he saw," she says. "Please make sure he does. They know she is missing."

Samantha nods and gestures towards the school again, telling her she'd better go. As soon as she has scurried off, Grace picks up her mobile and presses Nancy's number.

"Can we go now?" Matilda is asking.

"In a minute. I need to speak to Elodie's mummy."

"Why?"

"Because I need to check that Ethan is okay."

"Why do you need to check Ethan is okay?"

Grace holds up a hand to quieten Matilda as she listens to the ring tone. She can't focus on what she wants to say to the woman thanks to the image that fills her head: Anna at Crayne's Cliff. Only Grace doesn't see Anna as an adult, but as a teenager in faded jogging trousers and a purple hoodie, with bright pink trainers.

"Hi, Grace." Nancy's voice brings her back to the present. "Everything all right?"

"Well yes, except I was under the impression I was picking Ethan up from school today," Grace replies. "Only I hear you have him."

"That's right," Nancy says, her words clipped. "I spoke to Ben earlier and offered to pick him up."

"But I was having him. For tea."

There is a pause before Nancy says, "Well, I'm sorry, Grace. I didn't know that."

Grace bites her lip. Of course she knew that. She doesn't believe one word that comes out of this woman's mouth. "Have the police spoken to you?" Grace asks.

Again there is a moment's silence before Nancy replies. "Yes. They did." She pauses and then, "I'm sorry, Grace, I take it you haven't heard?" The words are uttered so quickly that Grace can tell there's something wrong.

Her fingers wrap tighter around her mobile as she says, "Heard what? What's happened?"

"Anna's been in touch."

"What?" Grace says, confused, for this was the absolute last thing she'd been expecting. "What do you mean she's been in touch? With you?" she spits out.

"No. Not with me," Nancy says coolly, and with the right tone to suggest Grace should already have known that. "With Ben."

"I don't understand. What's happened to her? Where is she?"

"I don't know all the ins and outs, but the good news is she's safe," Nancy replies.

"Why didn't anyone tell me?" Grace blurts. She feels a mixture of relief blended with anger that she has spent all day worrying over her friend and still is the last to hear.

For a moment Nancy doesn't respond. "It's good news, anyway," she says eventually. "Isn't it?"

"Yes. Yes, of course it's good news," Grace says, staring out the window as her daughter proceeds to kick the back of her seat again. Her mind is busy trying to process it, though. That Anna has been in touch, that she is safe, which of course is what she wants, but she's still none the wiser, and Nancy isn't telling her, and *why the hell did no one pick up the phone and tell her?*

As all these thoughts buzz around her head, Nancy is saying, "Okay, well, I have to go. We'll speak later." And it takes Grace a moment to realize she's hung up the phone.

Grace clicks off her own and throws it onto the passenger seat.

Yes, of course it is good news. If Anna is safe, then that's all that matters. It shouldn't matter that she didn't know, she tries to tell herself, though of course it does. How could it not?

But despite this, something still feels off. She has no more answers, and until Grace hears it for herself from Ben and knows for sure that Anna is okay, then she is not going to take Nancy's word for it.

That afternoon a group of mothers had clustered around the mobile class-room of 4C at least ten minutes earlier than usual for pickup. Not that any of them would admit it, but they'd been hanging around, waiting to leave the house, conscious they didn't want to be late and miss out on any news.

They had gathered at the gates before they were opened, where there'd been no sign of Nancy, Rachel, Caitlyn, or even Grace.

They saw Nancy first, rushing past as soon as they were allowed up the path that led to the classrooms. They wanted to call out but her head was down and her fur-lined hood pulled tight, and she was clearly not linger-ing to speak to anyone.

Nancy was going so fast that she reached the classroom door before any of them, apparently asking for Ethan, too, because he and Nancy's daugh-ter, Elodie, were let out first. And then, with her head still down, she took a hand of each of the children and scurried off the opposite way, towards another gate, which meant she didn't have to pass them again.

Her oddly frantic movements meant no one felt it appropriate to catch up with her and ask if there was any news. Especially not when Ethan was clutching one of her hands, practically being dragged out of the school.

A few of them glanced at each other, wondering if they were thinking the same thing: it didn't look good.

And then suddenly Caitlyn was alongside them in the gathering throng, waiting for her child, and one of the mums turned and asked if she'd heard anything about Anna. One by one they stopped their conversations to hear the answer, their faces all wearing the same expression of grave concern.

"Oh, well . . ." Caitlyn faltered. "Er, actually I think Anna is okay," she said. Her face was unreadable; she looked neither happy nor relieved about this fact.

"Oh?" someone said. "Well, that's great. I mean, thank God."

Caitlyn nodded in response.

"But . . . so . . . what happened, then?"

"Well, I don't really know all the facts," she replied. "But she's been in touch. And she's fine."

"Oh, brilliant," someone else piped up. "That's such a relief. I mean, I was beginning to think the worst."

"Absolutely," another agreed.

Caitlyn smiled. She looked as if she wanted to add something else, though she never did.

"So have you spoken to her?" They weren't keen to drop the subject just yet, not when still they had no idea what had happened to Anna Robinson, and especially not now that they knew she was safe and it sounded likely that she must have gone off on her own accord. Now that they could be thankful she wasn't hurt, they wanted the gossip.

"No. I haven't," Caitlyn said, shaking her head. "She's been in touch with Ben."

"He must be relieved, anyway," one of them pressed.

"Yes. Of course."

"How did he sound?" someone asked her.

"I haven't actually spoken to him," she replied. "Nancy did. She agreed to pick Ethan up for him, so he, you know . . ." Her words fizzled out.

"Right, yes, of course," they murmured, but they didn't know, and they certainly didn't understand. In fact, now everything seemed a lot more confusing and they were even keener to get to the bottom of it, but at the same time they weren't sure Caitlyn had any more answers than they did.

"Well, at least she's safe," someone murmured.

"Yes," Caitlyn said. "Exactly." She gave another small smile, and when she turned away, the others looked at one another and raised their eyebrows and silently agreed that something wasn't adding up.

10

Grace

Matilda is still going on at Grace from the back seat, rhythmically kicking into the small of her back. Grace is trying to block out her demands, but eventually the white noise coming from her daughter gets to be too much.

"Matilda, will you stop," she shouts, turning round, grabbing her daughter's shoe again and holding it in her hands this time. "I am trying to think. And I can't while you keep going on at me."

Matilda pauses, her eyes gradually narrowing in defiance as she says, "I want to go home."

"Well, we're not going home," Grace snaps, turning back and starting the engine.

"Where are we going?"

"To Ethan's."

"For a playdate? Why are we going there? Are we going to stay for tea?"

"Enough with the questions," she says. "We're going there, that's all you need to know."

This silences Matilda, who stops kicking and seems content in the knowledge she's going to get her playdate after all. Not that Grace has any idea if Ethan will be there—as far as she knows he is at Nancy's—but even that would be preferable to having Nancy at Anna's house too. She wants to speak to Ben, and it will be much better if he is there on his own.

Grace is relieved there's no sign of Nancy's Land Rover when she arrives outside the Robinsons' house. She waits for Matilda to climb out the back, then they go to the door and ring the bell, and eventually Ben opens it.

"Hi," he says awkwardly, his gaze traveling from her to Matilda and then back to her again as his fingers tap nervously on the doorframe.

"Hi, I was just checking that everything is all right. I thought I was collecting Ethan but then the school told me he'd already gone, so . . ." She glances over his shoulder at the hallway behind him. She doesn't want to let on what Nancy has told her, she wants to hear it from Ben.

"Can I play with Ethan?" Matilda asks in her most serious of polite voices, and Grace is grateful for her daughter getting to the point and inviting themselves into the house.

"Er, no, sorry he's not here right now," Ben answers, furrowing his brow as if he's finding the whole interchange completely confusing.

"Why not?" Matilda asks. "Where is he?"

There are plenty of times when Grace admonishes her child for her abruptness, especially when it verges on rudeness, but today isn't one of them because she wants the answer, too.

"He's at Nancy's," he says, before turning back to Grace. "I'm sorry." He shakes his head, his eyes wide with something that resembles less confusion than anxiety. He seems more on edge. "With everything going on . . . and then Nancy offered . . ."

"Oh okay, well, not to worry," Grace says as calmly as she can, though inside she is boiling at the thought that he didn't even think to call her. She waits to see if he is going to tell her that he has heard from his wife. When he doesn't, she asks, "Is there any news?"

"Er, yes." He rubs his chin. "Yeah, she got in touch with me this afternoon."

"Oh?" Grace feigns surprise. "You've spoken to her?"

"I did," he says, shuffling his feet as he seems to hop from one foot to the other.

"What did she say?" she persists, trying to read Ben's expression. His eyebrows arch into a point and he is still rubbing at his stubble, and the fact that he's in no rush to answer makes her wonder if he doesn't actually know what to say. She resists the urge to reach out, grab his hand so that he'll stop that bloody rubbing, and tell him to spit it out and just tell her what Anna said to him.

"Look, I'm sorry, Grace, this isn't a good time right now. Anna's fine, that's all you need to know. I'm sure she'll be in touch with you at some point."

"Wait," she says as he begins pushing the door closed. "That's it? I've been going out of my mind worrying about her all day. I need to know more than just that she's fine. Where is she? What happened last night?"

"Grace." He says her name with an elongated sigh. "I don't need to go through all this right now."

She hesitates, scanning his face, looking for a clue. Have they had an argument? Is this just about Anna and Ben? If so, then of course she should back off and give him some privacy, but she's certain that's not it.

Her mind is working overtime, because still nothing makes sense. Ben doesn't look comfortable one bit, and she is sure he is hiding something from her.

Grace bites the corner of her lip, not knowing how far to push it. "Has she messaged you?" she asks.

"What? Yes," he says, "I've had a text."

"Can I see it?" she says.

"What?" He laughs, incredulous.

"The message. Can I read it?" What she really wants is to see his phone, see it for herself.

"No. No, you're not—" Ben shakes his head, and while Grace knows that maybe she shouldn't push him, she can't ignore the nagging voice inside her head that reminds her Anna is missing and she would never forgive herself if she didn't ask questions of the people who clearly don't want to answer them.

Beside her Matilda steps closer, and she can feel her daughter's body pressing into her side. "Have the police been to see you?" she asks him. "I went to the station this morning. I told them about Anna."

"Yes, they've been here," he says. Does he seem tired of the conversation now?

"What did they say?" she persists. She can see from the way he is breathing, from the whites of his knuckles as his hands curl tightly around the doorframe, that she is pushing his patience, but she mustn't allow herself to care. When she knows for sure that Anna is safe, then she can explain herself, and surely her friend will thank her for not giving up.

Ben gives a semi shake of his head, one sharp movement to the right. "They're happy that Anna is fine. There's no case, Grace."

"What do you mean there's 'no case'? They've closed it?"

"Of course they have. They've seen the text, they're happy she's okay. Now please—" He closes his eyes briefly. "This has got nothing to do with you. So if you don't mind, I need to collect my son now."

Grace opens her mouth, then clamps it shut again. She is sick of everyone telling her that it has nothing to do with her. But she has tackled it wrong, got Ben defensive. She would start again if she could. For now all she can say, her tone softer, pleading, is, "Ben, aren't you worried?"

He looks at her then, his eyes narrowing, and in that moment she believes he is about to admit that yes, of course he is worried, because he's had a text from his wife that sounds nothing but out of the ordinary and either there is something seriously wrong with her or, worse, the text is from someone else.

But in the end, he shakes his head slightly and only says, "Like I said, everything's fine."

That night Grace can't concentrate on Matilda or the spelling homework her daughter has to do, which needs to be in the next day as it will be the end of the week.

Matilda has been firing questions at her since they got back from seeing Ben, a constant barrage about Ethan's mummy. Where is she? Why hasn't she come home? Has she had an accident?

As much as Grace can't truly answer the questions, she tells her daughter there is nothing to worry about, Anna is fine. She lies to her later in the evening that Ben has messaged her and assured her Anna is all right, although Matilda seems more inquisitive than distressed.

It's a relief to finally get her daughter into bed, but Grace can't settle and finds herself searching out photo albums from the past, pulling out snapshots of her and Anna, poring over them as she lays them out on the living room carpet.

She wakes on the sofa when it is still dark outside. The clock on the wall above the modern, faux fireplace tells her it is twenty past five in the morning. Photographs litter the carpet, strewn as if they are pieces of some crime scene, a puzzle for her to work out, and yet Grace knows they were never going to give her answers. She'd just wondered whether the clue was in there somewhere, hidden in the past.

She has spent the night dreaming of Anna and of Crayne's Cliff. The words of Samantha, the mother whose husband had seen Anna there at two o'clock yesterday morning, taunt her.

When Matilda walks into the living room an hour later, Grace is sitting on the edge of the sofa. Her daughter eyes the mess on the floor suspiciously, asks her if she can have Shreddies for breakfast, then proceeds to sit next to her and switch on the television.

All this time Grace doesn't move. She just wants to drop Matilda at school and get back to the police station, because she will not rest until she knows for sure that Anna is safe.

November

Four weeks earlier

Anna

Sally doesn't have her notebook on her lap today. It is closed and placed on the side table next to her. She is leaning forward, a serious expression on her face, her hands steepled in front of her. "We've been talking for six weeks now," she says softly, "and still sometimes I think we're only scratching the surface."

I pretend I have no idea what she is getting at, and yet my heart beats with a heavy thud.

"And so I guess I'm wondering why," Sally goes on. "Because I think you could be holding something back, and yet at the same time it might be the very reason you came to me in the first place."

One of my hands is fiddling with the seam of my jeans, which is beginning to come apart. If I poke at it too much I will make a hole, but I carry on regardless. Sally is waiting for a response, and I stop picking and shuffle forward in the chair, then back again. I can't get comfortable. Today it had been a thin line for me deciding whether or not to keep my appointment.

When I start digging my fingers back into the hole again, Sally asks, "How's it been with your friends lately?"

I think to myself that it hasn't been the same since Ben's party. There are new undercurrents within the group.

I tell Sally that Nancy and I had an argument at the school gates five days ago.

"You're not being a good friend to me, Anna," she had said as she prodded a finger against my chest. "You're putting her before me."

"Can you tell me what it was about?" Sally asks.

I give a slight shake of my head. I don't want to go into it.

"Is it sorted?" she asks instead.

"I—" I break off. "Kind of," I finish.

In reality, it is far from sorted. But while both Nancy and I know this to be the case, we've found an unspoken way of making believe it is. Of pretending—for now, at least.

"Your friends are incredibly important to you," Sally says. "I've picked up on this a lot during our sessions."

I nod.

"What else is it, Anna?" she persists. "Something is worrying you, making you nervous." Her gaze drifts back to my fingers, which are stretching the fabric of my jeans apart, pressing into the hole that I'd been consciously trying not to make.

"Last time I was telling you about my friend Heather Kerr?" I say, a question, making sure she remembers.

Sally nods at me to go on.

At the start of the summer in 1997 the days were hot. A short heat wave had exploded and the evenings were humid and drawn out.

Grace was coming for a sleepover. She hadn't been to our house in a long time and I hadn't been to hers. Our friendship was waning, and yet neither of us had discussed it, though I knew Grace must have noticed. I'd wondered if she were too afraid to mention it, for fear I'd tell her I didn't want her as a friend any longer. Would I have done that? I don't think I would, but then I was so wrapped up in Heather that I'd begun to begrudge Grace hanging around.

I also felt sorry for her, though, because I knew she had no one else to hang out with. And so when she'd been going on at me, saying she'd love to stay over, that she knew Heather had been and why wasn't I inviting her, I told her to come.

Heather was someone I was on par with. That was how I justified my growing distance from Grace. Heather had had an unusual upbringing too, being in foster care from the age of six, and I never felt that I was always looking up to her, or that I was missing out on a family like I did when I was with Grace.

Maybe that was one of the reasons I'd accepted her dare that day, even though I knew Grace was coming over to spend the night. It was possibly our riskiest move yet, and I knew Grace would be tagging along too, but I liked the idea of showing her I was different now.

Heather had caught up with me earlier in the day and said, "I dare us." That was the way we always started.

"What?" I'd giggled with a fizz of excitement.

"Tonight, when it's dark, we creep out and meet at the cliffs."

"Crayne's Cliff?" Now my excitement was beginning to melt into trepidation. "But it's taped off. After the accident. The ground slipped away; someone nearly died," I protested. "No one can go anywhere near the cliffs at the moment."

Not least, my dad would kill me if he found out I'd gone there. Somewhere so dangerous.

"So?" she said. "It's tape, not a six-foot wall. And anyway, *I dare us.*"

I wanted to say no. The cliffs had started to slide a week ago and had taken a walker with them, though thankfully the coastguard had managed to save him. And what would Grace have to say about it? She was currently walking across the field towards us, an overnight bag flung over her shoulder.

So, yes, it was risky and we shouldn't be doing it, but that was also the whole point of our dares. "Okay," I said, a nervous smile beginning to creep onto my lips. "What time?"

"Ten thirty," she said, and left before Grace reached us.

"We're going to sneak out and go to the cliffs tonight," I squealed to Grace as soon as she arrived at my side. "Oh my God, can you believe it?" I knew she was about to dampen my excitement, but I wanted her to know it was a done deal. I was going with Heather with or without her.

Grace just stared at me, and I waited for her to say no way was she going to the cliffs, but she didn't say a word. I was wrong-footed as we walked home and went about our evening. I asked my dad if we could put up the tent in the garden. It would make it so much easier to sneak out if we were sleeping outside. I watched him shake out the canvas onto the grass, muttering that two of the poles were missing, and that it meant a trip to the hardware store the next day, and reluctantly I laid out the spare mattress from beneath my bed instead, opening the window wider to let what little breeze there was into the room.

I doubted we'd get much sleep in the heat, but then sleep was the last thing on my mind as we ate sandwiches and crisps, played netball in the garden, and watched a movie. Still, Grace didn't utter another word about going to the cliffs until ten p.m., when she eventually said, "We can't go; you know that, don't you? It's madness. She's mad."

I knew it was coming and yet I still said, "Are you serious?"

Grace nodded. "I don't want you going, Anna, it's dangerous."

I wanted to yell at her, but at the same time I needed to keep my voice down. Dad was dozing in the living room, but he was only below us. "You are not my mum, Grace."

I could see she was taken aback but I didn't care. I'd spent years being cared for by Grace and her family; all I wanted was to make my own choices and take my own risks, and Grace wasn't going to stop me. Heather understood what it was like to have a dysfunctional childhood. Grace didn't.

The hurt on her face was almost palpable, but right then I was desperate to break free and make my own mistakes. "Fine. You can stay here, then," I told her.

I grabbed a purple hoodie and a pair of joggers that I slipped on, aware that Grace was watching me out of the corner of her eye. Eventually she got up from the mattress and said, "I'll come. I don't want you going on your own."

Heather was waiting at the end of the road, and we were nearly with her when Grace had another change of heart. She grabbed my arm and said, "We can't do this. It's stupid. What would your dad say if he caught you?"

For a moment I allowed my best friend to clutch tightly onto my arm because now that we were outside in the humid night air, I was losing some of my bravado.

In that moment I was torn. Between right and wrong. Between Grace and Heather. It went on forever as I deliberated which way it was greater.

Finally I pulled my arm away from Grace's clutch and said, "Go home, then. I'll see you later."

Grace's face fell. She looked gutted to the core, but as much as I felt guilty, I couldn't ignore that there was a slither of satisfaction from being able to show my friend I didn't need to be looked out for anymore.

I want to tell Sally that the night didn't end well. How I had gone home afterwards, tears streaking my face, desperate for Grace to still be at my house and not to have gone back to her own. I wouldn't have blamed her if she had, but how I had needed her right then, more than I ever had.

"Anna, are you okay?" Sally is asking me, pressing forward, handing me a tissue.

The relief of seeing my best friend asleep on the mattress in her Forever Friends top, a thin sheet draped over the lower half of her body, had been immense. I'd sobbed as I sank onto the bed with her, wishing I had listened to her and had never gone to the cliffs that night.

Just reliving the memory gives me palpitations. I grab my bag and coat and stand up. "I need to go," I say hurriedly.

"Anna?" Sally asks, but I don't reply as I leave the room and her house, grateful for the freshness of the cold air outside.

That night I had waited for "I told you so," but Grace wrapped her arms around me instead and promised me she was there for me.

Neither of us could have known how awfully the night would end, and yet Grace did something for me I could never have expected. She gave me an alibi. She said I was lying in the bed next to her all evening. That I never left the house.

11

Friday, 13 December

Grace

Two hours later and Grace has dropped Matilda at school and is now back at the police station, parking in a space on the road opposite. In her mind she runs through the conversation she had yesterday afternoon with Ben about Anna's supposed message, dwelling on how detached he was and how keen to get rid of her. His refusal to show her the text. Whether there is something he is covering up.

Every so often a voice reminds her that of course everything could be exactly as he says. Anna is fine and Ben is just embarrassed. But then she remembers how he'd looked so awkward, his desire to shut the door and stop her from asking questions, and she thinks that none of these are the actions of an innocent man.

Whatever, she is right to come here now. This time there is a woman behind the desk in reception, with tight curls on the top of her head and a pair of glasses that hang on a string around her neck. She has a slash of bright blue eyeshadow smeared across each eyelid and is nodding at an old man who is talking to her across the counter, reporting a stolen wallet, which he apparently left on a park bench. The woman patiently speaks with him, but the wait feels interminable.

When he eventually shuffles out of the station, Grace steps forward. "I was here yesterday and spoke with Peter Samson about a missing person," she tells the woman.

The woman fingers the beads of her glasses before putting them on the edge of her nose and peering through them.

"Is he here? I need to talk to him again."

"Can I take your name?" the woman asks. "And the person who is missing?"

Grace gives her both and waits for her to pick up her phone and ask if he is around.

"He's not in today but take a seat over there and someone will come out to see you."

"Great, thanks," Grace says and retreats to the seat, where she waits for another five minutes before another woman appears in the doorway and calls her name.

Grace nods as she gets up, following her to the interview room she was in the day before.

"I'm DCI Bethany Barker," the detective tells her. "I followed up on your report about your friend yesterday."

This is great. At least she is seeing a detective now, Grace thinks. "It was you who went to see Ben Robinson?" she asks.

Bethany nods, and Grace is relieved to be sitting in front of the right person.

"How can I help you?"

"Anna is still missing," Grace says. "I know that she's apparently texted her husband, but I still think something is wrong."

"Wrong in what way?"

"I'm not sure," Grace replies. "But her husband was particularly cagey with me, and he wouldn't show me the message."

"I saw it myself, Mrs. Goodwin," Bethany says. "And as far as I'm concerned, your friend just needed some time out."

Grace gives a small shake of her head. "But how do you know it is her?"·

The DCI leans back in her seat and crosses her legs, smoothing her hands across a black pencil skirt. "People take time out for all kinds of reasons," she explains. "You'd be surprised how many adults go missing from their usual routines and lives every day. It isn't a crime."

"That's as may be, but Anna isn't *many adults*," Grace says, feeling her pulse quickening at the thought that she's about to be passed off again. "I know she would never walk out on her son. I told your officer, or whoever he is, this yesterday. She wouldn't do that. I know she wouldn't. Because it's what her mum did to her, and there's no way Anna would do the same."

Grace spots the slight inclination of Bethany's head, acknowledging what she has just told her, and she knows, too late, that she has said the wrong thing. She might know, beyond doubt, that Anna wouldn't leave Ethan, but to the detective and anyone else who doesn't know Anna like she does, the fact that her mother left her when she was a child is enough reason to believe she is likely to do the same.

DCI Barker tells her she is certain there is nothing to worry about, and they aren't investigating Anna's disappearance any further. And as much as Grace protests, she is aware she is fighting a losing battle.

Outside the station, tears prick her eyes. They are tears of frustration that make her want to open her mouth and scream. She slams her hand too hard against a brick wall, feeling the sting shoot through her skin.

"Hello again," a male voice says.

She snaps her head to the side and finds the man from yesterday who was sitting behind the station desk with his bouncy hair and tattooed arms. He smiles at her, his whole face lighting up, and she sees again just how handsome he is. "Hello," she says.

"Everything all right?"

Grace shrugs, then shakes her head. "No. None of your colleagues believe me."

"Oh?"

She turns and looks down the street, eyes narrowing as she wonders how much to say. "My friend is still missing and yet apparently you've closed the case. Your detective in there seems content that Anna is absolutely fine and just having a little time out for herself."

"Which you don't believe?" he asks.

She turns back to him. "No."

He holds her gaze for a long moment. She wants to look away but can't quite bring herself to do so. "I remembered last night when I got home," he starts, "where I know your name from."

At this she notices his smile falter, the light in his eyes darkening. "It was my first case. Twenty-two years ago. Clearly you've changed a lot since then, as you were only a child. I wasn't much of an adult myself, I suppose, which is why the case is branded into my head." He taps himself on the side of his hair. "Your school friend. Heather Kerr."

Grace opens her mouth, her eyes trawling his face again for recognition. He was the policeman with the friendly face who had come to her parents' house and stood on their doorstep, telling them that Heather was missing. Anna had been sent home shortly after he arrived, back to her dad, Catherine insisting he needed to be present if Anna was to speak to the police.

Eventually Grace nods. "I remember," she says quietly. She remembers, though she doesn't want to.

Back in the car she slams her hands against the steering wheel, reaching for her phone and calling Anna's number, but the call diverts straight to voice mail again. "Anna, I'm worried about you," she says. "Please call me. If you're okay, just let me know. I want to hear it from you." She hangs up and tosses the phone onto the seat beside her, drumming her fingers now, not knowing where to go next.

The police officer's name is Marcus Hargreaves. She still remembers his name. She remembers that she'd sat on a beanbag in the living room while he sat next to her, asking her about school. *Did she like it? What was her favorite subject? Does she know what she wants to do when she leaves?* He'd told her back then there was nothing to be worried about. They would find Heather, he'd said. It is why she knows she cannot trust them when they tell her not to worry now, because he might have kept to his word. They did find her in the end, but it was too late.

As soon as he told her who he was, Grace made an excuse to go and left him standing on the corner of the road outside the station. She could feel his eyes on her back as she crossed over to her car, but Heather Kerr is not someone she wants to talk about, and especially not with the officer who was on the case.

She tries to push Marcus Hargreaves to the edge of her mind and focus on the here and now: Anna has supposedly messaged to say she is fine; the police aren't looking into her disappearance. There is still a gap in Wednesday night between when she left the pub and when the others did, and maybe if Grace knew what had happened after she left, she could work out what to do next.

Caitlyn is her best option. If Grace can get her on her own, then she has a chance of breaking her down and getting her to say what she knows. She will turn up unannounced. It'll be better that way. She'll drive to Caitlyn's house and just hope the woman is alone.

Caitlyn doesn't live in the new-build estates like her three friends do. Hers is a terraced town house on the eastern edge of Clearwater, where the property prices are cheaper. It's also a stone's throw from Anna's childhood house, which Grace has driven past a few times since she's been back, each time memories flooding back as if they were only yesterday.

In contrast, she has only driven past her own childhood home on a couple of occasions. Her parents' old house sits farther out of town still, and the years haven't been kind to it. The road, which was once deemed up-and-coming, has been abandoned to the thrill of the arrival of a housing estate. Her dad's once-pristine driveway and immaculate garage have been overtaken by weeds and peeling paint. It's hard to imagine him out front proudly polishing his new Mazda in front of the neighbors when looking at the house in its current state, so she is better off remembering it in her head.

When Matilda started at St. Christopher's, the mums had asked Grace, "What's it like to be back again after so much time?"

She told them it was like coming home. What she didn't add was if that was a good thing or not. Grace had always considered her childhood a happy one; she certainly hadn't wanted for anything, but as soon as she'd set foot in Clearwater again, the thought had hit her that she couldn't remember if she'd been actually *happy*.

She is coming up to Anna's old house now as these thoughts fill her head, and she finds herself slowing to a crawl as she approaches it, peering out of the passenger window. *Was* she happy? It's an unnerving thought that she may not have been, and one she has never wanted to address. She should have been. She had more than Anna ever did: two parents who were there for her all the time, at least, not an emotionally absent father like Anna's.

Grace slams a foot on the accelerator, speeding up too fast, eyes back on the road ahead and away from the house. Her mum was certainly there for her, anyway, too much most of the time—"a helicopter parent," she would be called now. But Grace knows the same couldn't really be said of her dad. Not even, she thinks now, as much as Anna's father had been there for his daughter. She has never been able to admit it before, not even to herself.

It's a thought she quickly dismisses as she turns onto Caitlyn's road and pulls up outside her house. It is the only one on the road with brand-new Velux windows peeking out of its roof, and whereas all the other front gardens are paved with ornate rockeries, this one has an unsightly climbing frame in the middle.

Caitlyn's car is parked on the road out front, and with none of the others' cars in sight, Grace feels some relief as she raps on the knocker and waits for someone to come to the door. When Caitlyn appears she is wrapped in a thick cardigan that reaches her mid-calves and her hair is tied back in a scruffy knot. Her face has panic written all over it when she sees Grace on her doorstep.

"Do you mind if I come in?" Grace asks.

Caitlyn nods and stands aside, looking down the road as if she expects someone to be watching them.

"The police have said they've closed the case," Grace says as she follows Caitlyn through the short hallway and into her front room. The table is covered in craft material. She can't even see the top of it for pots of glitter and tubes of glue. Pieces of colored card stock are strewn everywhere, intermingled with tiny felt Christmas trees, and there is a pile of paper chains dumped on the carpet.

When Caitlyn sees Grace eyeing it, she says, "Sorry. It's a mess." She begins to push some of it together but doesn't make much effort. When she stops she adds, "I make cards to sell in my sister's shop."

"I didn't know that." Grace picks one up. "They're good."

"Thank you. It's just a hobby, really, but for some reason she's already sold all the Christmas ones I made." Caitlyn smiles sheepishly. "You can sit down," she adds, gesturing to an armchair near the window.

Grace nods and sits as Caitlyn slides a wicker chair out from beneath the table for herself, looking at her expectantly.

"I didn't even know your sister has a shop." Grace smiles.

"It's a florist on the main road, but she sells other bits, too. I don't do it for the money," Caitlyn tells her, "which is good as they don't sell for much."

"Your husband works at the boatyard, doesn't he?" Grace goes on, sensing Caitlyn is beginning to feel a bit more comfortable in her presence.

"Yes. Alan's been there for as long as I've known him. As was his father and his grandfather, too." There is a hint of pride in her voice. "But it's Alan who's grown it into the business it is today," she says. "Eric will tell you that. It's turning more money now than it has in decades."

"Eric?" Grace asks. "Nancy's husband, Eric?"

Caitlyn nods. "He works for Alan now. He does the books."

Grace's eyes widen in surprise. "Oh?" she says, and immediately Caitlyn understands she has said something she likely shouldn't have said, for her cheeks flush red. "I mean, you know he used to have a very big job in London, but—"

Grace brushes the comment aside with "Of course." She smiles, but the information is interesting and she files it away to think about later, because it is just another little thing about Nancy that makes her not the person she presents herself to be.

"Anyway," Caitlyn starts, clearly about to change the subject, "you know Anna texted yesterday, don't you?"

"I know she supposedly did," Grace replies.

Caitlyn opens her mouth as if to protest, but in the end she doesn't say anything, clamping it shut again as if she doesn't disagree.

"Do you think she definitely has?" Grace asks her.

"Why would they lie?" Caitlyn replies.

Grace shrugs but doesn't take her eyes off Caitlyn. Finally she says, "Please tell me what happened on Wednesday evening after I left." She leans forward in the uncomfortable chair. "What happened when you left the pub?"

Caitlyn reaches for one of the pots of glitter and draws it towards her, fiddling with its plastic lid, pushing it up with her thumb and then pressing it shut again. Grace tries to ignore the irritating popping sound it makes each time it opens, and she wishes Caitlyn would just answer the question. "I don't know what you want me to say," she says eventually.

"I just want the truth."

"Nancy told me Anna had already gone," Caitlyn says. "I assumed she must have done, but I honestly didn't know if she had or not. I didn't see her for at least fifteen minutes before we called the cab, so she could have done, and by then it was almost two a.m. and I just wanted to get home. I'd told Alan I'd be home by one, so I had this panic he'd worry."

"Why would Nancy tell you Anna had left if Rachel says she was still there?" she asks. Grace has no interest whatsoever in Alan. She just wants Caitlyn to answer her questions.

"I don't know." Caitlyn shrugs. "I don't, Grace. Whatever you think you're going to get from me, I don't have the answers you want. Why aren't you speaking to Nancy or Rachel?"

"Because I don't think they'll tell me the truth," Grace admits.

Caitlyn peels her gaze away and studies the pot in her hand.

"And I want to know why not." When Caitlyn doesn't speak, she goes on: "What happened before that point?"

"Oh, I don't know." She shakes her head but carries on. "Anna was gone for ages with Rachel. They were outside smoking, I suppose. That must have been when they had the argument, because when they came back in I don't remember them talking to each other again. In fact, as soon as Anna came back, Nancy got up and dragged her to the bar and they were there for a really long time, because Rachel kept asking me what they were doing. But like I say, I have no idea, because none of them told me anything."

"Okay," Grace says, sensing some irritation at this. "And then what?"

"Anna was upset. I wondered if it was because of the argument with Rachel, but . . ." She shrugs.

"The one Nancy professed she knew nothing about?"

"Yes," she admits. "But I don't think she did know about that, because when you left Rachel's yesterday Nancy was demanding answers from her. I don't think she had a clue that they'd been arguing. So whatever her discussion was with Anna, it must have been unrelated."

"And what did Rachel say?"

"She wouldn't tell her. At least, not while I was there."

"You feel it too, don't you, Caitlyn?" Grace presses. "Like you're being kept out of something."

When Caitlyn doesn't answer, Grace asks, "So do you think that was why Anna was upset, or do you think there was another reason?"

"If you're asking me if I think her argument with Rachel was enough to drive her away from us at the end of the night then no, I don't see it. How can it be?"

"So there's something else?"

"Probably." Caitlyn finally releases the pot of glitter and absent-mindedly pushes it away. "The thing is, Anna was really . . ." Caitlyn pauses. "Well, frantic, I suppose. At one point Nancy was practically shaking her, telling her she was making no sense." She looks up at Grace. "But you have to remember how much everyone was drinking. I don't think we can look too far into any of it."

"Of course we can," Grace says. "Because Anna still isn't home. And she's your friend, Caitlyn. All of what you're telling me means there was something wrong, and by the end of the night, by the sounds of it, she'd fallen out with both Rachel and Nancy."

Caitlyn's brow furrows. "Do you think she's in trouble?"

"Do you?" Grace asks, her eyes narrowing as she cocks her head. There is something about Caitlyn's expression that concerns her, and yet it excites her at the same time, because it makes her think she is on the right track, and that finally someone agrees with her. "I want you to tell the police what you told me."

"I did. Yesterday," she says.

"Then I want you to come back to the station with me and tell them you're still concerned about Anna and they have to open the case back up."

"But she's texted Ben," Caitlyn says. "I can't."

"Why not? Because you're too scared to go against Nancy?"

"No. Of course not."

"For God's sake," Grace mutters, "what the hell has that women got on you all?"

Grace sits in the car outside Caitlyn's house. Rain has now started to drum on the windows and she can no longer see much but the increasing circles it creates as it thuds on the screen, disappearing before new ones emerge.

She has no idea if Anna is safe or not. If she texted Ben, or if someone else did. All she knows is that her friend is still missing, and even if Caitlyn is prepared to sit back and do nothing, *Grace* isn't.

As thoughts of the last two days slip in and out of her head, something strikes her from her first conversation with Ben. Anna has been seeing a therapist, a woman called Sally Parkinson, who lives in a place called Lewen Close.

Grace types the name into Google on her phone, expanding the map to show the address clearly. Then she calls the number and makes herself an appointment, using her mother's name to protect her anonymity, for Monday morning.

She has no idea what might happen in the next two days, but at least she is doing something.

December

One week earlier

Anna

"I'm pleased to see you, Anna," Sally says. "It's been three weeks. I have to be honest, I was worried you wouldn't come back. Not after last time. You seemed very upset when you left."

"I wasn't going to come," I admit. The fact that I had so nearly told Sally that Grace had given me an alibi that night weighed heavily and made me afraid. I had been waiting for Sally to chase me, press me into making another appointment, and had rehearsed what I was going to say: I didn't need any more sessions right now and I'd be in touch again if I ever did. I was up-to-date on my payments, I wasn't letting Sally down. I had decided it was the right thing to do; I didn't need to tell anyone what had happened.

But the call never came. And as the days and weeks passed, I wondered if it was because of this lack of contact that my fingers began to itch to pick up the phone. To speak to Sally again.

"Why weren't you going to come?" Sally asks.

Because I've said too much already. Because I'm afraid that if I tell her the rest, then everything is going to come crashing down. Because I could lose everything I love.

"Anna?" she persists when I don't respond. "How come you're back here, then?"

"Because I have to tell someone." This is the conclusion I had come to. I have to tell someone before I am driven mad.

Sally nods slowly. "Do you think you can tell me what happened to your friend Heather?"

That night I watched Grace turn into my driveway and disappear back into my house, all the while feeling sick with nerves that I'd chosen Heather over her. What was she going to say to me when I returned? What if it was the end of our friendship? Would she be upstairs on the mattress when I got home or might she have even gone back to her own house?

"Come on, then. Let's go," Heather was saying casually.

I tried to put the questions to the back of my mind as I turned and followed Heather up my street, before going down one of the lanes that led towards the seafront. Every so often I'd look back, waiting to see Grace reappear. I wasn't sure if I wanted her to or not; it would undoubtedly be easier without her, but it worried me that Grace was going to be at Dad's house alone. What if he woke up and asked where I was? Would Grace tell him the truth? He would be mad, but Catherine would never forgive me for going to the cliffs against her stark warnings, and likely even more so when she learned I'd left Grace behind.

We carried on, picking up our pace down the narrow lanes. It was a ten-minute walk to get to the coast road, and Grace hadn't reappeared. To our left, Crayne's Cliff loomed ominously. In the dark it looked like a chalk mountain, its face flat and imposing against the dark sky. It took us another fifteen minutes to climb it and reach the point where the moonlight got sucked up behind the canopy of the trees.

Soon we could make out the police tape tied between the trunks.

Heather was making her way over to it, pushing it down with her foot and climbing over. "What are you waiting for?" she called back to me.

Catherine had told us many stories over the years. My dad had, too. The cliffs had taken their victims. Anyone who had lived in Clearwater for long enough knew not to go near the edge, and especially now that it was out of bounds. You never knew when the earth could slide away and take you with it.

Heather was staring at me, though, and so I tentatively joined her. It was eerie at night, so dark, and hard to see your footing and what lay ahead. But now I was here, on the other side of the tape, and yet Heather was on the move again, picking her way towards the cliff edge. I followed her until my legs buckled. "Heather, stop. We've gone far enough," I said.

When she turned back her mouth was twisted into a smile. "A dare's a dare, Anna."

The dare was to cross the tape. We'd done that, hadn't we? We could go back now. "It's too dark, and the cliffs—you know, they can give way at any minute."

"Oh God, you're worse than Grace!"

"I'm not. I just—"

"I'm going." She waved her hands out, palms splayed upwards, grinning as she stepped backwards away from me, once, twice . . . She was at the edge now. Behind her the ground disappeared into darkness, the drop only a foot from where she stood. If anything happened out here we were going to be in so much trouble. Even stepping past the police tape felt worse than I'd imagined it would.

"Will you just come back?" I cried.

She laughed at me again, mockingly, and I wanted to cry like a baby. I stood rooted to the spot, unable to move as Heather shuffled farther back again. She must have been inches from the edge now. All it needed was one misplaced footing, a slip, or the earth to crumble beneath her, and she would be gone.

"If you don't come back, I'm leaving you here," I screamed. My whole body was shaking. My arms and legs felt like they didn't belong to me. All I wanted in that moment was to be wrapped up in the soft cotton sheet of my bed and not out on the cliffs in the dark with someone I'd thought was my friend but who was acting mad.

"I left her," I tell Sally, as warm tears slide down my cheeks. "I walked away. And then I heard a scream and I ran back, but by the time I got to the cliff edge she was gone. I couldn't see her. She'd fallen, gone over the edge."

"Oh, Anna," Sally murmurs, reaching into her box of Kleenex yet again and passing me another tissue.

I clutch it in a ball, shredding tiny pieces from it as each memory slices through me. Desperately trying to see Heather over the side of the cliff. Running home, every heartbeat a sharp knife in my chest. The following day, when Heather didn't turn up at school. When the police arrived at Grace's house the following evening and I was sent home to answer their questions.

Did I know where Heather was? Had I seen her at all that day? When was the last time I'd spoken to her?

"I lied," I whisper now to Sally. "I was so scared, that I lied. I didn't tell anyone I'd been to the cliffs, and Grace lied for me too. She told the police we were at my house, that the last time we saw Heather was at school earlier that day. It took them a week of searching before they found her." Through my sobs, my gasps for breath, I speak the words I have never told another soul in twenty-two years.

"Her foster mother turned up on my doorstep a day later, begging me to tell her if I knew where Heather was, asking me to let her know she wasn't in trouble," I cry. "But it was too late," I tell Sally, sucking in too much air as I breathe. "I was too caught up in my lies by then that all I did was stare back at her and tell her that I didn't have a clue where Heather was."

Sally continues to watch me silently. I glance up at her, trying to find the judgment I deserve, but I can read nothing in her eyes. "I let her foster mother, and the rest of Heather's family, believe she might still be alive. I never told anyone what had really happened that night."

12

Monday, 16 December

Grace

Monday arrives. It's been four days since anyone has seen Anna, and Grace's anguish is rising with the passing hours.

Still Ben tells her that Anna is fine. "Yes, she has messaged again," he says with increasing impatience at Grace's numerous calls. But Anna isn't answering her phone. Each time Grace has dialed her friend's number it goes straight to voice mail. She has lost count of the number of times she has called, but she doesn't care. Until she sees Anna for herself, she won't relent.

"Maybe she does need some time for herself," Caitlyn tells Grace, in what feels like a 180-degree turn. "I think we should leave her be."

No. Grace cannot believe this. She *knows* without a doubt Anna would not walk out on her son unless there was something seriously wrong, a life-or-death situation. And you don't spend an evening with your friends in the pub, laughing and drinking, to then decide at the end of it that you need space from your life.

She has told Caitlyn this a number of times over the weekend, but it is like banging her head against a brick wall.

Having Matilda around means Grace has tried to pretend there is nothing to worry about, but her daughter has been asking questions. "Who are you calling now, Mummy?"

Ben. Anna. Caitlyn. Nancy. Rachel. The police.

She has been calling all of them. She is pestering them, Nancy tells her.

Will you stop bloody pestering me, Grace? I have nothing else to say.

Their reluctance to talk to her and their refusal to agree that something isn't right makes her even more anxious that Anna isn't safe. Even more angry with them all.

Grace has sat in the car, with her daughter in the back, outside Ben's house, when he has neither let her in nor answered any more of her questions. She knows, she just knows, there is something he isn't telling her.

She has walked up and down the coast road, past the Old Vic, stood in its car park and stared over the wall at the cliffs to her left and the sea in front.

"Why doesn't Ethan's daddy want to speak to you, Mummy?" Matilda has asked her. "Why do we have to keep driving here? Can't we go on to the beach? Why can't we walk to the top of the cliffs?" Her daughter's questions are as relentless as the ones inside her own head.

"Will *you* stop pestering *me*," she has said to Matilda. Grace knows she is driving herself mad, but it isn't just the not knowing that is doing this to her, it is that someone close is hiding the truth.

But now at least she has safely deposited Matilda at school and she can focus on her upcoming appointment with Sally Parkinson. It is a half-hour journey and she is there by twenty past nine, so when she arrives she doesn't have long to wait.

Outside the therapist's house Grace leans across the seat to look out her car's passenger window. It would be ideal if she could tell Sally the truth about who she is and that she is worried about Anna, but any good therapist wouldn't tell her a thing. It isn't like the two of them could sit down and figure out what's been going on in Anna's head in the days and weeks before she disappeared.

No, the reason she is here is to see if there is any other way she can find out why Anna has been visiting Sally Parkinson for the last three months, and whether that will tell her why Anna has vanished—and if there is any chance she can get her hands on Sally's notes herself.

Sally leads Grace to a small two-seater sofa before sitting down in a wing-backed armchair that looks far too small for her. She has a notepad and a pen with an annoying gemstone that bounces from side to side as it moves, and a hairband that she is constantly fiddling with. Already Grace feels irritated, sitting in this small room with only one window to look out of. Not that there is much to see anyway, but the room could do with some daylight.

"Maybe we could start by you telling me what has brought you here today, Catherine," Sally says. Grace notices how strange it is to be addressed by her mother's name.

"I'm having problems with a friend," Grace says. "It seems silly me talking about it as an adult, but . . ." She lets the sentence hang for a moment, trying to gather some steam in her thoughts. She doesn't want to veer too close to the truth, but while she's paying for the therapist's time, she may as well get something out of it.

"What kind of problems?" Sally asks her. The pen with its stupid wobbly bit keeps dangling, waiting for her to give it something to write in the book.

"It's a friendship that feels very toxic." An image of Nancy fills her head, in her tight skinny jeans and the blazer she was wearing the night Anna disappeared. All puffed up with shoulder pads and faux importance, living the lie that her husband's job is so much more than working part-time for the boatyard.

While she is talking, Grace scans the room. There is a filing cabinet tucked into the corner, which must hold Sally's notes. The small window, which is marginally open to let in some air, is attached to a flimsy latch. Outside the room is a downstairs bathroom tucked under the stairs. She presumes the bathroom window looks out on the side path.

It is all a long shot, and Grace knows she isn't being rational, having thoughts of breaking in and searching through personal files. If she were caught, she'd be in a whole heap of trouble. But as she talks and the therapist makes vague noises, she wonders what other choice she has.

After Grace has managed to speak for forty minutes, she asks if she can use the restroom, and leaves the room wondering what sort of help Anna could have gotten from talking to a woman who has given so little. She has vivid memories of speaking to a counselor when she was a teenager, a woman her mum had dragged her to see in the weeks after Heather Kerr had been found. Grace had resisted it, protesting that she didn't need to speak to anyone, but in the end she endured three long sessions before her parents acquiesced that she was wasting their money if she wasn't going to open up. Not once did they appreciate that Grace simply didn't need the help.

As she expected, the bathroom looks out onto the thin pathway that runs up the side of the house. She unlocks the window and peeks out before pulling it shut again.

Her fingers linger on its clasp as thoughts flitter like butterflies through her head. She could climb through if she doesn't catch it properly. If Sally used the bathroom she would think it was still shut.

Carefully Grace closes it as tight as she can, without shutting it properly. She rests the catch to one side, making it look as if it is locked, while running a finger under the wooden frame to check she could open it from the outside. If she has the guts to.

What choice do you have? The thought plays on a loop once her session is over and she leaves Sally's house. What other option does she have if she wants to find out what has happened to her friend? Everyone else either is lying to her or has given up.

She will come back, because the truth is, she will do anything for Anna.

13

Grace

Back at home, Grace stands at the front of her apartment and stares out the large window with a mug of tea clutched in her hand. From the third floor she has an uninterrupted view of the sea on one side and Weymouth on the other.

If her dad could see her now. Back in Clearwater. He likely would have had the same words for her as her mum had when she'd announced she was retuning in August, but with a very different meaning.

"What are you doing going back there, Grace?" Catherine had said. Grace detected the panic in her voice and rolled her eyes in frustration. Her dad would have wanted to know because he'd never had a nice word for Clearwater when they'd left. As far as he was concerned, it was a dead-end town with no prospects.

"What are you worried about exactly?" she'd asked her mum. She had put up with her mother's neuroses for as long as she could remember. How her father put up with them she had no idea, and yet he seemed to tolerate her, love her, even. More than he loved Grace, because it was no secret Henry hadn't wanted children. Grace had once overheard him telling a customer in his office. An odd choice for someone to tell something so personal to, she'd thought, but then her dad was strange in that way.

Grace imagined her mum sitting in her square box of a front room, looking out onto a cul-de-sac of retirement houses exactly like hers, waiting for something to happen that would ping her out of her chair, like the arrival of the postman or a neighbor mowing their lawn.

It saddens Grace to think that her mum's life has come to this, and yet she has point-blank refused to move back to Clearwater.

"What are you worried about?" she had asked her mum again.

She imagined all the things Catherine might say and settled on it being her usual vague, "You know there's something unsafe about that town." But in the end her mum's voice, so quiet it was barely audible, had only uttered the words, "I'm worried about you, Gracie."

Grace had reeled back in shock and pressed the phone closer to her ear. She could hear her mum's breathing so clearly she could imagine the warm air on her neck.

Grace had wanted to ask what she meant, but her mum was saying, "You should never have gone back there, Gracie."

In the end, Grace had cut the call short. There was something eerie about her mum's words, and she really didn't want to think about what they meant.

Taking another sip of her now-cold tea, she drains the cup and takes it through to the kitchen. Since coming back from Sally's, she cannot get her head around the idea of breaking into the woman's house, and yet at the same time she's consumed by her need to know why Anna has been seeing a therapist.

She picks up her mobile and dials Ben's number again. When he doesn't respond, she sends him a text: *Have you heard any more from Anna?*

As she waits for his reply, Grace is unable to find anything to occupy her mind, and so eventually she grabs her car keys and takes the lift down to the underground car park.

Grace knows that Ben is at home because there is movement at his bedroom window. She can't see him clearly but notices a shadow as it passes through the light. It has been twenty minutes since she sent him a text, and she still hasn't received a reply.

Climbing out of the car, she paces up the driveway. There is no longer movement in the window above, but as she approaches the front door, she sees him descending the stairs through the glazed glass.

Grace presses her finger against the doorbell. When there is no answer, she stabs it again. It is definitely working. She can hear its ring shrilling inside the house. Eventually he opens the door, keeps it slightly ajar and says, "What is it, Grace?"

She sidesteps to see him better. "You know what it is. I want to talk to you about Anna."

"There's nothing to talk about." He begins to close the door.

"Yes there is." She holds her hand on it, pushing against him until the door eases back and exposes the hallway beyond and a figure behind him, standing in the doorway to the kitchen.

"Anna?" Grace gasps as she tries to take a step forward, but Ben's hand is still on the door and there is only so far she can get. "What are you doing here? Are you okay?"

Grace tries to take in what she is seeing. Her friend is alive but her face is streaked with tears and smudges of black mascara. If it is possible, she looks thinner than she did five days ago, more gaunt, and she is wrapped in a thick wool cardigan that she clutches around her body. Her eyes look haunted as they stare back at Grace.

Anna takes a step back and Grace pushes against the door, but Ben is pushing back equally hard. She has been hurt, Grace thinks. Is it Ben?

"I'm here, Anna." Grace holds out a hand to reach out for her, willing her friend to come to her, but she seems too scared to move. "God, what's happened to you?" She pushes back again, but Ben is too strong for her. "Anna?" she persists.

Anna shakes her head and opens her mouth, and Grace nods to encourage her, but when she finally speaks, she says, in a voice that doesn't sound hurt or scared but firm, "Just go, Grace," and Ben slams the door shut.

December

One week earlier

Anna

I wonder how Sally can listen and not pass judgment. How she manages to look sympathetic at the fact I have lived with this dreadful secret for so many years, rather than appalled that I never told anyone what happened.

"Heather's body was found a week later," I say. "It was washed up by the jetty. No one ever questioned us again after that. I guess there was no reason to believe I was with her.

"It has never left me," I go on. "It's always been there in the back of my head, that what I did was wrong. Because it isn't just the fact I lied. If I had called for help at the time, then I might have saved her. That's what is unbearable. That Heather might still be alive if I'd done the right thing."

"Why didn't you?" she asks me. "Why didn't you tell the police what happened?"

I turn away and consider how to answer, but before I do I say, "Grace coming back has opened this wound up again. I guess I learned to live with my guilt somehow. At times I've been able to convince myself there was nothing I could have done anyway. And as the years passed, I just got on with my life and focused on the important things—Ethan and Ben. And Zadie . . ." I pause. "Oh God, you see, this is what I can't cope with: that it could all be taken away from me."

"Why do you think that might happen?" Sally asks me.

"That Ben might leave me. Or that he'll stop me from seeing Ethan. I don't know. At the least, if the police ever found out, I'd never be able to adopt."

"Grace is the only one who knows?" she asks.

I nod.

"And you're worried she might tell someone?"

"The day Grace turned up four months ago I'd just got back from clearing out my dad's house," I tell Sally. "To find her on my doorstep was what I needed in that moment. I was thrilled to see her. She told me she was just over here visiting, not that she'd moved back. I didn't know I would see her again, but a week later I walked Ethan to school and there she was, standing in the playground, telling me Matilda was in the same class. I knew in that moment," I say, "that the life I'd so carefully protected was about to crumble around me."

"Anna, what are you actually saying?" Sally asks.

"You asked me why I didn't tell anyone. I need to tell you what happened when I got back to my dad's house that night."

I stood on the edge of the cliffs, shaking with fear as I leaned over as far as my body would allow. It was too dark to see much. The small flashlight I'd brought barely reached a few meters below, and even though I swept it back and forth across the cliff face, there was no sign of Heather.

I got down on my knees in the soil, tears of panic filling my eyes. My heart was racing so fast I thought it would burst out of me as I called Heather's name over and over, but in return the night was silent.

I had no idea how long I'd been on the ground before I eventually scrambled to my feet and stumbled backwards. It could have been two minutes. It could have been half an hour. Time had slipped from reality like the whole evening was fast doing.

I turned and ran, back through the trees, down the cliffs, until I was on the coastal path. I passed phone booths, where I could have made an emergency call, and yet I kept running because I just needed to be back in the safety of my own house. All the time my mind spun with images of Heather: standing on the cliff edge one minute; gone the next.

Soon I was at the end of an alleyway, a cut-through that was only around the corner from my house. I didn't even know how I'd gotten there, my run had been a daze, thoughts of anyone lurking in the shadows hadn't entered my head like they usually did.

When I reached my front door, I let myself in and raced up the stairs, praying Grace would be in my bedroom. I was so relieved to find her there. She looked the picture of innocence in her Forever Friends pajama top. How I wished I'd listened to her.

Falling to my knees on the end of her mattress, I shook Grace awake.

"What's happened?" She woke, startled.

"It's Heather," I spluttered. "She's fallen off the cliff."

"Oh my God." Grace held me against her as I sobbed and told her how Heather went too close to the edge, how I started walking away because I knew I shouldn't be there, and how she fell.

"And that's all that happened?" she asked me.

"Of course," I said, startled by her question, though my mind had filled with the argument Heather and I'd had only moments before. "I need to call the police," I cried. "And an ambulance. But oh God, my dad's going to kill me."

"Shhh," she whispered in my ear, still rocking me.

My hands were cold and shaking violently as she took them in her own.

"I'm going to be in so much trouble," I said.

How desperately I wanted Grace to tell me I wasn't going to be, that when she eventually did I felt myself slump deeper into her arms. "You won't be in trouble," she told me. "I won't let anything bad happen to you." How could she be so certain? And yet she told me this over and over until I almost believed her.

"You don't tell the police anything," my best friend said. "You were here all night. We both were. You were never on those cliffs."

I pulled away then and looked up at her calm face. "What? I can't . . . you mean . . . ?" The words weren't coming out. She meant I should do nothing? I shouldn't make a call? "But she might need help," I eventually said. "We can't leave her."

"*You* can't, you mean," Grace said, oh so quickly, before she moved on, making me wonder if I had heard her right. But I knew I had. A definite yet quick reminder that it wasn't "we" who had gotten into this mess, just "me."

Only now "we" were getting out of it together.

"Anna, if Heather fell over the cliff, she'd have no chance of surviving. And if you tell them what happened, this could become a murder inquiry." The thought turned me to ice. "We can't help her now. We just need to think of you," she kept telling me, and eventually my fourteen-year-old panicked self let Grace convince me this was the best thing to do.

Sally's face is creased into what could be sympathy or disgust, I have no idea.

"Grace always kept to her word," I say. "That night she promised me she would lie for me and she did. After that, we went back to being the best friends we'd always been before, only now our relationship was more one-sided than ever. Now she had something to hold over me."

"You think that's why she did it?" Sally asks.

"I didn't know at first, but later I'd wonder why she was being so kind to me when I'd chosen Heather over her that night. Grace always hated me being friends with anyone else. It was always just supposed to be her and me, 'sisters,'" I say. "I knew the moment I chose Heather over her she would be furious, so how did she manage to forgive me so easily that night?

"The fact is, she didn't," I continue. "She wasn't forgiving me by being there for me, she was taking care of it by making sure I would never leave her again."

"And then Grace went away? To Australia, for many years?" Sally says.

"I know, and over time I grasped just how oppressive our friendship had been. It took having that space to understand how I couldn't think for myself, couldn't breathe when she was around me. But now she's back again . . ." I turn away and look out the window. There is a clear, bright blue sky outside.

"I've tried to keep her at bay, but she wants more from me and she isn't happy about my friendship with Nancy and the others."

I turn back to Sally, thinking of the last conversation I'd had with Grace two days ago. *Do you think of Heather, Anna?* she had asked me. *Do you ever think about that night like I do?*

"No one knows Grace like I do," I tell Sally. "No one has a clue what she is capable of."

The truth is that if Grace wants it to happen, then there is every chance a murder inquiry might open up.

part two

Someone's friend who has twins in year one lives on the same road as Anna and saw her walk into her house. The information hit WhatsApp within minutes.

A tsunami of questions followed. What did Anna look like upon her return? Was she accompanied by anyone else? So she just waltzed back into her house like nothing happened?

She looked pale and tired, apparently. And she was alone, but her husband was at the door before she even started up the driveway, as if he were expecting her.

But what was even more strange was that half an hour later a woman had turned up at the house, and when they wouldn't let her in, she started shouting through the letterbox that she was the ONLY ONE looking for her, the ONLY ONE who cared. They emphasized it in capitals on the message, just to make the point as the woman had done in person.

"What did she look like?" someone asked.

"Auburn hair. Black BMW."

"Sounds like Grace," someone else suggested, yet it also didn't sound anything like her from what they'd seen before. Why on earth would she be shouting through the letterbox?

"And they didn't answer the door to her?" came another message.

"No. She just snapped at Anna's elderly neighbor and then stormed off," came the reply.

Well, this was odd behavior. And so unlike the Grace they knew. They couldn't imagine her raising her voice, getting angry, when she had been so placid and patient in the school playground.

But regardless, they all agreed that it made the anticipation of pickup even more appealing than it had been at the end of the previous week.

14

Anna

It has gone quiet now that Grace has stopped yelling through the letterbox. My hands are still shaking, tapping against my thighs.

"Is she still there?" I ask Ben.

He glimpses through the frosted window. "I'm not sure. I don't see her."

I am waiting for the doorbell to ring again. I know how persistent Grace can be when she wants something, and over the last few days Ben has learned this too.

"She won't go away, Anna," he says to me. "At some point you're going to have to face her." He cocks his head to one side as he looks at me. Ben has been generously patient with me since I came home this morning, but at some point he is going to want more answers than I've given him. "She's going to be at school every day. You can't avoid her."

"I know!" I cry. God, how I know. The time before Grace first arrived at St. Christopher's feels like a distant memory now. Nancy is collecting Ethan for me today, but I will have to be back there soon. "I think she might have gone," I tell him. "Please can we just . . ." I beckon to the kitchen.

Ben nods as he follows me through to the back and heads straight for the kettle, which he fills with water. Since I've been home, this is the first time we have been in a room together with nothing but the pressure of needing to talk hanging in the air, so densely stifling it feels almost too heavy to breathe.

"It's good to be back," I say again. "I've missed you and Ethan so much."

"I've missed you too." Ben's back is to me as he opens cupboards and fishes out a teabag, and so I can't see his face. His words are flat, though. "What kind of tea do you want?" he asks.

"Peppermint if we have it. I can't wait to see Ethan."

I will Ben to turn round. I just want to see his eyes, to know that there is love in them rather than the anger I'm fearing.

We have spoken a handful of times over the last four days, after I realized that my text to him at 4:13 a.m. on Thursday morning never went through. It was supposed to explain where I was going, that I didn't want him to worry. But by the time I had managed to charge my phone and see the text still sat there, unsent, I knew it was too late for that.

I'd nearly thrown up at the sight of the red exclamation mark—the message "Not delivered!" displayed like it was actually quite funny. By then it was almost midday and I knew Ben must have been going out of his mind. What had he told Ethan? I'd called him straightaway, at least put his mind at rest that I was alive.

"Where the hell are you?" he'd yelled down the line at me.

"Ben, I'm sorry," I pleaded. "I'm so sorry. I sent a text, I promise you. I didn't want you to worry." I was crying, though no tears were coming out. I was too filled with panic that whatever I told him might not be believed, that he might never forgive me.

"What's happened?" he growled. "I've been going out of my bloody mind, Anna."

He was angry, as well he should have been. I would have been the same, which made my apologies even more pathetic. I should have done more to make sure he knew I was all right, but I had fallen asleep, my phone had died, and I'd told myself it didn't matter because he'd have received the text and I'd call him as soon as I could.

I told him where I was and he laughed down the phone. "You're kidding, right?"

"There are things you don't know, Ben, but you have to trust me right now," I said. "I promise I'll tell you all of it later." I gave him sketchy details then, told him I didn't trust Grace, asked him not to talk to her. It all sounded so cloak-and-dagger, but at that point I was planning to be home by evening. I just had things I needed to find out, things that Grace had said to me on Wednesday night that made me think there was more to the night Heather died than I might ever have known. And if they were true, then I really had no idea how far she might go.

But I didn't want to get into any of this with Ben over the phone. It was too big, too important. And so I begged him to trust me until I came home later.

"Grace has already been here," he told me, and I felt a shiver run down my spine. Of course she had, she would be right there in the middle of this, turning over every stone. "She seemed worried about you."

"Don't talk to her again," I hissed, "whatever you do. Don't tell her where I am."

"Anna, you're lucky I haven't been to the police yet," he said.

I closed my eyes, shook my head. This could have been so much worse if he'd done that. "What did you tell Ethan?" I asked.

"I said you were staying at a friend's. I didn't want to worry him."

"Thank you," I breathed. Thank God Ethan didn't think anything was wrong. "Tell him I love him. I love you both, Ben, you know that, don't you?" When he didn't answer, I said, "Ben?"

"Yes," he replied eventually, resigned, reluctant. I had no idea how he was truly feeling. "What do I tell Nancy?"

I mulled it over for a moment. "Tell her what you know," I said. "But ask her not to say anything to the others just yet. She can tell them I needed some time out."

I told Ben again that I'd be back later that evening, though that wasn't how things panned out. When I knew I had to stay, I sent him another text telling him I loved him, that I would be back soon.

Now Ben is turning round and placing a mug of peppermint tea in front of me. He takes a chair and sits down, watching me expectantly. "I need you to start at the beginning," he says.

The beginning? I don't even know when that was. It could have been twenty-two years ago, when I was fourteen, or it might have been further back than that, when I was five and little Grace Goodwin first stuck her head into the playhouse and asked me why I was crying.

"Don't worry, I'll be your best friend, Anna," she had said so simply. "I am already best friends with Katrina Moore, but I'll be yours instead." Then she dipped plastic bowls into the plastic sink and rinsed them out with imaginary water.

I don't have a clue what happened to Katrina Moore after that, I barely remember the girl, but Grace had stuck true to her word and had indeed dumped Katrina in favor of me.

It made me feel so warm inside that someone cared about me. It had been one long hot summer since my mum had walked out, and this was a feeling I didn't want to lose. I clung on to Grace like a life support, and in return she included me in everything she did. But in return for that, I soon learned that I owed her the same. When in year four Julie Butcher asked me to Paultons Park with her family for the day, Grace told me that I'd be hurting her feelings if I went. "That's not fair, Anna. She's not inviting me and so what am I going to do? And we take you everywhere with us and your dad doesn't take me anywhere."

Grace was right, I decided. Of course it wasn't fair to her. As much as I would have loved to go to Paultons Park with Julie, because she was a nice girl and it was so nice to be noticed and asked, I ended up saying no. Four weeks later Catherine had acquiesced that she would take us, no doubt after badgering from Grace.

But right now I don't think Ben needs to hear stories from the past. Instead I tell him what happened on Wednesday night when our pre-Christmas drinks took a turn for the worse.

We were all already there when Grace arrived. Through her smile I saw that she was put out by this, but I didn't care because I had never wanted to invite her in the first place. It was supposed to be drinks for the four of us, but Grace had been lingering close to our conversations in the playground, eavesdropping and commenting on our plans.

She had sidled up to me in the playground and said, "Ooh, drinks out on a school night. Sounds very naughty." Her smile had lingered for too long to be genuine. "When are you going?"

"Wednesday night," Rachel told her. Caitlyn appeared as awkward as I felt as she nibbled her thumbnail, and I could see Nancy fast approaching us. The silence that followed was excruciating, and all eyes landed on me to make a decision. "I didn't think you'd be able to get a babysitter so . . ." I bit my lip, waving a hand in the air.

"Of course I can." Grace beamed. "I'd love to come with you."

I'd spent three months keeping Grace onside, dancing around between her and my three good friends, none of whom particularly liked her. It was Nancy who had seen through her the most.

"Anna, you need to tell me what it is about her," she had persisted.

"What do you mean?" I'd asked.

"I can see there is something about your friendship with her that doesn't make you happy. You act differently around her; you do things you don't want to do." She was right that I didn't want to go to Grace's for macaroni cheese, but how could I admit this? How could I tell anyone the truth when Grace knows the worst thing I have ever done? I'd had no choice but to play it carefully; I knew what Grace was like.

I'd seen it a lot more clearly after she left for Australia. One day the sense had struck me as fast and as hard as a lightning bolt: I had lied to the police and not done anything more for Heather that night because I had listened to Grace.

All the blame I'd been putting on myself—that if I had called the police and sent someone to help as soon as I'd gotten home, she might still be alive—had been controlled by Grace.

I push my mug of tea away, across the table. I chose peppermint to soothe my nerves, but even the smell of it makes me feel sick now, as my mind has already begun darting from five nights ago to all the events that have changed its course.

Over the last three months I have lived on edge, fearing that Grace might tell someone about that night. But it has only been over the last couple of weeks that she has been dropping it into conversation again. *Do you ever think of Heather, Anna? Do you ever think about that night like I do? Do you regret what we did? I know I do.*

"Go on," Ben is pressing me, and I need to focus my thoughts on last Wednesday.

"I drank far more than I should have," I start. "I should have kept my head clearer, because I had a feeling things might get a little out of control." It was the first night we'd all been out since Ben's party, and after a few drinks I imagined there would be words, secret conversations, questions, and so far Ben was the only person I'd told what I saw that night.

I drag the mug of tea towards me again and take a small sip, grimacing. The teabag has been left in too long and it tastes bitter, but my mouth is dry and I need something.

"I thought Grace might leave earlier than she did. I could see she wasn't enjoying herself and she didn't want to be there. I didn't care that she was being left out because I wanted her to go." I glance at

Ben, searching his face for disapproval, but he looks more anxious than anything.

"She didn't join in the first round of tequilas, so I kept buying more on purpose, but she wasn't going anywhere. Her eyes were on me all evening, watching me, judging me." I stop short of telling Ben that Grace had quizzed me about smoking because Ben doesn't like my occasional habit. I don't either, but that night I'd smoked more than usual because I needed time outside away from her and I needed to calm my nerves.

"I think I kept drinking more because I was so on edge. All evening Grace was watching me. I felt like I might slip up at any moment, only the more I drank the more I didn't care. I just wanted her to leave."

Eventually Ben asks, "Why did you never tell me she was this bad? I mean, I got the impression you hadn't bothered to see her since she's been back because you've hardly made time for her. I just thought you no longer had anything in common?"

I wrap my hands around my mug again and say, "I can't drink this. I'm going to make a normal one."

"I'll do it." Ben pushes his chair from the table to get up. "You carry on talking."

"Grace didn't go home that night," I continued. "And then at one point she followed me to the ladies' room and started questioning me." I replay the conversation in my head as I tell him.

Grace had said, "You know you really don't seem yourself tonight, Anna." On their own the words didn't sound like much, but I knew the tone and had seen the darkness of Grace's eyes too many times to dismiss them. She was pressing closer to me until I was backed up against the sink. She managed to keep enough distance though, so she couldn't be accused of threatening me, but I felt threatened all the same.

"You don't have to look after me anymore," I had spat, emboldened by the tequila running through my veins. I'd avoided speaking to Grace so harshly since she had been back in Clearwater. In fact, I don't think I'd spoken to her this way since we were fourteen and I was emboldened by Heather. After that I've always been too afraid of what she knew, what she might tell people.

But I didn't care on Wednesday night. My words had come out in desperation as much as anything. I wanted her out of my life. I was sick of dancing to her tune, of inviting her for drinks out of what Nancy called a misplaced loyalty, but what I knew was fear.

After our conversation in the ladies' room, Grace found me in there again later. It was possibly only ten minutes before she finally left the Old Vic. Her eyes were narrowed into thin slits as she stood behind me in front of the mirror and said, "Nancy has a hold on you."

I looked up at her reflection. Here we were again. A twenty-two-year cycle that had gone full circle, and it still managed to conjure up the same feelings inside me—I was being manipulated, only there felt like little I could do about it.

Grace had leaned in closer, her words eerily soft as she said, "Nancy controls you."

Nancy controls you.

Heather controls you.

No Grace, you control me.

"You're kidding me, right?" I'd cried.

She stepped back, wrong-footed. "No, I'm not kidding," she said as she proceeded to tell me how she had been watching Nancy and the way she was with me and I had eventually told her that I always felt like I had to come and talk to her.

"It's you who controls me," I had said eventually. "You've been doing it from the moment you found me in the playhouse when we were five."

Grace's mouth curled at its edges. She didn't like what she was hearing. The plan she had no doubt set out for our friendship over the last three months clearly wasn't working. She wouldn't have factored in the kind of close relationships I'd forged with Nancy, Rachel, and Caitlyn. Likely she'd thought we could pick up where we left off.

"Doesn't she have any other friends?" Nancy had once asked me in the playground. "Why is it you she's clinging to?"

"I want to be with my friends, Grace," I said, making a move to step past her. "Whatever we had in the past, that was a long time ago. I'm a different person now." I was hoping she didn't see that despite my efforts, my hands were shaking at my sides. I still stopped short of saying I didn't want her in my life.

But Grace stopped me, pressing a hand against my chest. "I still worry about you," she said, her eyes flashing with something that looked more threatening than worried. "And you must know why. Because I've seen it before, haven't I, Anna? This isn't the first time I've picked up the pieces."

She wasn't pushing me, but the touch of her hand made me stumble back against the basins. The air was getting hot in the small bathroom. I just wanted to get out.

But Grace was shaking her head, her cheeks reddening. "I was there for you when you needed me most," she was saying. "And this is how you repay me. You've spent three months pushing me away, ignoring me. You and your friends acting like I don't exist."

"Grace, I don't—"

"Do you have any idea how much it's hurt me, Anna? How for once I needed you, only you couldn't be there for me, like I've always been for you. We were best friends," she was saying, her eyes wide, tears glistening in their corners. "We were like sisters." She slapped the palm of her hand against her chest.

"You know, I should never have done what I did that night," she went on. "Giving you an alibi, lying to the police and my parents and poor Heather's foster mother for you. You can't have forgiven yourself?"

"No," I said, "I haven't." I was close to tears too, but I begged them not to fall. "But you can't keep holding this over me, Grace."

"I just need a friend," she cried. "Like you needed one then. But you weren't even honest me with me that night, were you? There was plenty you didn't tell me."

"What are you going on about?" I said.

"Your argument with Heather?" she spat. "You think I didn't know about what happened just before Heather fell over the cliff?"

"I don't . . . how do you—"

"I *know*, Anna. I know exactly what happened."

"You weren't there," I said, shaking my head, the hairs on my arms were standing on end.

Was she?

Grace's lips contorted into a smile.

"Tell me," I said as she turned her back on me and started to walk out of the restroom.

She must have followed me that night. She must have been there. There when Heather and I had argued, when I'd walked away, when I'd left Heather hanging at the edge of the cliff.

I'd heard a scream and it had taken me at least a minute to get back to the spot where she had been.

My mind started whirring over the events of that long-ago night. "Grace, what did you do?" The bathroom door slammed behind her, leaving me alone in the stark light of the restroom.

Bile rose up my throat, into my mouth, and I turned to spit it into the sink, the sharp burn of tequila stinging my tongue. I'd barely had to wake Grace when I got back to my house. She must have just had time to get home and climb into bed. And she'd been so persistent about me not calling the police.

"What did you do, Grace?" I whispered again into the empty bathroom.

15

Anna

I didn't dare speak to Grace again that evening. I left the ladies' room and went back into the pub, allowing Rachel to spin me around in a drunken haze of a dance, and Nancy to ply me with more wine.

I ignored Grace, though I watched her out of the corner of my eye, and she watched my every movement in return.

She left at midnight. I felt sick. Numb. My hands were shaking, only the others didn't notice as we carried on drinking. Nancy brought up the subject of Ben's party with me, then later Rachel did too—both hushed, secret discussions between them and me that expanded into arguments, which I couldn't handle and didn't even care about in that moment.

My head was too full of the idea that Grace did so much more that evening than give me an alibi. I had to know what I was dealing with. I needed to understand how far she might go to get what she supposedly wanted right now, which appeared to be me.

Ben places a fresh cup of tea on the table. I have given him the gist of my conversation with Grace but I need to tell him the rest. About

Heather and my part in what happened to her. About Grace's alibi and the fact that I ran away on Wednesday night because I'd needed to talk to someone about what had happened twenty-two years ago. I couldn't carry on playing Grace's games. Who might I lose next?

"I need to show you something," I say to Ben. I go upstairs and dig in the back of a wardrobe for a box that I bring back down. I have kept it since I was a child, locked with a combination: 0706, the night of Heather's accident, 7 June. I'd chosen the numbers to taunt myself, a stark reminder of something I'd never be able to forget. The box hasn't been opened in a long while. Still, its contents are as etched into my memory as if I had only placed them there yesterday.

I take out a newspaper clipping and pass it to Ben.

"This is the girl who went missing in ninety-seven?" he asks as he taps the paper. "I remember you talking about this. Didn't you once say you were at school with her?"

I nod. I had passed it off once in general conversation.

"I don't understand," Ben says as he skims the cutting and then looks up at me. "What has this got to do with anything?"

"I was friends with Heather," I say, "for a short time, but we became close. She used to stay at my dad's sometimes because her childhood was even crazier than mine."

"It says here that she was in care."

"She was. She had a lovely foster family who—" I break off as an image springs into my head of her kindly foster mother on my doorstep. "Anyway, Heather was fun, but she also got me into a lot of trouble."

"You?" Ben laughs. "I thought you were a goody-goody? I thought you always said you wouldn't say boo to a goose."

"Yes, well, when Heather came along, she opened my eyes for a while. I think she showed me what kind of person I might have been if I hadn't been swept up by Grace and her family. I was more influenced by them than I was by my own dad."

"Okay," Ben says cautiously. He pulls his own mug closer now, though it is long empty, but he needs something to do with his hands and wrapping them around a mug must offer some comfort. "So you were close to Heather. I still don't see what this has to do with anything."

"I was with her," I tell him. "I was at the cliffs the night she . . ."

Fell. I will myself to finish the sentence. The night Heather fell. Not was pushed. Instead I say, "Disappeared."

"You were with her?"

I sense Ben's anxiety as I nod. "She dared me to go to the cliffs with her late at night. We crossed the police tape, which was there because someone had had an accident a few days earlier.

"I didn't want to go," I continued. "But I did. I followed her until she got too close to the edge of the cliff, and . . ."

"Wait," he says when I pause again. "Are you saying you saw what happened to her? That you were there when she fell?" His face has paled, grayer than I've ever seen it. "And you never told anyone?"

"I didn't see what happened. We had an argument; I told her to get back from the edge but she refused, and so I walked away." Tears fill my eyes as I relay the story. "And then I heard a noise, and when I went back she was gone." I don't tell Ben more about the noise: that it was a scream—a scream that the years have elongated and turned into a sickening, blood-curdling shriek; a scream that has woken me from many a nightmare. Thankfully he doesn't ask, either.

"But you didn't tell anyone?" he says, unable to get his head around why I would never have done that. "You didn't even know if she was still alive?"

I try to explain what happened when I ran home, how Grace had held me until I stopped sobbing, and how she'd told me she would take care of it and what we would do.

It is the second time I've ever told this story, and telling Ben is so much harder than telling Sally.

"Jesus, Anna," he says as he pushes his mug away and reels back in his seat. He adds nothing more for a moment, and I imagine where his mind might be taking him. To a place where he believes that he has never known his wife. That I sicken him. That he can't trust me again. Will I ever be able to get him to understand how caught up I was in Grace's web?

"There is more I need to tell you," I plead. "About Grace. I need you to understand what she was like."

I didn't understand myself for a long while. Not until Grace was safely packed away on the other side of the world was I afforded the space to look back over those fragile years of childhood and adolescence. And only later, when I formed friendships that left me feeling better about myself rather than inadequate or incapable, could I finally fit the last piece of the puzzle into place.

But how can I explain all this to Ben? He wasn't there to see firsthand the intricacies of our relationship, or to understand how much more difficult it is to break up with a friend than a lover. How hard it was to cut a friend out of my life, particularly one who was entangled in it as much as Grace had been. Especially when she knew the worst thing about me. I cannot possibly explain in such a short time how I've still managed to end up with Grace in my life.

I catch Ben checking the time. We have an hour before Nancy will be bringing Ethan home from school. An hour in which we at least need to reach a level of acceptance before our son is back, because I cannot let Ethan know there is a problem. I must protect him from that.

I tell Ben what Grace said to me at the pub that night, my fear about what it might mean.

"I don't understand," he says. "What exactly are you worried about now?"

"I'm worried about what else she could do," I tell him.

Ben has clenched himself into a tight ball. I want to reach out and ease the knots that must be in his shoulders.

Grace knows too much about that long-ago night, more than I ever appreciated. Was she responsible for Heather's fall? If she was, then who else might she hurt? She will use what she knows to hurt me more, I am sure. To take away the people I love, the chance of adopting Zadie.

"But you still don't know that she did anything," he says. "You still don't have the answers."

"I have more of them now than I did twenty-two years ago," I tell him. "That's why I had to go and see Grace's mother. She's the only other person who can help me."

16

Grace

Grace lets herself back into the apartment, tossing her keys so they skitter across the kitchen counter. She turns the tap on full before grabbing a pint glass to fill, gulping its contents down, and slamming the glass into the sink.

All she can see in her mind is Anna's face. At first she'd thought her friend was in trouble, but then she'd spat the words, *Just go, Grace.* Like she hated her.

She picks the glass out of the sink and hurls it onto the kitchen floor so that it splinters into tiny shards. The noise is more satisfying than the mess that lies in front of her. The fragments sparkle like crystals under the bright spotlights. They are how she feels. Broken, crushed—the emotions make her want to scream, and so that's what she does. In her perfect kitchen, she screams because of her imperfect life.

Grace has never felt so alone. Even when she was shipped across the world to a place she didn't want to go to, having to leave her best friend behind. At least then she hadn't been abandoned by Anna. Her best friend had cried as much as she had at the airport, both of them howling and clutching each other. They were sisters being ripped apart. They needed each other like the breath in their bodies.

Grace knew that when she was old enough she would one day return to Clearwater. When she didn't have to answer to her parents or do what they told her. When she had enough money for the flights on her own. Or enough to live on when she got to England. There were many "whens" that made it impossible for a long time—it wasn't as simple as the plans she had mapped out—and for years she was angry at her parents for making the choice for her.

"Oh, Gracie, but it's so lovely here," her mum was always saying to her. "Why would you want to go back to Clearwater?"

Because she had no one there except for a mother who fussed around her and a father who talked over her at dinnertime when he didn't even notice she was speaking. Grace remembers the way her mum would smile at her then, her forehead creasing into a stupid little frown as if she was saying, *I know, Grace. He's just got something else on his mind, that's all.* But she never said anything. She never said, *Henry, your daughter is trying to tell you something.*

Grace was invisible to her father. She has always known it, and yet now, as she stands in her apartment with its white walls and clinical kitchen units, she feels it more than ever. All she wanted was his attention, an acknowledgment that she'd done well at school or work, or anything ever in her life. All she wanted was what Anna got from her dad.

She shakes the thought from her head. No. That can't be right. Anna's father wasn't there for her, either. And yet he loved her. He overcooked fish fingers for her tea because she preferred them crispy, and carefully slipped his glasses on to read her school reports as if they were the world news, and always ruffled her hair when she walked past him. Grace saw it all. She saw it and she envied it.

She had nothing in Australia. And the only person who'd always given her the attention she needed was on the other side of the world. Grace found it bloody hard to make new friends. Or at least proper ones that stuck around and weren't just people to talk to at the watercooler at work.

She'd been mulling over the idea of moving back to England in her early twenties when she met Graham one day at that same watercooler. Suddenly he was filling the empty space that Anna had once filled, giving her time, attention, making her feel special and wanted and important. And so even when her parents moved back five years later, Grace was in a different place.

Graham. The waste of space she married. The pointless father. The man who has called her only once since she told him Anna had disappeared. She picks up her mobile now and stabs her finger on his name, holding the phone to her ear. It is 8:20 p.m. in Singapore. She knows his time zones as well as she knows her own. Graham should be in his hotel room.

"Hi, love," he says when she answers. "I'm going to have to be quick."

Grace grits her teeth, listening to a background noise that she can't quite make out as she resists the urge to slam down the phone. *How dare you*, she thinks. His priority will always be something else, and yet she keeps allowing it to humiliate her. But she won't give him the satisfaction of asking where he is.

"Everything okay?" he is asking in his irritatingly jolly voice.

"Are you not even going to ask about Anna?" she says to him.

"I'm sorry. I just thought you'd tell me if there was any news." Now he just sounds flat again, as usual, already tired by the conversation. "Is there?"

Grace bites her lip. She wishes she hadn't called him. She no longer gets anything from him. She is a ball of anger and frustration, and in a blind moment she'd needed to talk to someone about Anna, but not him. Not her bastard of a husband who doesn't give a toss about her or their daughter. Who is too wrapped up in his own life to care what she has been going through. "No, there is still no news," she lies.

"The police must be doing something about it now?" he asks. "When was it, Friday she went missing?"

"Wednesday," she says. "Wednesday night, Graham."

"Then they must be taking you seriously. Have you tried calling them again?"

She's squeezing the phone so tightly that her hand cramps. "I've got to go," she says, and as she hears him begin to say, "Wait, I need to tell you—" she ends the call and hurls her phone across the open-plan room, where it lands with a soft thud on the sofa.

Grace paces to the end of the living room and then back into the kitchen, her hands steepled in front of her as if in prayer, her fingers tapping against each other impatiently. For the last five days she has been going out of her mind with worry for Anna. More than Nancy or any of the others. She's the one who's been piecing together what might have happened to Anna, begging the police to believe that something is wrong. She's the one who has refused to give up when everyone else has seemed to, and for what? For nothing? For Anna to run off to wherever she is and not even have the decency to call and say that she is safe? Alive?

Grace's breaths come out short and sharp as she paces. She can almost feel the blood rushing through her veins, like it is building her into a crescendo and at any moment she might explode.

She cannot get Anna's face out of her head.

Just go, Grace, Anna had told her.

Grace stands in front of her full-length windows now and pushes her hands against the panes. The thought is there—the wondering how hard she would need to press, the force required to take a window out. She knows she doesn't have the strength to force its glass, and yet her hands push deeper, testing it, willing it in some ways to shatter.

Eventually she turns away, picks up the phone from the sofa and hurls it against the glass, watching it bounce off with a disappointing thud.

"God!" she screams, clenching her hands into fists.

All her life she has looked out for Anna, picked up the pieces when things were broken. She invited Anna into her own family, until Grace's own mother looked upon her as another daughter. There were many times when Catherine had refused to take sides if there was an argument between them. Even when everything was spiraling out of control between Grace and Anna, she didn't automatically stand by Grace.

There was a time, not long before Heather went over the cliffs, that her mum had asked her what was wrong. "I haven't seen much of Anna lately," she had said. "Is everything okay between you girls? I can't even think of the last time she was here for the night."

Everything had not been okay. And the reason Anna hadn't been there to sleep was because she was staying at Heather's and inviting Heather to her dad's, and all of a sudden the arrival of a new girl at school meant that Grace was no longer wanted.

"Anna's being a bitch," she had said.

"Grace, do not say things like that," Catherine had reprimanded her.

"Well, she is."

"What's happened?"

"She's decided she doesn't need me as a friend."

"Oh, I'm sure that's not the case."

"Actually it is, Mum. She's got it into her head that she's someone else now and I'm not good enough for her."

"What have you done?"

That was what her mum had questioned. *What have you done?*

"What have *I* done?" Grace had yelled.

"Oh, I don't mean anything—I don't mean it like that," her mum had said in a fluster. "But it takes two to have an argument, Gracie, I'm just saying—"

"She no longer wants to be here, Mum, is that not enough for you? She doesn't want to come to your house anymore."

"Oh, Grace, I'm sure she does—"

"Oh my God, just forget it."

Grace had given Anna everything: a share of her family, a portion of her mother. Yet still she was able to go home to her own dad and his fish fingers and his stupid reading glasses that were taped up on one side with a bandage.

Grace jumps when her mobile rings from the floor where it lays, and is more surprised when she picks it up and sees her mum's name flashing on the screen. Right now she really doesn't want to get embroiled in one of her mum's fanciful conversations about the goings-on in her neighborhood. But at the same time she hasn't spoken to her in well over a week, and it's unusual for her to call during the day when she is still under the impression that calls are cheaper after seven.

At the last minute Grace picks up. "Hello, Mum."

"How are you?" Catherine asks.

She can already tell there is something off in her mum's voice, her breath catching with each word.

"What's up?" Grace asks bluntly. "Are you ill?" Her mother often complains about various ailments, though they are never remotely serious.

"No, I'm not ill," she says. "Why would you think that?"

"You sounded like you might be."

"No, dear, I'm fine."

"Okay."

"I just wondered if . . ." Her mum trails off and then inhales loudly before finishing. "I just wondered how everything is going in Clearwater?"

Grace leans against the back of the sofa. "What do you mean how everything is here?" she asks. "Why wouldn't everything be fine?"

She is glad she never told her mum anything about Anna. She couldn't bear to see her pandering, panicking, drawing her own conclusions as to what is going on, conclusions that are likely so far from the truth they're ridiculous.

"Well, it's just—"

"Yes?" she snaps. A few times since she has moved back, she has felt her mum pushing Grace to tell her something that hasn't even happened.

How are things with Anna, dear? Are you sure everything is going well? You would tell me if there were any problems, wouldn't you, Gracie?

Grace cannot imagine what it must be like to live with such a sense of impending doom constantly hanging over you like a black cloud, but then her mother has always loved having something to worry about.

She almost wishes her mum would tell her something mundane about one of the neighbors and is about to ask about them when Catherine says, "I've been thinking long and hard about whether to tell you this, Gracie . . ."

"Tell me what?" she asks. "Mum, just say it. You are ill, aren't you?" Now thoughts of cancer and heart disease come crashing into her head, and Grace can feel her mind speeding back to the time when her mum called with the news that her father was seriously ill.

She grips the phone tighter. Her mum may irritate her to the ends of the earth, but she isn't ready to say goodbye to another parent.

"Well, if I'm being honest, I had a bit of a turn on Thursday but that's not why I'm calling, and I'm all right now, anyway."

"A bit of a turn? What are you talking about?"

"It's nothing to worry about, love. They said it was probably caused by stress."

"Who are they, the doctors?"

"The paramedics; but like I say, everything is fine now."

"You called an ambulance?"

"I didn't really want to be bothering them."

"Why would anything be brought on by stress, Mum?" she asks.

Her mother's life is so lacking in stress that she doesn't believe she is telling the truth, and still she is thinking that there is more to this turn, and that her mum is hiding scan results and tests from her, that she doesn't actually take in what her mother says next.

"Anna has been here."

After a moment Grace replies, "Say that again."

"Anna has been here," her mum explains again. "She arrived Thursday morning."

"What?" Grace is shaking her head, thoughts somersaulting over each other. "What the hell do you mean Anna has been there?"

"She came to see me, Gracie. She had some questions."

"Are you . . . ? I don't . . . Wait a minute, that can't be right?" she says. "You mean she came to see you last Thursday? As in five days ago?"

Her mum breathes out through her nose, a sound that loudly fills the line. "Yes."

"What time?"

"I don't know what time. I think she got here about eleven—before lunch, anyway. Why does that matter?" She sighs. "You don't focus on the relevant details, Gracie; you never did."

"It matters because everyone thought she was missing." Grace's mind flicks back to the day: Ben's panic that morning; the way it had subsided by the afternoon when he'd received a text. He wasn't lying. Ben knew by then where she was. Probably even Nancy knew, too, but they kept this important fact from her—that Anna was with Grace's own mother. "What questions?" she asks through gritted teeth. "You said she had some questions."

"I told you I was worried about you moving back to Clearwater," Catherine says. "She had questions about the past, Gracie. Anna wanted to know about the past."

Grace slides down the back of the sofa until she is sitting on the highly polished wooden floor, her knees bent, her head bowed forward. She closes her eyes, her pulse flickering like a moth as their last conversation in the ladies' room of the Old Vic flashes in her head.

"What exactly did you tell her?" she says.

June 1997

Grace stuffed the box under her bed when she heard her mum coming up the stairs, folding the valance sheet down so it draped on the floor.

"Gracie, didn't you hear me?" Catherine was calling. "Your tea is ready."

Grace heard her mum pause outside the door before it opened a crack and she stuck her head around. Her eyes scanned the room. The usually tidy bedroom was covered in clothes and scraps of paper where Grace had been attempting her chemistry homework. An empty bag of crisps lay on the bed that she had only just eaten from her packed lunch. Catherine didn't comment on the mess as she said, "No Anna again tonight?"

It was funny how those words always induced such bitter anger in Grace that her friend wasn't where she should be. She had been asked the same question every night for the last two weeks, as if her mother had the right to be gutted that Anna wasn't there.

Grace had told her last week that Anna was a bitch, but her mum hadn't wanted to believe her. Yet that was exactly how Anna was acting. Sometimes Grace considered telling her mum about Heather, the girl who had arrived at school with her too-short skirts and penned drawings on her arms that she pretended were tattoos like she was really cool, when really she just looked totally stupid. Surely if she did, her mum would have something to say about Anna, but then, she wondered, what if her mum talked to her father about it, and they decided Anna was now a bad influence on her? What if, when all this had passed and Anna and Grace were best friends again, Anna was no longer welcome in their house and on their holidays?

She wouldn't risk it. Her mum wasn't the kind of mum to give the advice she would want to hear anyway. Grace wanted someone to tell her *how* to get Heather Kerr out of the picture, and how to make sure Anna would never even consider not being her best friend again. Not deny Anna was doing anything malicious on purpose, but when she finally saw that Anna *was* being a bitch, to coo over Grace like she was five years old again and tell her she just needed to move on and would easily find another best friend.

And so she didn't say anything, and eventually her mum stopped asking what was wrong and stopped commenting that there was "no Anna again tonight" when it was perfectly obvious there wasn't.

In fact, two weeks later, by which time Anna had succumbed to having tea at their house on two occasions, Grace and her mother hadn't talked about anything more serious than the weather and local gossip.

Grace was spending the night at Anna's for the first time in months. Her mum had raised her eyebrows when Grace asked if she could go, a smile creeping onto her lips. Her pleasure sickened Grace. It made her feel pitied and pathetic, but she chose to ignore it as she folded her pajamas into her rucksack and packed a washbag and book.

She wasn't entirely sure how pleased Anna was about her staying the night, when Grace had more or less invited herself. "I know you've had Heather to stay," Grace had said to her the day before. "But you haven't invited me for as long as I can remember."

Anna had turned away, fiddling with the clasp on her bag that had always been a nightmare to close. Grace took it out of her hands and forced the catch together before handing it back to her.

"Have you any idea how it makes me feel?" she went on. "When you've been to mine so much and you never invite me in return? All the things I've ever done for you, Anna."

"Okay," her best friend had relented. "Come tomorrow."

She had gotten what she wanted but it didn't make her feel good. How could anyone feel *good* when they were clawing at the threads of a fraying friendship that had bound them together for the last nine years? She had no doubt that if she were a boyfriend she would be dumped by now.

Grace had one more thing to do. The next morning she waited for Heather Kerr to roll in late for school as she always did. As soon as she was near, Grace strolled out onto the path in front of her. "I know you think you're all that, Heather," she said. "But I also know there's one thing you'll never do that the boys are planning for tomorrow night."

Heather laughed. "Right. What's that, then?"

"I've heard them say they're going to the cliffs after dark."

"Oh wow." She widened her eyes theatrically. "Sounds terrifying."

"There's police tape all around the dangerous part where the man fell off the cliff last week, and they're going to climb over it."

Heather laughed again, but this time it was more of an intrigued chuckle.

Grace leaned in and added, "They say the tape is so close to the edge that when you're on the other side of it at night you can't even see where you're stepping. Sometimes you don't even know when you're on the edge until your foot slips off it."

"You think that would bother me?" she said.

I can tell it would, Grace thought.

By 3:15 the whispers that Anna was back had spread across the play-ground like wildfire. Most of the parents who were already huddled in the playground knew she had come home this morning, safe and unharmed. By all accounts she had left of her own accord, and not gone to another man's house like some of them had suspected.

"An emergency came up," Nancy told them. She was impatiently cran-ing to see through the classroom window, waving at the teacher. Can I get the children? *she was mouthing and pointing.* Ethan too?

The mums raised their eyebrows. It was still three minutes before the children were officially let out of school, and yet there was Miss Williams ushering Elodie and Ethan out of the chairs.

"What kind of emergency?" someone asked.

Nancy turned. "I think that's Anna's business right now," she said. "I'm sure she will tell everyone when she is ready."

"Maybe." The woman screwed up her eyes. "But she left everyone wor-rying she was missing. So what I mean is that it was odd for her to dis-appear like that in the middle of the night and not tell anyone where she was going."

Nancy gave her a long look before turning back to the classroom door, which was now opening. "Hey, kids," she said to Elodie and Ethan. "Come on, then, let's get you home."

"Is Mummy going to be there?" they heard Ethan ask as Nancy strode off across the playground, her hand pushing into Elodie's back to shimmy her along.

"Yes," Nancy told him. "Mummy's waiting for you."

"Really?" They saw the little boy's glee as he bounced in the air and raced ahead of Nancy, turning to face her. "She's going to be there?"

The parents all looked at one another silently. "That sounds bloody weird," one said.

"I bet Nancy knows exactly what's happened. There's no sign of Grace, is there?" she added. "I'm still keen to know why she was shouting through Anna's letterbox earlier."

They glanced around the playground in the hope of seeing the woman, but they couldn't find her.

Now Miss Williams was back at the door, as the children lined up behind her. One by one she called out for their waiting parents. Only a few were left as the other mums began sauntering back towards the path in a large bubble and their children ran in crazy circles around them.

There was no sign of Caitlyn yet, or Rachel—though that wasn't unusual if she was working—but as they approached the path leading out of the playground, they suddenly clocked Grace storming up it, heading towards them.

Grace looked straight through them as she plowed ahead. If they didn't get out of her way, she would barrel on through, so they stepped to one side, making a pathway for her. She didn't acknowledge any of them. It was as if she hadn't recognized or even noticed who they were as she channeled through and turned right, out of sight towards the classroom.

For a moment they all stopped where they were and glanced behind them.

"Wow. Someone's not happy," one of them piped up.

At the end of the path they lingered in a cluster for a while, talking about Anna. All of them were feeling a little peeved by the end result of the drama, but really none of them wanted to go just yet before they'd had a chance to see Grace again.

Eventually Grace reappeared with Matilda in tow, looking set to ignore them again, until one of them stopped her and said, "Hey, Grace, I hear Anna is home."

Grace paused as Matilda danced at her feet, tugging on her arm, telling her mother she was hungry. Grace ignored her daughter as her face fell into a smile. "Yes. Isn't it great? We're all so pleased she's safe."

They shuffled awkwardly. It wasn't quite the reaction they had expected. "Do you know where she's been, Grace?" the same mum asked.

She didn't respond for a moment as she seemed to contemplate what to say. Then eventually she replied, "Anna needed to get away for a while. But don't worry," she went on, "I'm going to be there for her. I'm just glad I came back when I did."

And as they watched her march out of the playground and through the school gates, all of them were momentarily at a loss for words. A fake smile and those odd words had been a chilling response, and it didn't feel like Grace was the person who Anna would actually want around.

They wondered if they'd just seen, for the first time, a different side to Grace Goodwin. One that they didn't particularly like.

June 1997

During the evening of the sleepover, Anna couldn't sit still. Even through the movie she was up, down, pausing it so she could chatter excitedly. Grace watched her with interest. She wasn't talking about anything specific; in fact, her conversation flipped from one topic to another, and half the time Grace had no idea what she was going on about. She was bubbling with nervous excitement but still hadn't said any more about Heather and her dare since mentioning it at school.

It wasn't until they were lying on their beds at ten p.m. that Grace brought it up. "We can't go; you know that, don't you?"

Grace needed to tread a thin line between acknowledging it wasn't a good idea and putting Anna off. Because Heather dragging Anna onto the cliffs in the middle of the night was perfect. All it needed was for something to go wrong—like Anna's dad to wake up and notice she wasn't there, for example—and that would be the end of Heather.

Anna sat bolt upright in her bed and leaned over the side of it. "Are you serious?"

"I don't want you going, Anna, it's dangerous." She knew this would get Anna's back up, and sure enough her friend looked like she were about to yell at her.

Instead Anna whispered, "You are not my mum, Grace."

Grace drew back with narrowed eyes. She could see where the argument was heading but she had to stay firm.

"Fine. You can stay here, then," Anna told her. "Heather says that—"

It was another punch, but Grace cut out the rest of her words. She'd do a U-turn and pretend that she wanted to go, because she wanted to ensure that Heather showed up, but she also wished Anna would stop parroting Heather in this way.

But then, Grace had already concluded that Anna needed people to tell her what to do because she lacked direction at home. Anna was always asking Grace's mum about periods and boyfriends and how much it hurt when she got her ears pierced. Sometimes Grace thought that Anna was desperate for anyone to be a mother figure in her life.

Grace had taken on that role herself for the past nine years, but now Anna was rebelling and withdrawing, and Grace could not bear the gaping hole it left as her friend pulled away from her when she knew she didn't deserve it. Who was Anna to de-friend her? Each time she asked herself this question, the more it twisted her and wound her up, and now she wanted to show Anna she was wrong.

"I'll come," Grace told her. "I don't want you going on your own."

Anna smiled at her, but she couldn't tell if her friend was truly happy that she would be dragging along too. It certainly didn't feel like it.

She watched Anna climb out of bed and slip on jogging trousers and a purple hoodie. An hour earlier, her dad had closed the door to the living room downstairs. Here he would watch mindless television with a beer resting on his stomach until he fell asleep in his armchair.

Grace followed Anna's lead and they crept down the stairs, peeking in on Anna's sleeping father before slipping on their trainers and going out the front door.

Anna quickened her step when she saw Heather waiting at the end of the road. Grace followed reluctantly, but this was as far as she was going. She grabbed hold of Anna's arm. "We can't do this. It's stupid. What would your dad say if he caught you?" This, of course, she hoped they would find out later.

Whatever was going through Anna's mind, Grace thought her friend looked petrified, and she doubted for a moment that it would take much to persuade Anna to go home. But for her plan to work, she needed Anna to choose to go with Heather, however hard it was to let her go.

Anna looked at her coldly, and thankfully said, "Go home, then. I'll see you later."

Heather was calling Anna, and eventually her friend turned her back on Grace and walked away, and it was all Grace could do to stop herself from running after them and punching Heather smack in the face. Instead she used her anger to drive her on, walking back into Anna's house, creeping upstairs to Anna's room, where she lay on the mattress, staring at the ceiling with its faded and peeled splotches where once neon stars had been stuck when they were kids.

It was barely ten minutes later that Grace flung herself up again and grabbed her sweater from the back of a chair and crept downstairs once more.

She couldn't lie there for hours, imagining what was going on without her. She needed to see for herself. She had to quicken her steps on the pavement, racing as fast as she could until she saw Anna and Heather in the distance. And then she held back as she followed them to the edge of Crayne's Cliff and the point where the light felt like it had been sucked out of the night.

Grace hadn't brought a flashlight, but both girls were in her sights, and she kept close enough that she could see exactly what they were up to without either of them ever knowing she was watching.

17

Anna

Ben pushes his chair away from the table and takes the mugs to the sink. He splays his hands on either side of it and bows his head, pushing back as he rolls his shoulders. "Go on," he says to me. "Tell me what happened when you got to Catherine's on Thursday."

I recall the way I'd stood outside Catherine's bungalow. I'd been there only once before, three weeks after Grace's dad, Henry, died, when I'd gotten back from holiday. I'd always regretted not being able to go to the funeral—I had wanted to be there for the woman who had practically brought me up.

My relationship with Grace's dad was nothing like the one I'd had with Catherine. He'd always been pleasant enough, though very formally so, but had never shown much interest in me. When we were younger I'd spent most of the time with Grace and Catherine. In later years Henry would take himself off to another room and Catherine would eventually follow him. Even on holidays he rarely looked up from a newspaper or a glass of Scotch. I was mostly happier when he wasn't around because he always managed to make me feel on edge, like I had to be on my best behavior.

I'd been nervous visiting Catherine after his death because I was clumsy with other people's grief and never knew what to say, but five days ago I felt even more nervous as I waited for Catherine to answer the door, hoping she was in.

"Oh my love," she said when she finally opened it. "I was upstairs, I only just heard the door. Come in, my dear, you look freezing standing out there in what you're wearing." My red-felt coat was belted around my waist, but it did little to hold off the biting wind. "What's happened?" she said, ushering me indoors. She held out her hands for my coat, but I shook my head. The bungalow was blasting heat out of its radiators, but I was tired and shivering and didn't want to reveal the sheer black top I had on underneath.

"Nothing's happened," I said, leaning forward and kissing Catherine on the cheek. She wrapped her arms around me and hugged me. "It's so good to see you," I went on. "You don't age."

"You're too kind," Catherine said, eventually. "But I know you're lying." She smiled. "I see myself in the mirror every morning and my mother is looking back at me."

I smiled back sadly. I would never know such a feeling.

"Let me get you a tea and I'll put the fire on in the front room; you can sit by that and warm yourself up." Catherine beckoned me to follow her and pressed the clunky button that eventually sent the fake coals bursting into flames. When she stood up she lingered by the fire for a moment. "I know you say nothing has happened, but you wouldn't be here for no good reason."

I looked up at her as the heat from the fire began creeping towards me and warming my hands.

"But I'll get you that tea first," she said, before turning away and leaving the room.

I was already feeling warmer by the time she returned, and had unbuttoned my coat, leaving myself exposed in the top that was much less suited to daywear in the middle of winter than for a night out.

Catherine's eyes were on me as she placed the mug of tea on the side table next to me, but she said nothing.

"How are you doing here, Catherine? Are you happy?" I asked.

"Oh, I am," she said with a smile. "I have everything I need around me. I come and go as I please," she added, raising her eyebrows slightly as if this were much of the attraction. That she was finally able to do what *she* wanted, though it had never seemed to bother her the way Henry took charge. "You look like you haven't slept all night," she added.

"I haven't had much; only a bit on the train."

Catherine nodded. She took a deep breath as she said, "Maybe you should just tell me what's brought you here, love. It's not doing me much good wondering."

"I'm sorry. I know I should have called you first." Turning up out the blue seemed ridiculous now.

"I think you must have had good reason," Catherine said.

I gave a partial nod.

"And I'm certain it is to do with Grace."

"She's not ill or anything," I said quickly.

"No." Catherine shook her head. "I wasn't thinking that. Tell me what's happened, Anna."

"That's just it. There's nothing I can tell you specifically. I'm just . . . I'm—" I broke off.

During the train journey to Leicester I'd gone over and over in my head what I wanted to say, but now that I was here, none of it felt sufficient. *I'm here because your daughter won't leave me alone. Because she doesn't want me having any friends.*

I'm here because she has been holding something over me for more than twenty years, and I think there is more to the night Heather fell than I know for sure.

I'm here because I'm frightened of your daughter.

Catherine was biting the corner of her lip as she studied me. "I told Grace never to go back to Clearwater. I didn't think she should."

"Why not?" I asked.

"I thought it was better for both of you if you kept some distance from each other."

"I don't understand." I sat in the armchair that Catherine had ushered me into. "You wanted to take me to Australia with you. You asked my dad."

"I know I did. At the time I couldn't imagine leaving you behind, if I'm honest. You were like a daughter to me—you know that, Anna. We were so close when you were growing up." She perched on the edge of a chair opposite, leaning her body towards me. "I should never admit this, but in some ways I felt closer to you than I did to Grace."

I sucked in a breath as she dipped her gaze away from me. Had I always known this? Had Grace?

"She was her father's daughter; they were much more similar . . ." Catherine drifted off, her brow furrowed. "Very determined, very . . ."

Controlling? I think, but I don't say anything.

"Anyway, I knew your dad would never agree. So I suppose it was something I just needed to do, to ask him."

"What if he had agreed?"

"Then I would have been delighted to have you with us. Still"— she shook her head—"it wouldn't have been right."

"Why not?"

"Well, I couldn't have taken you from your father, for one thing. Besides, I think you and Grace needed the space from each other to grow," she replied.

I opened my mouth to speak, but Catherine held up a hand.

"You were too entangled in each other's lives. You had been from such an early age. I always did say you were more like sisters than friends, and I know I treated you that way, but you were very different girls, Anna. I was surprised you didn't clash more than you did, but I think that was because of you. You were always so easygoing.

"There was a time when you were both maybe eight years old and Henry and I took you camping for a few nights," she went on.

"I remember. We went to the Isle of Wight."

"The weather was awful, and you girls ended up in this kids' club every afternoon. You made a friend," she said. "I think her name was Carla."

"I remember her," I said, thinking of a little girl with two blond plaits hanging down to her waist. "She had a new bike that she was always riding round our tent."

"She was a sweet thing, but only you were interested in playing with her. She was always asking if you could both come out to play and I could see how keen you were, but Grace . . . Grace was constantly telling me things about Carla, like how she would make you both steal things from other people's tents."

"I don't remember that."

"That's because it wasn't true. I knew Grace didn't want either of you to play with her, and so to keep the peace I made excuses so you didn't have to. Then one night there was a disco at the club and you had to get into pairs and for whatever reason you joined up with Carla. Grace was livid," Catherine explained. "The next morning I woke up to find she'd taken a pair of scissors to your favorite dress, the one you were wearing at the disco, and cut a hole right in the middle of the skirt."

"You told me it ripped when you were washing it," I said, remembering the pretty dress with its sequin flowers and netting that my dad had bought me for my birthday.

"I lied because I couldn't face having to deal with what Grace had done in front of you. I tried speaking to her—making her see that what she did was wrong—but there was such . . ." Catherine waved a hand in the air as she fought for the right word.

"Control," I finished this time. "She controlled me."

Catherine smiled thinly. It was a smile that didn't reach her eyes. Of course she knew this, and yet she allowed it to happen.

"Did Grace tell you why she cut up my dress?" I asked.

"She told me she was angry with you," Catherine replied. "I thought she just wanted to destroy something that was precious to you."

"But she let me think it was an accident. So she didn't even do it to let me know she was angry," I pointed out. It made Grace's behavior even more chilling.

"I think if you were both my daughters I might have handled things differently, but much of the time you always seemed so happy together that I chose to ignore it. I worried that if Gracie didn't have you in her life she might not have had any friends at all, and rightly or wrongly, I couldn't bear the thought of that.

"I was proven right when we moved," Catherine went on. "She never did make any true friends out in Australia—not like the friendship she had with you, anyway. I hated seeing her so lonely, and she was, for a long time, until she met Graham, but that's a whole different story . . ." Catherine trailed off. "Anyway, by then I also saw the way she was with people, much more so than I think I ever did with you. You were always more like me, Anna. You put up with a lot.

"Grace was like her dad in that they both wanted to prove something, maybe that they were always," she flung a hand around in the air, "in charge. On top. I don't know, however you want to say it. People like you and me, we just go along with things."

"I'm not like that," I protested. "Or maybe I wasn't given the chance to be different. I was just a child. I shouldn't have had to put up with it."

"I know, and like I say, I wish for your sake I had done more to stop it, but Grace was my daughter and I was scared for her. She had no one else, no other friends, neither of you ever did—" Catherine stopped abruptly as if something had swept across her mind. Was it Heather? But she continued speaking before I could ask. "So tell me, Anna, what has happened? What's gone wrong that's brought you to see me?"

"It's about what happened twenty-two years ago," I said.

Catherine waited.

"Heather Kerr," I prompted.

"Okay," she said cautiously.

"Did you know I was friends with her, too?"

She shook her head slightly, a faint movement that was little more than a flicker, but there was panic behind her eyes; I could see it in the way they darkened, and wondered what she was remembering right now. Was it the police officer who stood on her doorstep and told her a girl was missing? The way she quickly shunted me out of her house and told me to get back to my dad's so she could speak to Grace alone?

"Are you sure you didn't know?" I asked.

"I never knew anything for certain," Catherine said quietly.

But I felt sure there was more to it than that.

18

Anna

I look at the clock on the kitchen wall behind Ben's head. "Nancy will be back with Ethan any minute," I say. I cannot wait to see him, but I'm nervous about facing Nancy after the last few days; worried, too, about the words we had on Wednesday night.

"You need to keep speaking to me," Ben says.

"I know I do—" I'm interrupted by the sound of the doorbell and quickly I push my chair back and get up, but a thought comes crashing into my head. "What if it's Grace?"

"I'll go," he says, and as soon as he opens the door I hear Nancy's voice and the sound of Ethan's shoes as he runs inside. Ben is calling at him to take his shoes off, but he is clearly being ignored as Ethan is suddenly in the doorway to the kitchen, his face lit up with delight as he shouts, "Mummy!" and runs into my arms.

I drop to my knees in front of him and hold him against me. Tears stream down my cheeks. It has only been five days, but it feels like a lifetime ago that I held his little body and smelled his familiar smell.

"I've missed you," he says as he lifts up a hand to wipe away my tears. "Why are you crying?"

"Because I've missed you too, my angel."

"Okay. Can Elodie stay to play?"

"I told him probably not," Nancy says as she appears in the doorway. I push myself to standing. "Maybe some other time. It's good to see you, Anna." She smiles and holds out her arms and I go over to give my friend a hug. "You gave us quite the shock," she says in a whisper that Ethan can't hear.

"Please can I just show Elodie the Minecraft world I built?" Ethan is asking.

I laugh as I ruffle his hair. "Five minutes. If that's okay with you, Nance?"

"Of course it is." Nancy shrugs as she takes a seat.

"I'll leave you two to it for a minute," Ben tells us. "I need to make a work call anyway," he adds, but hovers briefly, clearly hesitant to leave the room.

"Thank you for picking Ethan up for me," I say when he's gone.

"Oh dear God, Anna, you hardly have to thank me for that."

"I know but I—"

"I'm just bloody glad we didn't have to scour the beaches looking for you," she goes on. "Honestly, when I got that call from Ben to say you'd been in touch I cried. Can you imagine that? Me, crying?" She gives me a wry smile. "You know I'm not expecting you to tell me everything right now," she adds.

"Thank you."

"Unless you want to, of course."

"I haven't spoken to Ben properly yet," I tell her. "What did he tell you when he let you know I called?"

"That you had some things to sort out from the past. He said they were to do with Grace, though I'm hardly surprised by that: the woman is clearly nuts."

I give her a thin smile.

"He asked me not to tell Rachel and Caitlyn the details, so I didn't.

That was a bit awkward, though. I think they believed I knew more than I was letting on. Caitlyn, anyway, the way she was pressing me."

"I just didn't want too many people knowing anything, not before I'd worked out what I was going to do. Grace was always very controlling of me when we were kids," I explain as I sit down. "Obsessive, almost."

"But why did you suddenly run off without telling any of us where you were going?"

"She said something to me on Wednesday night that spooked me. Something I needed to look into. I was drunk; at the time I didn't want to get into a cab with Rachel, and after I watched you all go and I was alone—" I break off. At two a.m. I had walked to the bottom of the cliffs and felt my whole life caving in on me. "I knew I had to see Grace's mum," I say. "Maybe it was the alcohol that took over my brain, but I just had to speak to her and I thought I'd get there and back in a day."

"You couldn't have called her?"

I shrug. "I needed to see her face-to-face." I know Nancy cannot understand my actions without knowing the depths of my worries. "I will tell you everything, Nance, but please, just not right now."

"That's fine," she says, though her shoulders sag as if she's reluctant to accept she has to wait.

"Thank you."

"What for this time?"

"For not saying anything to the others. For not pressuring me. For being such a good friend when there's still so much I'm not telling you and you must feel like you don't even know me. For everything."

"I do know you, Anna Robinson. And I knew something was eating you up. I didn't trust that woman one bit, and it kind of all makes sense now that you say she was obsessive when you were kids. I can see it, the way she watches me; she looks furious whenever you and I are together. Shit, should I be scared?" she jokes.

"No, of course not," I say, although that isn't the whole truth, because what if Nancy should be scared?

"That's good. I don't want to come home to find Elodie's rabbit cooking on the stove." She leans forward and runs her fingers absently over the table. "Anna, you and I spoke about stuff on Wednesday night. Ben's party? I half thought that had something to do with you running off, so I was bloody relieved when Ben told me it was Grace." She smiles sadly as her fingers stop moving. "Rachel's finally admitted what happened. She told me her side of the story, anyway: that Eric forced himself on her in your bathroom. And that you saw them."

"Oh God, Nance. I wanted to speak to you after the party, I really did."

"You knew I knew something was up, though. The way Eric was with me at the end of the party, how he was suddenly so angry, knocking back drinks before he dragged me away from your house. I mean, we all know he can get like that at the best of times, but I was sure something had happened," Nancy says.

"But it had to come from Rachel," I insist. "I told her she had to be honest with you, but she kept putting it off. She was scared it would change your friendship. That's why we argued on Wednesday night. I was giving her one last chance before I told you myself."

Nancy nods, though I'm not sure if she accepts this deep down. Whether I made a mistake in not telling her and if I would have been a better friend to her if I had.

"What did you actually see?" she asks.

I hesitate. I know she is asking for my version of events, whether she should believe Rachel or whatever her husband might or might not have told her. "I didn't really see anything but I could hear Rachel telling Eric to stop whatever it was he was doing," I admit. "When she came out of the bathroom she looked really upset and a bit disheveled. Rachel swears to me he followed her up there and that she hadn't locked the door properly. She says he forced himself on her. I don't know, but . . ."

"But you believe her?" Nancy says when I don't finish.

I do not know which is worse for Nancy to hear: that her friend is lying and has betrayed her or that her husband has pushed himself on another woman. But I owe her the truth. "I do believe her. I know she's always joked about fancying him, but she wouldn't do anything about it."

"I wish you had told me sooner," she says quietly.

"I'm so sorry, Nance, I really am."

Eventually she inhales a deep breath. "I need to grab Elodie, I suppose."

"Nancy?" I stop her. "What are you going to do?"

"I don't know," she says, her eyes welling up, though she is fighting against her tears. "I haven't spoken to Eric yet; I was waiting to speak to you first. Then I . . . I just don't know," she admits, deflated.

"I know you're not all right about this, Nance. You don't need to try to be."

"No." She laughs. "I'm not."

"I'm so sorry."

"Me too." She smiles, adding sadly, "But I don't think either of us is that surprised by my husband, are we?"

It's true, but it doesn't make it any easier. Maybe this will be a final straw for her, to give her the strength to move on. "We are still friends, aren't we?" I say.

"Oh God, Anna, of course we are." Nancy leans forward and hugs me. "I think I'm going to need you more than ever in the weeks to come," she murmurs.

"I think we're going to need each other," I say.

"You told me you were scared earlier," Ben says later that night, when Ethan is tucked up in his bed, fast asleep. I know because I have checked on him twice, reluctant to leave his room, longing to stay and watch him. "What exactly are you scared of?"

Later in my conversations with Catherine, I had been left with the feeling that there was more to Grace's story of that night. That she will stop at nothing to get what she wants—but what is that exactly? To keep me to herself?

While I don't know for sure if Grace pushed Heather, in some ways the uncertainty is more frightening. The very fact that she could have done it and hidden it from us for all these years. She keeps her hand so close to her chest.

And yet there is nothing to prove she was there. Only her word against mine, if it comes to it.

"I'm scared of what I might lose," I tell Ben.

I am scared because I have to find a way to get Grace out of my life, or risk losing everyone else.

September 1997

Catherine knew Grace kept some kind of diary, and she'd always promised herself she would never invade her daughter's privacy by looking at it, but right now she felt worried. It was tucked under Grace's bed, almost out of reach.

She'd taken Grace to see a therapist recently, a woman who had been recommended to her through a friend of a friend. It had been three months since Heather Kerr's body had been found, and she'd told the therapist she thought it was a good idea for Grace to talk about it. The police had searched for Heather for a whole week before her body had washed up farther up-shore from the cliffs. The little pink café on the front ended up closing for a fortnight. Its owner hadn't been able to face the constant questions from the press or supposedly well-meaning customers.

Henry told Catherine there was no need for Grace to talk to anyone about the incident because she appeared to have taken it in her stride and had come through it relatively unscathed, but surely that in itself, Catherine deliberated, was something to worry about. For once she went against him, finally making an appointment for her daughter.

The therapist was a kindly woman who danced around the subject of Heather Kerr, even though Catherine had prompted her from the outset that this was what Grace should be talking about.

Catherine had been watching both girls much more lately. The incident had been another turning point in Grace and Anna's friendship, which appeared to have resumed its normal course with Anna staying over again, coming for tea most nights. The girls were often huddled in the old treehouse in the garden during the long summer nights of the school holidays, chatting, sharing secrets.

Catherine had originally told herself that they were getting each other through it. Because surely they needed to talk between themselves about what had happened? Still, no one knew for certain what had led to Heather Kerr being washed up on the beaches of Clearwater. The assumption was that she might have fallen off Crayne's Cliff, where she never should have been in the first place.

While Grace appeared balanced and unnervingly calm, Anna's behavior had been a little more erratic over the last three months. Certainly more than Catherine had seen before. One minute she would be frantically speaking to her ten to the dozen about a plethora of different topics and the next she'd be quite somber, leaving Catherine unable to get a word out of her.

The girls had one thing in common, though, and that was their refusal to open up about Heather. Catherine had tried talking to both of them on a number of occasions, separately and together, and they would always clam up.

This was why she had sat Grace in front of a therapist, although Catherine had not been allowed to sit in. After three sessions, Grace told her she didn't want to go back. Catherine had at least got the woman to admit that Grace wouldn't budge with her one iota, and that in her opinion, Grace appeared indifferent to the tragedy that had shaken the rest of the town.

Grace's indifference made no sense. That's why Catherine was tearing her daughter's bedroom apart. She wanted more insight into what was going on inside her head. She would never admit this to Henry, but there was something about Grace that frightened her. But then there was something about her husband that sometimes frightened her too, the way she couldn't do anything without running it by him first.

Her hands felt for the shoebox at the far side of the bed. She pulled it out and slowly lifted its lid to peer inside. There was the diary, once locked with a padlock and clasp that now hung uselessly from the catch. Catherine sat on the floor, her back pressed against the bed, the book resting on her lap for a moment as her fingers softly tapped its cover. She didn't want to look, but at the same time she needed to.

Eventually she opened it and gazed at the date and then the words and pictures underneath. She flicked through its pages, the black ink drawings that made her shudder: girls holding hands, their eyes made of circles that were black holes, red Biro scrawled over their heads with such force that it had ripped through the paper. Catherine could feel her daughter's rage as if Grace were standing next to her, shaking her.

She didn't want to keep looking but she couldn't stop herself, the dates rolling on, each drawing as intense as the one before, until she reached the last few pages. The most recent entries were ten weeks ago. After that there was nothing except for blank pieces of paper.

There was something eerily calm about these final drawings, Catherine thought: the cliff face, the blue tape depicted so clearly she could imagine it flapping in the breeze. Even the body on the beach looked more rested than dead.

Catherine's hands shook as the book slid out of her grasp and hit the floor. What was she going to do?

But as she sat there, her thoughts whirring about incoherently, she realized that Gracie *had* seemed so much happier and calmer lately. Maybe this was because she and Anna were so close again. Maybe

Grace's diary entries were just her way of getting her emotions out and making sense of the tragedy. She had never been one to talk about her feelings. Maybe this was a good thing, Catherine told herself. It was Grace's therapy. And who was she to argue over how anyone chose to heal?

Catherine pushed the box underneath the bed again, out of sight, where she hoped she would never have to see it again. If she admitted it to herself, she would say she was too afraid to address her daughter's behavior for fear of what it might turn up.

But then she also couldn't deny that the weeks and the months, and even the years that followed had brought back a happier Gracie, and surely that was all a mother ever wanted for her child?

19

Grace

Grace notices that Anna isn't at school pickup this afternoon. She has the luxury of asking a friend to do the job for her and, unsurprisingly, it is Nancy she's chosen again. Grace has been watching Nancy as she sits in her car, parked across the road. In fact, for three months she has had to watch Anna cavorting with her new friends, abandoning her in the school playground, leaving her out of invites, lying to her about why she can't come to see her when really Grace knows that she has chosen the others over her.

This is what she cannot get past. After everything she has done for Anna. It is the unfairness of it.

Grace climbs out of the car. She has been sitting here so long that she is now late to pick up Matilda. The other class mothers are already ambling down the path, and she avoids their gazes as she rushes past them. They will be gossiping, trying to figure out where Anna has been and what she has been doing. How long before they all find out she was visiting Grace's own mother?

She has been betrayed by Anna. By Catherine, too. It had taken until today for her mum to call and let her know Anna had been with her for the last few days, and all the while Grace has been frantic with worry. Of course, her mum had protested she didn't have a clue that Grace would be concerned about her friend. Anna having told her she'd been in contact with her husband was enough to put her mind at ease over that one, apparently.

"Well, he didn't tell me, Mum," Grace had said.

Her mum hadn't said as much, but Grace could imagine her thinking, *Maybe he didn't, Grace, but then you are the reason the poor girl had to come here.*

"She's the reason you had to call an ambulance, isn't she?" Grace had shouted. "She made you ill."

"Oh no, love, I'm sure it was just coincidental. It wasn't Anna's fault—"

"Of course it was. Why can't you admit that? You had a bloody panic attack because of her."

Catherine had been momentarily silent and had then said quietly, "Anna stayed with me to make sure I was okay. She insisted she wouldn't leave me on my own until I was better and I'd seen my doctor."

"Because quite rightly she felt guilty," Grace had hissed. "She did this to you and if you can't see it, you're bloody stupid."

"I think we're missing the point anyway," Catherine had said.

Yes. The point. The point was that Anna was digging up the past, asking questions about a night that Grace took care of for her and lied to the police about just so that her best friend didn't get in trouble.

She should never have said anything to Anna about it, but how was she to know Anna was going to go this far? She'd just wanted to remind her of what she had done for her, that she knew Anna better than anyone else ever would.

Grace's rage continues to simmer as she reaches the classroom and sees her daughter hovering outside with the other kids whose parents are late.

"Sorry," she mutters to no one in particular as she holds out a hand for Matilda. "Come on, we need to go."

Miss Williams gives her a shifty look, but Grace resists the urge to snap at her. She waltzes her daughter back down the path to where the mums are still congregating, stopping her as she moves to ask her what she knows about Anna's return.

All evening Matilda plays her up. Sometimes Grace thinks her daughter knows exactly how to wind her up the wrong way until she gets to the point when she wants to blow. They are similar in many ways. Her daughter is strong minded and persistent. It is Graham who Matilda always manages to wind around her finger, but Grace doesn't give in like her mother always did with her. Catherine was too soft; even Grace could see she had no boundaries. She isn't like that with Matilda, even if it means they are often at loggerheads.

Grace puts her to bed at seven-fifteen, switching off the lights twenty minutes later, but still Matilda is calling out from her room that she isn't tired and demanding that Grace go in to see her. She ignores her. The problem with living in this apartment is that there is nowhere to escape to. However spacious the rooms feel when you walk in, the walls begin to close in on you soon enough.

It is two o'clock the following afternoon when Grace hears the buzz of her intercom. She takes a step back, shocked, when she sees who is waiting downstairs to be let in. Pressing the buzzer she opens the door to her apartment and leaves it wide as she retreats to the kitchen, waiting for the ping of the lift to signal its arrival on the third floor.

She hears the slump of his suitcase on the hallway floor and the door closing before she sees him appear around the corner.

"What are you doing here?" These are the first words out of Grace's mouth as she regards her husband. She folds her arms across her chest, stands feet apart, wanting him to know he can't just turn up in their lives whenever he fancies it.

Graham's eyes are heavy with fatigue. He's never managed to sleep much when he flies. "When we spoke last night I was about to tell you I had a flight booked. But you hung up on me."

She wonders if he expects an apology, which she is in no mood to give, and yet she is torn, because a part of her wants to feel her husband's arms around her. Just someone to hold her and tell her everything will be all right.

But she cannot forgive Graham for the fact he has only been here once in the last three months. So they remain standing in awkward silence until Graham eventually comes over to the breakfast bar and gives her a peck on the cheek. His hand rests lightly on her shoulder and she feels herself stiffen beneath his touch.

In return Graham pulls back. "Have you nothing to say?" he asks as he rubs a hand across his bleary eyes. He seems colder with her than usual, though possibly it's because she isn't giving him the reaction he was hoping for.

"I thought you weren't coming back until the twenty-third."

She watches him closely. For someone who has traveled for over thirteen hours to see her, he certainly doesn't look remotely happy. Already they have not gotten off to a good start, and she doesn't like the feeling of apprehension it is giving her. Usually Graham would be all over her, apologizing for one thing or another, but today he isn't.

She is about to say something more, maybe soften her initial reaction to his arrival, when he shakes his head and says, "You never change, Grace, do you?"

She lets out a short laugh. He has no concept of reality, no idea that he deserves a cold shoulder when he has treated her so badly. Did he really think he could waltz into the apartment and count on her to open her arms and welcome him back when he has made no effort with her or Matilda?

"I wasn't expecting you," she says, and knows she is making it sound like it's a bad thing, but she cannot help the tone in her voice. And yet at the same time she wants to scratch out the last five minutes and start again. For Graham to have at least walked in with a bunch of flowers and an apology so that they can reset, because then at last she'd have someone in Clearwater who is on her side.

Grace's mind is busy working through how they can move past this faulty start, whether she is able to relent *yet again* and put aside the fact he chooses to prioritize his work over her when he says, "There's a reason I'm back earlier."

"Oh?"

He takes out a stool and sits beside her. "Grace, we need to talk."

"Right." Her tone is stiff, she can hear it herself, but she thinks she knows what's coming. His eyes have no life in them; they have lost something and she cannot put it all down to an overnight flight. It makes her nervous.

"You must know this isn't working, Grace," he continues. "*We* aren't working."

Her heart pounds.

"I can't go on like this," he tells her.

"Then what are you going to do about it?" she finds herself saying, not particularly wanting to hear his answer. She quickly adds, "Are you going to move back to the UK? To be with us?"

"Grace." He laughs sadly, shaking his head. "I moved my job to Singapore to be nearer you. You know that." When she doesn't answer he says, "You upped and left Australia without telling me what you were planning. You took Matilda to live in another country without telling me. No sane person makes that kind of decision."

"I told you I was moving," she says.

"With two weeks' notice. The house was already packed up. You left me to sort out its rental. You'd planned it all and I wasn't a part of those plans, but as always I went along with it because—" He breaks off.

"Because why, Graham?" she goads.

"You know why," he says, as if he has the weight of the entire world on his shoulders. "Because it's too hard to keep fighting you, Grace. I can't do it anymore. I want a divorce."

She recoils from him, trying to make sense of what she is feeling. Should she have seen this coming beforehand? Over the months, the years even. Maybe, but in truth, she never expected Graham to *leave her.* If anything, if she ever thought about it, it was always the other way round. Graham was supposed to be devoted to her, and yet here he is, doing exactly that.

God, she actually wants to beg him not to do this. But how can she let him see her like that? She was always the one with the upper hand in their relationship; he was always telling her how lucky he was to have her.

"Is there someone else?" she asks. There must be. There can be no other reason. The thought that Graham has met another woman makes her want to throw up.

"No." He shakes his head. "There is no one else." He reaches out a hand towards her but she pulls away.

"Don't touch me," she snaps. She *will not* let him see how raw she is feeling.

June 1997

Every so often Grace caught a flash of Anna's purple hoodie and the bright green top that Heather was wearing as they wove off the path a little way ahead of her and through the trees towards the cliffs. It was dark now, the streetlights far behind them, and the intermittent flash of Anna's flashlight had stopped beaming, no doubt another of Heather's dares to make the night feel more dangerous.

Grace kept her distance as she twisted through the trees. At one point she could just make out the blue and white of the police tape ahead, marking out the area as unsafe. She and Anna knew well enough how precarious the cliff face was, her mum had drummed it into them over the last few days since the incident. The land could just slide away beneath your feet in an instant.

She stopped when they did, hiding behind a tree. Up ahead she could hear their muted voices, discussing something: what they were going to do next, no doubt. But then Heather stepped over the tape, pressing her foot to flatten it so Anna could hop over straight after. If Anna was anxious, she wasn't showing it, staying close on Heather's heels as they disappeared, momentarily out of sight.

Grace edged forward until she could make out their figures again. Two silhouettes against the dim moonlit sky beyond. She hated seeing her best friend with someone else. It was the worst kind of betrayal. And though she should be turning back now, making sure she got back to Anna's house either before Anna did or before Anna's dad woke up and found them both missing, she couldn't drag herself away. Something ferocious was brewing inside her.

"Are you in love with Anna?" Heather had asked her once, about three weeks ago, when she had crept up on Grace sitting on the grass banks outside school waiting for her friend to come out of her history lesson so they could walk home together.

"No. Of course not," she had snapped back.

That was the thing with Heather, she made everything so vulgar. Grace wasn't in love with Anna, their relationship was so much more than that, but Heather wouldn't understand it. Girls like her had friends for a season that came and went. Not like Grace and Anna, who would be connected forever.

But then sometimes Grace couldn't understand their friendship either, or at least not in a way that she could easily explain. How do you detail the intricacies that bind you to someone until you know their thoughts as well as you know your own?

She was closer to Anna than anyone. More so even than to her mum, who nervously fluttered between her and her dad and Anna, as if she needed to be there for them all. Only she flapped her wings far closer to Anna than she did to Grace, like a protective mother bird. Then as soon as Henry clicked his fingers, she would scarper his way, pretending to enjoy whatever he wanted to watch on TV, chuckling at his work stories that she likely didn't care about or understand.

And Grace didn't need anyone to point out that her own father barely acknowledged her existence.

So no, Heather, I am not in love with Anna, I just NEED her! The words reverberated in Grace's head.

Heather had laughed at Grace that day on the bank, as if she knew better. And now Grace was having to watch her lead her best friend to the edge of the cliff without so much as a thought for her. And what made it so much worse was that Anna had chosen Heather over her.

Grace needed to press forward again as they dipped out of sight, but when she saw them once more they were facing away from her, close together, their voices raised now, like they were arguing.

It wasn't until they grew louder that Grace began to catch snatches of their conversation: "This is ridiculous." "You're being so stupid." With each accusation their tones of voice got harsher.

Grace worried that if she didn't leave now she would soon be seen and then the whole evening would be wasted. She needed to get back to Anna's house and wake Anna's dad so he'd notice Anna had gone out.

But she couldn't move. She was rooted to the spot, unable to tear herself away from the scene unfurling in front of her.

"Fine," Anna was yelling. "Be like that, if you want." She was starting to walk away when Heather reached out for her. In turn, Anna grabbed her arm, and all of a sudden Heather lost her footing.

By reflex, Grace shot up from where she was crouching behind a tree, stumbled forward a step, cracking a twig beneath her trainers. Neither girl looked round, they were too engrossed in their argument as they tussled back and forth, too close to the edge of the cliff for anyone's liking, and Grace wondered if she needed to forget her plan and stop the girls going farther before one of them died.

The night hadn't turned out like she'd imagined it would.

She had only just made it back to the house before Anna did, ripping off her sweatshirt and tucking herself under the sheet when she heard the key in the lock downstairs.

As Anna climbed the stairs, Grace squeezed her eyes shut, forcing them closed, but Anna didn't notice as she stumbled onto the mattress and shook Grace's leg, sobbing at her to wake up.

Grace made a pretense of stirring and rubbing her eyes. "What's happened?" she asked as she sat upright.

Anna was shaking uncontrollably, her lip quivering. "It's Heather," she finally said. "She's fallen off the cliff."

"Oh my God," Grace replied. She automatically reached out her arms to Anna and held her, rocking her, the way she had done so many times before.

And Anna told her a story, though it wasn't the one she had seen on the clifftops earlier because it did not mention an argument, a tussle on the cliff edge. Still, Grace silently listened to her friend as she continued to hold her.

"What am I going to do?" Anna was crying, worrying about her dad and Grace's mum, of all people, worrying she was going to be in so much trouble and what they would say when they found out.

"I won't let anything bad happen to you," Grace told her firmly over and over again against Anna's cries. "We'll tell the police you were here all night. No one will ever know you were there."

They will be in this together, Grace thought. And Anna would always need her.

Her words soothed Anna until she fell asleep beside her on the mattress on the floor. As Grace watched her best friend lying there, she tried to make sense of her own feelings.

On the one hand, she had gotten exactly what she wanted. On the other, she was still furious at Anna for having ever tried to leave her.

The following morning Anna said nothing of her argument with Heather. For a few days Grace was trapped by a desire to let Anna know what she had seen. She didn't like that her friend was keeping secrets from her.

But by then they were bound by a different secret, one that would tie them together for life, and so Grace kept the knowledge to herself. Just in case she might ever need it.

20

Wednesday, 18 December

Anna

Another day passes before I summon the courage to take Ethan to school. I am flanked by Nancy and Caitlyn when I arrive, and we linger by the edge of the path, not quite inside the playground where the other mums huddle.

I can't see Grace, though I have a permanent eye on the gate for the moment she walks through it. What I will do then, I haven't a clue.

For now, my friends give me a certain amount of comfort, but I know I can't live like this, too anxious to take Ethan to school. It surprises me that I haven't heard from Grace since she turned up at the house on Monday. Her absence is more unsettling than reassuring.

Some of the mothers glance in my direction, offer me waves, but they seem to be giving me a wide berth. Nancy has told them I've had family problems, has reminded them the drama was short-lived—they all knew I was safe by Thursday afternoon, after all, even if some of them chose to believe that Ben hadn't heard from me.

It is a relief when the bell rings and Ethan runs back for a hug before lining up with his classmates, and this is when I catch sight of Matilda among them. I sweep the playground for a sign of Grace. "Where is she?" I mutter under my breath.

"I don't like that you're so nervous, Anna," Nancy says. "You can't be scared of standing in the school playground."

"Come on," Caitlyn adds, tugging on my arm. "Let's go." The children are already disappearing into their classrooms. "Why don't we grab a coffee?"

I shake my head. "I can't," I say.

All through the night I have been lying awake, thinking about how I can pass everyone off with a story. My friends know about Grace now, to some degree—about her possessiveness, her need for control—although I haven't told them about Heather. But it's Grace herself who has kept me awake. She is my true problem.

I have two choices: either I confront her or I do what I have always done and let her win. In many ways the latter feels like the simplest option.

"Why can't you have a coffee?" Nancy asks. "What are you up to?"

"I have things to do."

"Where's Ben?" she asks.

"Working. Why?"

"Then let us come to you."

"I told you I can't," I protest.

"Nonsense, we're—"

"Nancy, stop!" I cry. I know they want more of my story, but right now I cannot give them what they need.

"Okay." She holds up her hands. "I'm sorry. We're worried about you," she adds, "that's all."

"I know."

"We just want to help."

"You can't," I say. Tears pool in my eyes, and as soon as my friends notice them we pick up our steps again, walking up the street, away from the throng of other mothers who are fast approaching.

It might seem like the easiest option to let Grace win, but in the long run I know it isn't the right one. If she isn't at school, I need to find her.

It doesn't take long to get to her apartment. I am still wondering how I managed to miss her this morning as I park outside the front of the Waterview complex and make my way to the communal entrance, where I press a finger on her buzzer.

My stomach is fluttering, butterflies furiously flapping, as I wait for her voice. The thought of entering my old friend's flat and facing her makes me feel sick.

A man's voice answers and I apologize. "I must have pressed the wrong number," I say.

"Who are you after?" he asks.

"Grace Goodwin?"

"No, you've got the right place. She's not here at the moment, though. Who is it?"

I go to say *a friend*, but instead just say, "Anna."

"Anna?" He sounds confused. "But I thought you were—" He breaks off and then, "Anna, I'm Grace's husband, hold on, I'll let you in."

The door clicks and I push it open, all the while wondering what Graham is doing here when as far as I knew he was in Singapore. The lift takes me up to the third floor, where he is waiting in the doorway to Grace's apartment. His hand is held out in greeting, and I shake it as he stands aside to let me in.

"It's nice to finally meet you. But I have to say, I'm surprised to see you, Anna. Grace told me you were missing."

"I'm surprised to see you, too," I say. "I didn't know you were back." I have seen photos of Graham, but he looks older in the flesh.

His skin is puffy and wrinkled, and there are dark shadows under his eyes. He has wavy hair that is more gray than the light brown it must once have been. And yet he is smartly dressed in an open-necked shirt and dark jeans that look perfectly pressed.

"Only as of yesterday," he says. "Can I get you something to drink?"

"No, thank you, I'm fine. Will Grace be long, do you know?"

Graham rubs a hand on either side of his chin. "I don't know. She didn't tell me where she was going." His mouth contorts into a grimace, and now that I look closer, I see that it's as if something is making him anxious. "To be honest, we needed to talk, but she just told me she had more important things . . ." He trails off.

"Okay, well, maybe you could just get her to call me when she's back," I say, eager to get away from the awkwardness.

Graham nods. "I will do. It's nice to meet you, though, Anna," he says as I start walking back to the door, wondering why he brought me up here when he has no idea where Grace is. "It's just, like I said, Grace told me you'd disappeared."

"I had," I reply. "But I'm back now."

"So I see. That's good." He hovers by the door as I go to open it. "I'm sorry. It's just that I'm glad I've met you at last. I've heard a lot about you."

I pause, my hand resting on the door handle. I want to go home now that I know Grace isn't here, but there is something about Graham and the way he is looking at me. He is nothing like what I expected from the images Grace has painted of her hard, career-focused husband.

"I can see that you're reluctant to stay," Graham says gently. "I can understand that." He shakes his head and laughs softly. "You know, I was jealous of you at first," he admits with a shy smile.

"Jealous of me?"

"When Grace and I first got together, she talked about you a lot, about your relationship with her. But now . . ." He pauses. "Well, I'm pleased she has you."

"Pleased she has me?"

"I know she spoke to you before she came back to England, that you were worried about her being on her own," he says. "She's told me that it was you who convinced her to move back here, but the truth is I didn't actually know she'd made that decision."

"Sorry, what?" I say.

"Whatever she's told you about us," he goes on, "I just want you to know that I haven't been as bad a husband to your best friend as she might have painted me out to be."

I shake my head, confused. "But she didn't talk to me before she came back here," I tell him. "We never had any conversation."

Graham looks as surprised as I feel. "She said you begged her to," he says, "for her own sanity."

"Me?" I say, incredulous.

Graham nods. "She said you told her she shouldn't have to put up with being on her own." He hesitates. "You really don't know any of this, do you?"

"I didn't even know Grace was coming back until she called me and said she was standing on my driveway." I remember the call now with frightening clarity. To think that Grace had planned it all, had told her husband the idea was mine. "I hadn't spoken to her in two years."

"Oh God," Graham says, thinking it through. "I suppose I shouldn't really be surprised. Grace has told me enough lies over the years, but somehow she still manages to catch me out. The thing is, when I was originally posted abroad, to Germany, we talked about moving to the UK. I'm from London, and it's what we both wanted."

"Why didn't you?" I ask.

"To be honest, I never really understood why she changed her mind. Especially when she started telling me I was never there for her or our daughter. I couldn't get my head round it, when we'd made this decision together and it was Grace's choice to stay in Australia. Then the job came up in Singapore at the start of the year and I asked her to move out to be with me. She told me she didn't want to go, so I agreed I'd take it for a year and then move back to Australia.

"I don't expect you to believe me," he says, "when you've only just met me—"

"I do believe you," I say, still astounded at the depths of Grace's manipulation.

"I've never been able to make her happy. I've always known that, I suppose, but it hasn't stopped me trying. I want you to know that."

"It doesn't matter what I think," I tell him. "We aren't the best friends she seems to have made out to you we are."

"I'm beginning to see that," Graham says. "I imagine half of what she's told me about you isn't true."

"What has she told you?" I ask.

"She used to taunt me with the way you have this link that will bind you together forever. She loved telling me how you were wound together in ways I could never understand." He gives a small laugh. "She knew I used to be envious of your closeness, and it was as if she used your relationship to make me feel worse."

"We were just friends, as kids," I say. "You know it was no more than that?" The thought of the significance that our relationship still holds for Grace unnerves me; that so many years later I could still have so much importance in her life. "And now, well, we hadn't been in touch for a long while," I tell him.

"Dear God, Grace . . ." Graham raises his eyes to the ceiling. "So she has no one. I leave her, and she will have no one. It's sad, isn't it? It's bloody pathetically sad."

"I think I should go." I grapple for the door handle again. I cannot feel any sadness for Grace. The idea that she has traveled halfway across the globe with her daughter in tow because of me . . . It fills me not with sorrow, but with dread.

I drive home, too fast, my head spinning with what Graham has told me, so that I don't even notice Nancy's Land Rover parked outside my house until I need to slow down to avoid bumping into it as I turn into the driveway. By the time I get out of the car, Nancy is out of hers, too, and waiting by the gate.

"I'm sorry," she is saying, "I was only here to drop these off." She is proffering a large bunch of flowers. "They're a welcome-home gift."

I take them and smile my thanks, admiring the red petals, running my finger along a holly leaf as it presses into my skin. "It's up to me to get rid of her," I say.

"Grace?" Nancy asks.

"I have to tell her to go."

21

Grace

It must have been karma that led Grace to get a second appointment
with Sally at eight a.m. on Wednesday morning, a time she would never
usually have been able to make had Graham not been there to take
Matilda to school for one of the few times in their daughter's young life.

Sally had told Grace that she doesn't work Wednesdays when Grace
had phoned her the afternoon before, desperate to see her again.

"Please," Grace begged. "I need to speak to you urgently."

She could imagine the woman likely sighing as she heard her flapping the pages of a paper diary. "I can squeeze you in on Friday at
three thirty?"

That was three days away, and Grace wasn't prepared to wait. "Is
there nothing you can do tomorrow?"

"Well . . ." Sally paused. "I suppose I could do something early in
the morning. It would have to be eight; I need to leave by nine thirty."

"Thank you," Grace said. "That's perfect."

And it was perfect. Because having spoken to Sally for fifty minutes about the state of her marriage and anything else she could think
of, half an hour after the end of her appointment, Grace knows Sally's
house will be empty. She has told her as much.

During her session she has excused herself to use the bathroom and opened its window a crack again. She wonders if Sally noticed it had been opened on Monday. Now, as she leaves, she glances back at the house before getting into her car and driving to the end of the road, where she waits until she sees Sally pulling out of the driveway in her yellow Mini.

As soon as the car has turned the corner and disappeared out of sight, Grace gets out of her own vehicle and walks back towards the house. There is a side gate at the front of the path, and she opens the bolt and walks through.

The bathroom window is still ajar, though you wouldn't be able to tell if you didn't know. Grace drags a bin underneath and opens the window, climbing on top of the bin and hauling herself through. When she is inside she hesitates a moment before entering the hall-way. If Sally has set an alarm, then it will surely be triggered when she steps out.

But no alarm sounds and so, regardless of the fact she is alone in the house, Grace tiptoes across the hallway floor and lets herself into the front room as quietly as possible. The gray metal filing cabinet sits in the corner, and she makes her way over to it, pulling out unlocked drawers, rifling through the folders until she finds the one she is look-ing for in the third drawer down: Anna Robinson's.

Her best friend has gone behind her back, and Grace has no clue what she is up to and what she might tell people, but all of a sudden she is holding the evidence that will tell her what she needs to know: the therapy notes she had always planned to come back for anyway.

Grace lifts out the folder and flicks through the handwritten pages inside. There are notes that go back to Anna's first visit three months ago in September, a few weeks after Grace had returned to Clearwater.

Closing up the file she heads back to the bathroom, climbing onto the toilet to haul herself back out through the window and onto the path. It has been ridiculously easy, breaking into Sally's house, and with what she has come for tucked under her arm, she lets herself back out through the gate, bolting it up again, for what little use that does.

Grace gets back in her car, flinging the file onto the passenger seat as she starts the engine. Its contents are so tantalizingly close, but she wants to get away from Sally's before she opens them, just in case the woman returns to find her sitting at the end of her road. She has taken enough chances already.

She does not want to take it back to her apartment. Graham will hopefully be gone by now, but she won't risk it. She has a night of him staying in her apartment, having relented, when he begged her that he couldn't leave immediately, having only just seen Matilda.

She tells herself she is doing this for her daughter, although possibly there is still some part of her that wonders if he might apologize, recognize he has made a mistake and say that this is all his fault.

But he hasn't, and now she cannot bear to look at him, and so instead Grace finds herself driving through Clearwater and towards the bottom of Crayne's Cliff, which she knows at 9:45 a.m. on a blustery December morning will be pretty deserted.

As suspected, she easily finds a place to park on the side of the road, turning her engine off before picking up the file and opening it again. This time she reads Sally's notes carefully, absorbing every word that picks up on Anna's behaviors and mannerisms, what she has told her therapist and all the things she didn't say, too, as well as what Sally has inferred from what Anna has told her.

All of it paints a very clear picture of what has been going on inside Anna Robinson's head over the last three months. In a way, Grace is jealous of her friend for having spent so much time dissecting her thoughts; if she had spent more time with Sally, then she might have had some for herself, but in many ways it is more satisfying to read Anna's.

Grace keeps flicking through the pages until she comes to the transcript from Anna's last session, which took place not even two weeks ago. *I left Heather*, it reads. *That night I made a decision to leave her. For good. I've never told another soul what I did, but it's never left me. What I did was so wrong.*

Grace carries on reading, about how she herself had always kept to her word, which is of course true, because she has carried Anna's secret with her for twenty-two years, something only a good friend would do.

She is beginning to feel a tingle of warmth from such friendship when she sees Anna's next sentence: *Now she had a hold on me.*

Grace's fingers tap against the paper.

Grace always hated me being friends with anyone else . . .

I knew the moment I chose Heather she would have been furious . . .

. . . making sure I would never leave her again . . .

No one knows Grace like I do. No one has a clue what Grace Goodwin is capable of.

Grace turns the page, dropping it in her haste, scooping it up quickly to carry on reading.

How do you mean? Sally had gone on to ask her.

I think she might have done it.

A red pen has circled this last line, making three rings around the sentence. *Probed for more*, it states in a handwritten note. *Anna refuses to tell me. Does she think Grace killed Heather????*

22

Anna

I climb back into my car, tap out a text, and listen for the ping to signal that it has been sent. *Meet me*, I have written to Grace. *In fifteen minutes on the beach.*

I don't specify where, but Grace will understand. It is barely a five-minute drive to the coast road, and yet when I turn onto it and head towards the Old Vic car park, I see Grace's car already ahead of me.

I pull over as a reply comes through. *I am here x*

Surely it is coincidence, and yet it is an unnerving thought that Grace is always one step ahead.

I feel a burning apprehension as I climb out of the car. The beach is empty and no one else knows I am here. I didn't even tell Nancy when she left because at that point I still didn't know what I was going to do. But I shake any thoughts of danger out of my head.

Grace is smiling as she gets out of her own car and walks towards me. She is holding up her hand in greeting, but I don't wave back. Instead I turn and look out at the vast expanse of sea that seems to go on forever. Despite the waves that chop in frothy white fountains, it calms me to watch it.

"It's good to see you again," Grace says as she joins me. "You know you frightened me, Anna, disappearing like that."

It has been two days since Grace turned up at the house, and so unlike her not to have been in touch since, which, doubled with her cheery disposition, is disquieting. But then she always has had a knack for throwing me off course.

I fight an instinct to apologize as we walk towards the wall. It is lower on this part of the road, which means we can sit on it, and we do, our feet dangling over the side, the way we would when we were children, slowly licking Mr. Whippy ice creams, Grace always passing her Flake to me as she didn't like it.

"I reported you missing," Grace goes on. "Did Ben tell you that?"

"He did."

"You'll never guess who I saw at the station."

When she doesn't tell me, I ask, "Who?"

"Marcus Hargreaves. Do you remember him?"

"Of course I remember him." I turn to Grace. I have never forgotten his name.

"Well, he remembered you, too. Both of us, of course."

I continue to stare at her, but Grace adds no more on the subject. Instead she says, "We have so many memories here, don't we, Anna? Do you remember the time you wanted us to run away?"

There is a vague memory of something, but nothing I can put my finger on. "No," I say eventually.

"I do." Grace laughs. "You'd had an argument with your dad. You rang me in tears and said you'd packed a case and we were going to get coach tickets to London."

It is coming back to me now. "How old were we?"

"Thirteen. Or I was. It was a week before your birthday."

"I don't remember what the argument was about."

"You wanted a new pair of trainers and he told you he would sort it, but he bought a pair from some mate of his to give you. You were livid."

"That was it?" I say.

"Yes." Grace is beaming at the memory.

"Why would I want to run away over that?"

"I don't know, Anna. It blew up into something bigger, I suppose. By the time I met you here you were adamant he didn't care about you and that he never had."

I turn back to the sea, tears pricking the corners of my eyes. All of a sudden I feel an urge to tell Grace I miss him. That I know he always cared about me. That the thought of running away from him over a pair of trainers makes me feel sick.

"I know you miss him," Grace says, as if reading my thoughts. I can feel her eyes on me, her hand so close to my own. Any moment I might feel it on mine, and yet I don't draw away. How easy it is to slip back into what was once normality. Does that mean there is a part of me that still wants it? It is a frightening thought.

"We had happy times, though, didn't we?" Grace says. Her fingers are so close, I can almost feel them brushing my skin. Once, I'd known Grace's hands as well as my own. We would often clasp them together as we walked down the road, even as teenagers, and would occasionally hold hands instead of linking arms. It had always made me feel so safe.

"Like when we were kids and your dad took us digging for razor clams and you screamed when one popped out of the sand," Grace says.

Despite myself, I smile.

"And the time I nearly drowned out there because that tire he sent us out to sea in capsized and I couldn't get back up again."

"He refused to buy a dinghy, saying that would do," I remember. "He had to run in fully clothed to get you out."

Grace is laughing, and for a very small moment it feels like this is how it should be. Talking about the past, talking about my dad. It is something we rarely did, I realize. Usually Grace would put him down, and yet she must have been able to see how he was always there for me.

I shift on the hard wall and look away in the opposite direction. "Why did you come back?" I ask. When Grace doesn't answer, I carry on. "Graham says it was because of me. He says I begged you to come here." Now I face her.

Grace's eyes narrow and she doesn't ask how I know this, but instead says, "When I left, I felt like part of me had been cut out, not having you in my life. Didn't you ever feel like that?"

I want to say no, but that isn't true, because for a long while I did. For years I wanted Grace back, but it wasn't until later I understood that just because you missed something it doesn't mean it was good for you.

"The day I came back here and you found me standing on your driveway," she continues, "tell me honestly what you thought."

My mind drifts back to it for the second time today. Grace must have seen my immediate elation as I was swept up in the surprise of seeing her again. But I had spent the morning clearing out my dad's house. In that moment I craved having someone I could talk to again. Someone who knew him.

"Grace, why have you come back?" I ask her again. "You surely didn't return to Clearwater because of me?"

"Oh, don't flatter yourself, Anna," she mutters. "I came back because my husband left Matilda and me so he could travel round the world. I thought you would be there for me, but clearly your priorities lie with your *mum* friends."

I close my eyes and sigh. We will go round in circles, and so instead I say, "We need to talk about what happened the night Heather died." When I open them again, I see Grace's mock surprise. I'm grateful for the padding of my coat that hides my pumping heart, which races so quickly it almost hurts. The blood in my ears swishes loudly. I can no longer focus on the sound of the waves.

"Why?" Grace's face is blank. Her response surprises me.

"Because . . ." I search for the right words. *Isn't it obvious?* "I need to understand . . ."

"If I killed her?" she says. "Is that what you want to know?"

My lips part but I don't answer.

"Only I saw *you*, Anna. *Your* argument with Heather, which you never told me about. Why didn't you?" she asks. "Because I heard all of it."

I open my mouth, but she's already saying, "You really think *I* killed her? After everything I did—and you can sit here and suggest it was me? I saw you and her, Anna. I saw what happened."

I shake my head. The day has turned sour, as it was always going to.

"So shouldn't I be asking you that question?" Grace says. "Did *you* kill Heather, Anna? Did you push her off the cliff?"

"You need to go, Grace." I want the conversation to end now. I don't think I want to dig any further into what happened that night.

Grace laughs.

"I mean it. I don't want you in Clearwater. I don't want Matilda at the same school that Ethan goes to. You should never have come back."

"You're telling me to leave?"

"Yes. You came back thinking we could be best friends again, but I don't want that, Grace. I don't need you in my life anymore."

Grace opens her mouth to answer, but when no words come out, she clamps it shut again.

I shuffle onto my hands, which have been shaking by my sides, pushing them under my bottom to still the nerves. In some ways I do wish it could be different. We have so many memories that have bound us together, closer than possibly anyone else in my life, bar Ben or Ethan. It shouldn't have had to be this way, and yet it needs to be.

There is nothing I can do but cut Grace out of my life once and for all.

23

Grace

Grace watches Anna drive away. In the space of two days her husband and her best friend have told her they don't want her in their lives any longer. Both of them have broken up with her, dumped her, whatever you want to call it.

Graham has told her that he will never be good enough for her, will never be able to do anything right. His friends, it turns out, warned him of this at the beginning of their relationship but he chose to ignore them because he loved her. In many ways she shouldn't be surprised. This is why she had come back to England.

She finds herself pacing the pathway alongside the beach, in the direction that Anna has just left, heading towards the roundabout at the end of the road. Grace doesn't know why she is still walking, but she doesn't want to go home, not until she knows for sure Graham will have gone.

"All this a week before Christmas?" she had asked him. "What kind of Christmas is this going to be for our daughter?"

"What do you suggest, Grace?" he'd said. "That we play happy families until the new year?"

Yes, she supposes, that is what they should be doing, or at least that is what he should want to do. But the thought of him continuing to live in her apartment for the next few weeks is unimaginable. This is his doing, and when their daughter doesn't get over this and in years to come remembers her father for what he is—a selfish coward who has always put himself over her—Grace will not contradict her.

Opposite the roundabout the rowing club's stupid Christmas fairy lights are flapping in the wind as they twinkle dimly against the dull gray sky. Her husband might as well have punched her in the gut, but Anna has reached a hand in and squeezed so tight that Grace can hardly breathe.

It is Anna, Grace realizes, whom she'd expected would pick up the pieces. Be there for her in a way no one else ever could. It was only ever Anna who made Grace feel noticed, listened to, important.

"You've always needed me," she would say to Anna when they were younger, and Anna would agree with her and tell her yes, she did need her and she was so grateful for Grace being there.

Only deep down Grace has a feeling—a horrible, horrible feeling—that maybe she needed Anna more.

"Grace Goodwin?"

A man's voice is calling her and she turns to try to identify him, but it takes her a moment to acknowledge Detective Marcus Hargreaves ambling along the pavement across the road.

She stops but she doesn't answer. Her heart is beating like she has run a marathon when she hasn't even walked half a mile.

"Hello?" He is calling to her. He is crossing the road now, skipping between the sporadic traffic as he makes his way round to her. "Hi," he says when he finally stands beside her. "Is everything okay?"

"Yes. Fine," she tells him.

"Only you don't look . . ." He waves a hand in the air, gesturing for a word that he doesn't end up using. She knows she is staring at him blankly, but she feels blank. Her whole body is numb. It is shock, she presumes, although now that she has stopped she is beginning to feel something that more resembles anger, hatred, a desire to explode with rage.

But she is far too composed for that, and with the detective staring at her oddly, she ignores the sensations she's experiencing and says, "Sorry, I was miles away."

He smiles, but there isn't the twinkle in his eyes that she saw when they first met last Thursday. He is worried about her, she thinks. It is nice to have someone worrying about her. "I just wanted to catch up with you to see if there is any news?" he asks.

"News?"

"Your friend, Anna . . ." He clicks his fingers, searching for a surname.

"Anna Robinson."

The detective nods. "Have you heard from her yet?"

"I have," Grace says. "Yes."

"Oh, great." He pauses as if he is expecting more. "And so everything is okay?"

"Yes, I suppose everything is fine."

"Right. Listen, Grace, I really wanted to say I'm sorry, you know; I can see you were worried about your friend last week, but I'm glad everything has turned out well."

"You're sorry for what?" Grace asks. "For not listening to me?"

"Well, yeah, but it wasn't my call. DCI Barker's an experienced detective and . . . well, thankfully it looks like she was right."

"Not to be worried?"

"Yeah. Are you sure everything is okay?"

"Only just because Anna is back, it doesn't mean there isn't anything to worry about, does it?"

"No, I suppose not always, but it's not a crime to disappear, and . . . Listen, Grace, do you want to talk? I have time to grab a coffee if you like?"

"Why are you being so kind?" she says to him. "You don't owe me anything. Like you say, it wasn't your call to decide whether or not to listen to me."

"I know, but—" He breaks off, and once again she cannot help but notice just how handsome he is, and suddenly she feels like she is being a complete bitch to him when he doesn't deserve it. "I guess I just remember you so well when you were younger and I came to your house that time. It's like I said to you before, the case has never left me. And when you turned up at the station last week it all came rushing back." He is squinting at her as if he doesn't expect her to understand, when she understands only too well.

"I do have time for a coffee," she tells him with a smile. "I'd like that, thank you."

"Good. That's great. There's this place up the road over there, on the high street, that does the best lemon drizzle cake. Actually, it's my sister-in-law's café," he says with a grin, "so I'm a bit biased. But it's my treat if you're happy to go there."

"Perfectly happy," she tells him. "It sounds lovely." Grace follows him, over the road again and towards one of the small alleyways that will take them up towards the café.

"I'm glad I've bumped into you, Marcus," she says as they walk. "I haven't spoken to anyone about Heather Kerr in a very long time."

Because, Grace thinks, there is no harm in having a little chat to the detective about what happened all those years ago.

June 1997

The detective sat in the living room. Grace was curled up on a bean-bag. He was perched on the edge of the sofa, leaning forward, his hands clasped together as they hung between his knees.

"Gracie, darling, move out of there," her mother told her quietly. "Go and sit on the chair."

"It's fine, Mrs. Goodwin," the detective said. "Grace is fine where she is."

He had big eyebrows that just about met in the middle and a pair of sunglasses that were pressed into the top of his bouncy hair. He'd introduced himself as DS Hargreaves but told Grace she could call him Marcus.

Grace had heard her mum in the kitchen, talking to her dad, worrying that she didn't think he looked old enough to be running an investigation this important, but he must have been at least twenty-five, and to Grace that felt really old.

"Do you like school?" he was asking her.

Grace shrugged. "It's okay, I suppose."

"Do you have any idea what you want to do when you leave?"

"Not really."

"What do you enjoy?" he asked.

"Art."

"She's forever drawing," her mum butted in. "She's actually very good at it."

Marcus smiled and nodded. "Grace, I want to ask you some questions about Heather Kerr. I believe she is in your class?"

"Yes. She's only been there since Christmas. Is she in trouble?" Grace asked.

"No. She's not in any trouble."

"She's always getting caught. Doing things she shouldn't be."

"Is she?" he said. "What kinds of things?"

Grace told him some of Heather's exploits and knew she had said the right thing, as he seemed particularly interested in her take on the girl.

She could feel her mum shuffling about in the corner of the room. "Gracie, the girl is missing. I don't think you should be talking about her like this." Her expression was pained.

"No, no," he said. "It's very useful."

Grace smiled to herself. She was glad she was being useful. She appeared to have struck the right chord with him.

"Grace, can you tell me about the last time you saw Heather?"

"Yes," she said. "It was yesterday."

"Can you remember what time?" he asked.

Yes, she can remember exactly what time she last saw Heather. It was 10:55 p.m., when Heather disappeared over the edge of the cliff.

Grace had been thinking about this all day, wondering what time the police would start investigating what had happened to Heather, whether it would be when they were all still at school, or maybe not until the following day. And she'd thought about what she was going to say, because she was still so very mad at Anna for the way she had treated her, and there was a part of her that thought her friend didn't deserve to get away with what she had done.

But then Anna was her best friend. And being a best friend

trumps everything else. And sometimes that means that you have to lie for your friends and do whatever it takes for them not to get into trouble.

Grace told Marcus Hargreaves that she had last seen Heather in school, and she went on to tell him that she had been at Anna's house all night, but she tucked some truths away for now, in case, one day, she might need them. Grace knew that she was very good at playing a long game if she needed to.

part three

24

31 December

Two weeks later

Anna

It is the first time I have been back in the Old Vic since the night of our pre-Christmas drinks. It wasn't my preferred choice, it wasn't anyone's, but we left it so late it was the only place Nancy could book a week before New Year's Eve. She'd reserved a table in the corner of the pub—a table for seven, as Eric is missing from the group. Nancy has told everyone they couldn't get a babysitter at late notice, but this isn't the real reason her husband isn't here. Nancy just needs to work things through in her own time. Lately I've understood how much good friends allow each other to do this.

Personally I am glad of Eric's absence. It is more comfortable without him and his rallies for so-called debates that are really just alcohol-fueled arguments. Nancy seems calmer herself tonight, too, happier and more relaxed, and besides, it would never have worked with Rachel sitting at the same table.

At the last minute the thought of the whole evening became too much to bear and I wanted to call off our own babysitter, a seventeen-year-old girl who lives opposite and hasn't yet had any inclination to go out partying with her friends. The thought of going back to the Old Vic was too much; but as Ben pointed out, I shouldn't stay away from the places that are our haunts. Grace mustn't drive me out of our hometown.

"And anyway," he reminded me, "we haven't heard from Grace. As far as we know, she's already left Clearwater."

I know this isn't true. Grace may have been uneasily quiet in the two weeks since our conversation on the beach, but this doesn't mean she has left town. I haven't told Ben that I have seen her on a couple of occasions when I purposefully drove past her apartment block.

I had started counting each day that I hadn't heard from Grace after we last met, wondering what her silence meant. It was Christmas Eve when I took the car for some last-minute shopping and detoured past her apartment block, spotting her leaving with Matilda and Graham in tow.

I questioned her motivations for not being in touch with me, because her deathly silence goes against everything I would have expected from her. But then isn't that also so clever of her? A way of keeping me on my toes? One thing I know for sure is that she is not gone from my life yet.

Later that day there was a card addressed solely to me lying on the mat. Inside it read, *Happy Christmas, Anna. Missing you, G x*

I'd ripped it up and put it straight in the bin and restarted my count of the days that I hadn't heard from Grace. Today it is seven.

Alan places a tray of drinks on the table and sits down next to Caitlyn, wrapping an arm around his wife's shoulder. I smile warmly at his jacket, the little handkerchief peeking out of its pocket. Despite the fact it is New Year's Eve, the night is subdued and none of us rush to grab our drinks like we'd usually do.

In the corner three guys are setting up a band. It is only nine thirty and I'm already wondering how quickly Ben and I can escape after midnight. "We should have booked a taxi," I say to him as I reach for my wine. "Maybe we should order one now?"

"For what time?" Rachel is calling over the table. "I hate knowing I have to be gone by a certain time."

"I don't want to be too late for the babysitter," I say.

"I know, but tonight . . . ?" she protests. "It's New Year's Eve."

"I know," I say, but I hadn't wanted to leave Ethan. I'd still rather be at home with him because there is a feeling of disquiet hanging over me. All day I've had a sense of foreboding and deep down I wish I hadn't come out, but I fought against the impulse because it is New Year's Eve and Ben has told me our lives mustn't stop.

"I think I might just phone and check everything's okay," I mutter to no one in particular.

"Anna, what's up with you tonight?" Rachel asks as she takes a large glass of Chablis and twists the stem in her fingers, glass poised to her lips before she takes a gulp. "This is supposed to be a celebration. It's New Year's Eve, guys: time for new starts and resolutions; but look at us. We all look miserable," she adds this quietly, glancing at Nancy out of the corner of her eye. "Okay, I know we've had an odd couple of weeks, but we're here together. Shift around," she commands. "Come on, girls, let's take one end of the table and the boys can have the other."

We obediently move seats until Rachel is on the other side of Nancy, and Caitlyn is perched next to her. The band begins to play and I don't get around to calling the babysitter and checking that everything is okay at home.

For a moment I forget everything is far from right as we drink our wine and the four of us laugh at a joke Rachel shares, and maybe we are all desperate to recognize the importance of our friendship, even though it has shifted in the last two weeks.

They don't know everything about me, my best friends. Though I tell myself they never have, it seems different now, more poignant.

What they do know is that I went to see Grace's mum to find out why she had come back. They know the depth of Grace's control over me, her obsession. But they know nothing of what she can do that really scares me.

It is Ben who worries me most. From the other end of the table I catch him looking at me, and I smile, but he barely gives one in return before he turns back to his conversation with Alan.

Three days before Christmas he had turned to me and said, "I think we need to talk about the adoption."

"Zadie?" He could not even say her name. "You're not serious?" I had gasped. We were meeting Zadie on 6 January. *Let's get Christmas out of the way first*, the agency had said to us. "Ben?" I had pleaded. "You can't mean we don't go ahead?"

But of course this was what I'd feared. Ben brushed a hand away and dismissed the subject, and I'd been so anxious about bringing it up again that in the end I decided it would be better not to do so. If we could get to the sixth without any drama, there's no way he'd want to turn her away, surely?

Ben's remarks and questions have come at unexpected times in the last two weeks. I was peeling sprouts on Christmas morning when he approached me and said, "You must have known that what you were doing was wrong. When Grace told you to lie, you must have known." It wasn't the first time he had asked, and it wouldn't be the last.

"Of course I did," I said, dropping a sprout into the colander, my hand resting the knife against the sink. "But you don't know what she was like, Ben. She had this way of persuading me, like it was the only option."

"No, I don't know what she was like," he replied. "That's what I still don't get, Anna." He reached into the cupboard for a wine-glass and poured himself a large glass of red. Each of his movements brought with them a slam or a bang. I hadn't ever known him to start drinking before midday, even on Christmas Day.

It wasn't for want of me trying to explain to him, but I'd hit a wall with Ben, his reaction always one of anger and what appeared to be jealousy.

His accusations seem to twist away from what I'd done to the reason behind my having done it: Grace. I pointed out that I wasn't having an affair, he had no right to be envious of someone who had manipulated my life the way she did so many years ago, and yet somehow, instead of offering sympathy for what I'd been through, he seemed angry with me.

"To us!" Nancy is saying as she raises her glass, and we all copy. I catch Rachel squeezing her arm, and Nancy nods in return. I have been filled in on their conversations of the past two weeks: the tears, more of Rachel's apologies for not having said anything sooner, her protestation that it wasn't her, that she didn't lead Eric on. Yes, she might have been a bit flirty with him, but it had only gone as far as what Nancy had seen.

Nancy has chosen to believe Rachel, though I can see how much it pains her in the smile she gives as Rachel's hand lingers on her arm, how desperately she wishes it had never happened.

We carry on drinking our wine, and two glasses later, I am feeling pleased that we came out for the evening and that I am here with my friends, bringing in the New Year as we have done every year for the last five.

Just over an hour later, I am standing in a short queue for the ladies' room and my phone pings with a text notification. I take it out of my bag and click on the screen.

I want to see you.

Grace. My breath catches, tight in my throat, as my thumb hovers over the phone. I should have expected this, I think, as I glance over my shoulder to where the rest of our party is drinking and laughing obliviously. I should ignore it. I do not want to answer to Grace tonight. I should put my phone away and not keep checking it, but when I am here and Ethan is at home, I can't do that. What if she is standing outside my house right now?

I can't see you tonight, I text back, pressing send and then holding the phone as I stare at its screen. Three dots appear, vanish, reappear—Grace is texting, and already I know this toing-and-froing will go on all evening.

You owe me, Anna.

And now I am already caught up in Grace's game, which is exactly what she wants—to monopolize my evening and make sure she has my full attention. There is no chance of enjoying the night now, I may as well go home. Though what will Ben say? I glance in his direction as I subconsciously step forward in the line.

I should text *I don't owe you anything,* but then maybe I do. I expected some fallout from our conversation two weeks ago, and I must have known Grace would have chosen her timing carefully; this, I have to admit, is pure bloody perfection on her part. Instead I reply, *Okay, we can speak tomorrow.*

No. Tonight. I can come to you, Anna, if you prefer?

Again I glance around the pub, because it is likely Grace knows exactly where I am, though even that is preferable to the thought of her standing on our driveway, Ethan's only protection a seventeen-year-old girl who would be no match for Grace.

Ben will tell me Grace wouldn't do anything to harm our son. "What do you think she's going to do, Anna? Hurt him? Take him?" He'll tell me I am pandering to her again.

Oh, but Grace could do anything if she thought it was the best way of getting to me.

It's in your best interest pops onto my phone screen.

Someone in the queue behind me says, "Do you need the loo? There's one free at the end?"

I apologize to the woman and lock myself in the end cubicle where I sit slumped forward, my phone gripped between both hands. There is something oddly calming about being contained in this tiny space, as if the rest of the world can carry on while I hide.

There is no way I can leave the pub to meet Grace, and no way I should, and yet if I don't, the messages will go on all evening and then there will be calls, and I cannot afford to turn my phone off for fear of not being in contact with our babysitter, in case she needs to reach me. It is only my number she has, and I don't want to ask Ben to call her. I don't want to ask anything of Ben, because of Grace.

It feels like the only possible way to cope this evening is to go home. I will tell Ben I don't feel well; he can stay here if he wants.

With this decision made I am feeling calmer already, when another message pops onto the screen.

I've spoken to the detective today.

Then another: *I've been speaking to him a lot recently.*

And straight after: *You know who I mean, the one who questioned us when Heather went missing.*

Despite my grip on my phone, it slips out of my hand and lands on the floor. There is a crack in the glass, but Grace's last message continues to taunt me.

I have seen that detective sporadically over the years but have never spoken to him. After a while, I doubted Marcus Hargreaves would recognize me. I haven't been in the station since that long-ago time, but it's easier for me to spot him, knowing he still works there.

I bend down to pick up my phone and start to type, *What have you said to him?* But I end up deleting the text, letter by letter.

Grace has me trapped. I know this already, and I also know she won't wait until morning because she has likely had her response planned for days. She isn't going anywhere tonight. And I have no choice but to meet her.

Where? I text.

On the cliffs. Where else?

Of course on the cliffs, but at least I am not far, and so maybe I can escape for half an hour, I think, heading back to the table, my mind whirring with excuses. In the end, I bend down next to Ben and whisper, "I have to go out for a bit."

"What are you talking about?" His face contorts into one of angry confusion that I have come to know well.

I don't want to explain, but I have to give him something. "Grace is outside."

"Shit, Anna. No way." He shakes his head. "You're not going."

"I have to Ben," I plead quietly. "I want this to be over. I want her out of my life. I think she wants to say goodbye," I add optimistically, though I'm sure he doesn't believe this, either. "I'll be fine. I'm just outside," I lie. "I just have to do this and then . . ."

"And then what?" he snarls. He is holding on to my wrist, unwilling to let me go.

"And then she'll go. For good."

He shakes his head, but eventually he releases my arm, shrugs, and waves a hand. "Fine."

I waver for a moment and then turn to leave as he calls, "Anna?"

I look back.

"Call me if there's any problem," he says. "And I'll come out in ten minutes to check."

"There's no need to do that," I tell him, though I know he will and I will just have to cross that bridge later.

I glance at Nancy, who is eyeing me carefully. I smile at her, and walk out of the Old Vic.

25

Grace

Grace sees Anna leaving the pub. She has her red coat on again, pulled tightly around her. She watches her walk across the car park and turn left, starting towards the cliff path. As soon as Anna is nearer she spots her, and so Grace turns and starts walking, knowing Anna will follow up and up the path and then into the trees.

It is amazing how much sound the trees can suck up. Only a few feet in and already the noise of laughter and celebration coming from the pub is dissipating into the night.

"I *am* here," Anna calls behind her. "You don't have to keep walking."

Grace ignores her as she wraps her own coat tighter. It is after eleven on New Year's Eve and there is a biting cold wind in the air.

She has no idea if anyone has followed Anna, but Grace wants them to be alone. Her friend owes her that much after telling her to leave Clearwater and get out of her life. Did Anna really think Grace was going to walk away so easily?

For two weeks she has been dealing with Graham and the fallout from the breakdown of her marriage. She cannot wait for him to leave in two days and go back to Singapore. If she never sees that man again it will be too soon. Why he has chosen now to hover around his daughter's life she has no idea, but he has been nearby, tempting Matilda with his presence over Christmas, showing her what it is like to have a father in her life. Of course, it is Grace who will pick up the pieces when he leaves. It is as if he doesn't know they would have been better if he hadn't come back in the first place.

But then today he announced that he wants joint custody of their daughter. That he is going to ask to be transferred to the UK because he doesn't think it is right for Matilda to be living with Grace full-time.

"Not right?" she had screamed at him. "Not right? When I am the one who has been bringing her up like a single parent?"

"I don't want Matilda caught up in your games any more than she has to be," he had told her.

Games. Grace had laughed at him. These weren't games. She was just trying to deal with the people in her life who kept letting her down. All she has ever wanted is for someone to be on her side, but she's never had that—not even her from her own mother, who had always pandered to Anna, a girl who isn't even related to them, just like she did again recently. And certainly not from her father, who barely looked up when she talked to him.

"Grace, will you just stop!" Anna is calling out from behind her now.

Grace pauses and turns around. They are in the dense thicket of trees now, the thrum of music from the Old Vic a distant murmur. As soon as she stops, Anna does too. Her face is a picture, Grace thinks. Despite the makeup she must have so carefully painted on for her night out celebrating, she looks ghostly and ill.

"What are we doing here?" Anna asks.

"Well, clearly we need to talk," Grace says, "because for starters, I'm not going anywhere. Clearwater is as much my home as it is yours, Anna. I don't really think you can tell me to leave, do you?"

Anna shuffles from one foot to the other. She is clearly nervous, but Grace goes on, regardless. "Do you have any idea how upsetting that was for me to hear? To know that you must hate me as much as you do to tell me to get out of town?"

When Anna doesn't respond, she says, "I don't get how you can treat me like this after everything—"

"After everything you've done for me?" Anna breaks in with some sudden bravado. "Like you always say? What do you think you did for me, Grace? On that night, which I assume you're referring to."

"I lied for you. You know that. I told the police you were with me all night."

"Only, you lied too. You admitted to me that you saw me, didn't you? You followed me, Grace, so you saw what happened."

"Yes," she says, "I saw exactly what happened. I saw your argument. I saw Heather fall." She pauses, waiting for it to sink in.

"You know I didn't kill Heather," Anna says, as they both hear the sound of a twig cracking behind them. She looks around and Grace steps forward, trying to see what has made the noise.

"Who knows you're here?" Grace hisses.

"No one," Anna says when she turns back. Her face is even paler now. Eventually she adds, "I didn't kill Heather. You know I didn't."

Grace raises her eyes. She should tell Anna about the conversations she's been having with Marcus. How he's been so caring towards her, so open about the investigation when she started talking to him in the café after Anna told her to leave town. It seems like they both had things they wanted to get off their chest.

"I've been speaking to that lovely police officer," she tells Anna. "Marcus Hargreaves. He's very handsome."

Anna doesn't respond.

"We've become quite friendly." She takes hold of a branch and snaps a twig off into her hand, which she twirls in circles like a majorette's stick. "Did you know he always thought he missed something on that case?"

"Missed what?"

Grace can tell that she has piqued Anna's interest at last. "He always found it odd that no one particularly knew Heather. He said he thought at least one of the girls was hiding something."

"Why would he tell you that?"

Anna is still shuffling from one foot to the other, her eyes wide in a panic. *Good*, Grace thinks. She hated having to drag her best friend here from her celebrations with all her other friends. It shouldn't be like that. *She* should be celebrating New Year's Eve with Anna, not having to bribe her onto the cliffs to be with her. "Oh, I almost forgot," Grace says, and she swings the bag off her back and throws it to the ground in front of her, unclasping the catch.

"What are you—"

"I've got this," she declares, producing a bottle of champagne. "I thought we could toast the New Year together."

"Are you mad?"

"Maybe only mad enough to think you might want to spend some time with me, Anna Fallow, like you once did," Grace spits.

"I'm Robinson now," Anna says, "and I'm not staying here. This is crazy. *You* are crazy. I'm going back to my husband and my friends."

Grace flicks out a wrist and looks at her watch. It is nearly eleven thirty. She thinks Anna will still be here at midnight, whether she plans to be or not, because despite her threat to leave, she isn't actually moving.

"Marcus was very interested to hear that Heather *did* have friends," Grace says.

Anna is shaking her head, her mouth hanging open like a carp.

"I told him *you* were good friends with Heather," Grace adds.

"No."

"I told him this today, as a matter-of-fact," she recalls, thinking back to how Marcus had so kindly agreed to meet her before his shift, just after Graham had advised her that he wanted to take her daughter away from her.

It has been nice to have someone listen to her, someone to talk about the past with. "Come on," she goes on. "Let's go to the edge of the cliff and have this." She waves the champagne bottle. "I've got glasses too," she adds cheerily.

Grace turns and starts walking in the direction of the cliff edge. She is risking Anna turning back to the safety of the pub, but she knows her best friend better than that. Anna is going to want two things tonight: the truth about the night Heather died, and what Grace has told Marcus Hargreaves.

"It'll be midnight soon," Grace calls over her shoulder, and sure enough, she can hear Anna following her.

26

Anna

I have no choice but to follow Grace, even though I long to turn and walk away. She holds all the cards, just as she always has since we were five years old. I didn't see it then, of course—that the little girl who had proclaimed she would be my best friend would impact my life to such lengths.

Grace knows I can't walk away. There is something about her and the game she is playing tonight that scares me. Rachel's words still ring in my ears, about how this is a time for new starts, because one way or another she will surely be right.

I follow Grace, dancing between the trees as if we are playing some kind of hide-and-seek, though she is slowing now as I knew she would be because she is reaching the part of the cliffs that were once cordoned off with police tape, and this has to be where she wanted to bring me.

I haven't been to this spot in over twenty years. I have walked along the path with Ben and Ethan, but never this far, never back here. But now that I am, I'm taken back to that awful night as if it were only yesterday. All of it crystal clear and carved into my memory so deeply.

Grace is sitting on the ground, running her finger under the foil of the champagne bottle. She has set two glasses beside her. There is a sudden pop as the cork flies out, which makes Grace laugh. She pats the ground next to her. "Come on. Sit down."

Obligingly I sit and absently take a glass that Grace is passing me, waiting for her to fill it. The whole idea of us sitting here on the edge of the cliffs, drinking champagne, only twenty-five minutes before the New Year, is farcical, and yet I have been lured here so frighteningly easily.

"What shall we drink to?" she asks. "I know, how about Zadie?"

"What?" I gasp. "How do you know—"

But it seems Grace can't be bothered to explain how she knows about the adoption as she interrupts me. "I followed you that night," she says, "because I couldn't bear the thought of you being there without me, Anna. I was looking out for you," she adds, beginning the story.

June 1997

Anna was still yelling at Heather to come back from the edge when all of a sudden Heather's foot slipped and she tumbled over.

Grace shot up from her spot behind the tree. In an instant Anna's shouts stopped and the air was filled with an eerie silence except for a twig that cracked beneath Grace's trainers. It hadn't been enough to catch Anna's attention, thankfully. She was too absorbed in what had happened to Heather as she sank to the ground, the air seemingly sucked from within her.

Grace deliberated whether she should run over to see what had happened or race back to Anna's house to ensure she got home first, but in the end she did neither. Instead she watched as Anna shouted Heather's name, which was quickly followed by the sound of Heather's laughter.

She hadn't gone far, just out of sight. Grace saw that she hadn't fallen off the edge of the cliff at all. Now she could see Heather curled in a ball, one leg hanging over the edge. She and Anna must have known that could have been it for her, a fatal slip, but she had only gone far enough to stop Anna's screeching.

"It's not funny," Anna was crying.

"Yes it is. Your face is a picture." Heather couldn't stop laughing as she rolled onto her back.

"I thought you were going to fall."

"Oh, don't be so dramatic." She laughed harder still. The sound rippled through the trees to Grace.

"Oh my God, Heather, I'm not. Will you just come up now?"

"No!"

"What do you mean, no?"

"Join me down here. It's beautiful." Heather's voice sounded all hazy and dreamy as she spoke, her arms stretched out wide on the ground.

"Come up now." Anna was scared. Grace could hear the tears in her words. "I mean it. I want to go." Heather had obviously given her quite a fright. "Fine, I'm going anyway. You can stay here," Anna cried.

Heather continued to laugh as Grace watched Anna stomp away. She pulled back for a moment. Strangely, Anna wasn't heading in the direction of her house, but instead was weaving through the trees.

Grace dragged herself out from her hiding place. It was time to leave; she knew she had to go now if she was to get back before Anna, so why was she so drawn to Heather, who was making snow-angel shapes with her arms in the rough ground?

Maybe it was Grace's anger that pushed her on until she was almost on top of Heather, hovering over her.

"What the hell are you doing here?"

Grace didn't answer.

Slowly Heather pushed herself up, but she winced when she tried to move her leg. "My ankle's caught," she said, reaching forward, trying to dislodge her foot. "Help me, for God's sake; don't just stand there." Heather tried to reach for the twine that was caught around her ankle, having to move herself closer to the edge of the cliff. "It's hurting," she said in a panic, her hands fiddling with the twine, but still Grace was silent and still.

It happened so suddenly then, the ground beneath Heather giving way. She slid farther from Grace, her hands grappling to clutch at clumps of soil or rock, anything that would give her purchase.

"Help me, Grace," she yelped, as Grace hopped back by instinct to avoid the crumbling soil. "Do something, Grace!" she screamed. "Bloody help me."

Heather's fingers continued to paw at the ground. She was managing to shake her ankle free from its trap when Grace stepped forward again. All she needed to do was reach down and take one of Heather's hands and she could pull her to safety. But instead she just continued to watch as the ground slipped away again beneath Heather's grasp, and this time it took Heather and a bloodcurdling scream with her.

Grace stumbled back. In the distance she could hear Anna's voice calling Heather's name in panic. Anna would have heard the cry for sure. Any minute and her friend would be back, and so Grace did what she had to do. She ran as fast as she could, all the way to Anna's house, where she slipped out of her clothes and back into bed and waited for her best friend to return and tell her what the night had taken.

27

Anna

It must be almost midnight.

The air is still and cold and yet I don't feel it. I am warmed by the champagne that cruises through my veins, putting me in a kind of trance, though at the same time I am alert to every sound, every crackle of twig and hoot of an owl in the distance.

"You let her die," I say, not in disbelief because I have been imagining this, but still it shocks me. I turn to Grace. "How on earth can you believe you were looking out for me?" I ask. "How can you justify that to yourself?"

"Heather wasn't good for you," she tells me seriously. "She led you astray."

I stare at her. "Do you know what?" I say eventually. "I *know* you don't believe that. You're not even trying to convince yourself; it's just bullshit, and you know it."

I numbly push myself to my feet. Grace is watching me. "You let her die," I repeat, "and you let me feel guilty for it. All my life you've held this over me. How could you ever have called yourself a friend?" I say. "How could you—"

But there are no words to finish the sentence and no point arguing with her because there is nothing worse than fighting with someone who does not even see reason.

"I've always been a good friend to you. Always," Grace is saying. "Do you remember that time—"

"Oh, shut up, Grace!" I cry. "Just shut up. I can't bear to hear another memory."

Grace turns away and looks out to the sea, slowly taking a sip of her champagne.

"All my life you've tried to control me, Grace, and you're doing it again. Getting me up here, away from my friends. Well, this is where it ends."

"I haven't tried to control you," she says plainly. "I've looked out for you, there's a difference."

"Why me?" I ask. "How come after twenty years you travel across the world because of me?"

"I didn't come back because of you," she mutters.

"I think you did."

"No." She laughs. "I didn't."

"That's what Graham told me."

"Yes, well, you can't believe a word my husband says."

"Only I *do* believe him, Grace," I say, taking a step closer. "I believe *him* and I don't trust *you*. You let Heather die because you were jealous. You let me believe you were being a good friend to me so you always had something over me. I look back at our childhood and see it all so clearly now, the way you manipulated me right from the start. Your mum told me how you cut up my favorite dress because you didn't want me playing with someone else."

"Oh, I bet she did," Grace says. "You were always her bloody favorite, weren't you, Anna? She always took your side over mine."

"No she didn't—"

"I had to share her with you; but I didn't complain because I loved you like I would have loved a sister."

"No," I protest, "you didn't have to share me, you wanted—"

"You really think I wanted it? Of course I didn't. She was my mother, but she treated you just the same as she did me."

I shake my head. It isn't the way I see it, but then what if Grace is right? Did I take a part of her mother away? I cannot ever imagine treating one of Ethan's friends as Catherine did me. No one could come anywhere near as close to my son.

But I cannot give Grace any more ammunition for her twisted beliefs. "You need to leave Clearwater," I tell her. "I don't want you in my life, Grace."

It is ten to midnight. I have been gone for an hour. Ben must be worried sick by now. Even if I hurry I won't make it to the Old Vic in time to see in the New Year, but I start walking, regardless.

"You seem to be forgetting what I've told Marcus," she calls out as she stands, too.

I pause, turning back. I want to ask, I really do, but I know I just need to keep on walking.

"Don't you want to know?" Grace screeches at me. "I'm never leaving, Anna, you know that. I'll be back at school next week."

"No!" I shout as I turn and fly at her. "I don't want to see you again. I don't want you at our school." I hurl myself forward, pushing my hands against Grace's chest. It is the thought of this I cannot bear the most, of seeing her every day. Of her being in Ethan's life.

"Anna!" I hear someone calling from behind us. "Anna?"

It is Nancy who comes running through the trees, followed by Rachel, and then Caitlyn. "What's going on?" she's asking.

"What are you all doing here?" I say.

"Ben thought you might be somewhere on the cliffs." Nancy is panting, out of breath from running; she has stopped now, her hands on her hips, bending forward slightly as she inhales deep lungfuls of air. "He's been going out of his mind. He went outside to find you and when there was no sign of you we all started looking. The boys went one way . . ." She throws an arm in the opposite direction.

"You needn't have come," I tell her. "I was heading back anyway."

"What the hell are you doing here?" Rachel asks.

"We were just talking about old times," Grace butts in. "Weren't we, Anna? Maybe we should fill them in?"

"What's she talking about?" Nancy asks, straightening up. "And will you just come away from the edge, both of you?"

Neither Grace nor I move. I know we are both precariously close to the point where the cliffs disappear into the sea, and yet I don't want to step away first because as soon as I join Nancy and the others, Grace will tell them everything.

"No one's going to listen to you, Nancy," Grace is telling her. "This isn't your night tonight. It's mine and Anna's."

"What the hell is that supposed to mean?" Nancy says. "Anna, what's she talking about? And will you come back from the edge? You're far too close."

"We've been reliving our past, haven't we?" Grace is saying. "Sharing secrets."

"Anna?" Nancy stares at me; her voice is quieter now, less strident.

"Did you know that once upon a time Anna had a friend called Heather?"

"Stop, Grace," I tell her. I feel the tears swelling in my eyes, a wave of anger beginning to uncurl from within me. Whatever I tell my friends, it needs to be my version of the story, not Grace's.

"And one night they came here to this very cliff, right about where we are now."

"Stop it," I say, turning to face her. "Just stop, Grace."

"And that night, Heather died."

"Shut up!" I scream as I push my hands into Grace again.

Nancy leaps towards me, drawing me back. I feel her grip on my arms but I won't let go. My fingers dig into Grace's skin, and I am pushing at her and Nancy is tugging at me, pulling my hands off, and Caitlyn is here now, urging me to get back, and Rachel is here too, I notice, because we are too dangerously close to the edge. All of us. Just like Nancy said we were. Too close. So close that something was bound to happen. One of us was bound to fall.

28

Anna

Across the water in Weymouth, fireworks light up the sky. Midnight has come and gone. It is a new year now. A new start.

My whole body is so frozen in shock that I cannot move it, but then none of us is moving. I realize this when I do eventually step back and fall to the ground. It is too reminiscent of what happened before, I think, as I lean over the edge and cry out Grace's name.

Now Nancy is beside me, using the flashlight from her phone, which does little to shed any light on the cliff face. Still, I know already, I don't have to be told that Grace isn't alive. We heard her scream as it petered away while she tumbled to the bottom. There is little chance of survival.

All four of us crouch on the ground. My own fingers paw at the earth. I swear I can hear each one of our separate heartbeats over the rhythmic thud of the waves as they crash onto the pebbles.

Eventually I rock back, folding my knees tightly against me. "Oh God," I groan. "Oh my God."

I'm going to be sick. I roll myself over until I am on my knees throwing up, hanging my head, my eyes unfocused, my head spinning.

"Someone needs to call 999." I am pretty sure it is Rachel who says this.

"I'll do it." This from Caitlyn, in no more than a whisper.

I can hear the beeps of a phone as the three digits are pressed. "There's been an accident," Caitlyn is saying, her voice cracking under the strain of each word. "Crayne's Cliff. Someone has fallen."

I wipe my mouth, close my eyes. Everything is still rocking and spinning, which makes me feel like I might be sick again. But it is good that they are doing this, I think. In contrast to how we handled things all those years ago. Someone has already called the police. There has been no discussion about it; it has not crossed their minds that we might walk away without saying anything. My friends are good people. It is a thought that hits me sharply, just how much I wasn't. Good.

"What happened?" Rachel says. "What actually happened?"

My heart gallops. It reminds me of the sound of Ethan's heart when he was in my tummy. "What do you think I'm having?" I had asked the midwife.

"Well, if I had to guess I'd say you were having a girl," she had replied. "Or a very excited boy!"

I find myself thinking of my placid, calm Ethan now, and wishing beyond anything that I was cuddled beside him in his bed, not out here on the cliff edge.

"What happened?" Rachel is saying again, her voice clipped with panic. It is Nancy who is oddly mute. "I mean, I didn't . . ."

Didn't what? Didn't see or didn't do it?

I want the answers too, but like Nancy, I don't utter a word.

I know this wasn't my fault, or at least not directly, because my arms had been ripped away from Grace. At the last minute maybe, but in time, and I had taken a step back, I wasn't touching Grace in the moments before she went. Only I don't know who had their hands on her and who didn't.

"Did she fall?" Rachel asks. "Did she just slip?"

Come on, Nancy, say something, please. Put all of us out of our misery. What happened?

"Because I wasn't . . ." Rachel must want to say she wasn't anywhere near Grace either, only as soon as she does so she is implying someone else was, and right now all four of us are trapped in this tragedy together. We must not fracture or turn on one another. Not yet.

"We need to go down there," Caitlyn says. She has finished the call. "The police will want to speak to us." How strange it is that Caitlyn is the one taking charge. It is so not the way I would have written it.

"What did you tell them?" Rachel asks her.

I feel a hand on my arm, pulling me up, so I obligingly stand because I need to do what they are asking of me. Be there for them as they are for me.

"I told them there was an accident," she says. "They haven't asked anything more yet."

"But they will," Rachel says. "And I don't even know what happened. Who does?" She is searching all of us for a clue, desperate. "One of us must know."

"Honestly, I don't," Caitlyn tells her. "I didn't see. I was too busy pulling Anna off her."

Caitlyn is right; I remember how she urgently spoke to me as she told me to get back from the cliff.

"So . . ." Rachel pauses and looks at Nancy, and I am standing now, facing her too.

But I don't want to know. I do not want to know who might or might not have pushed Grace, because the fact is it doesn't matter. We are all in this together, but worse than that, the only reason my friends are here is because of me. So whether Nancy pushed her too hard or not, ultimately it is my fault, and this is what I must tell the police.

"I didn't touch her," Nancy says. "I swear I didn't . . . I didn't touch her." She holds up her hands, her face is ghostly. Shards of moonlight catch her pale skin and make her look haunted. "She just . . . One minute she was there, the next she wasn't."

"So it was an accident?" Rachel asks, nodding. There are distant sounds of sirens. Whether or not they are getting closer it is hard to tell. "It must have been an accident. Because Anna wasn't near her and all of us are saying we weren't touching her, so she must have slipped. She should never have been that close to the edge in the first place," Rachel cries, as we begin stumbling back through the trees, towards the woods.

Now someone else is shouting my name. Ben is here and is coming our way.

"We've just got to be honest," Rachel says. "All of us. We just have to tell the police exactly what happened. It was no one's fault," she reiterates. "We just have to tell them the truth."

Wednesday, 1 January

As Marcus Hargreaves reaches his car, he pauses and looks back at the cliffs, wondering if anyone else at the station will be asking themselves the question that he is taunting himself with. *Could they have known something like this might happen?*

Three weeks ago Grace Goodwin had stood in the station and tried to report a crime, but the officers she spoke with had refused to believe she was right to be worried. And yet his first call this morning hadn't been to wish him a Happy New Year, but to tell him there was a dead body.

His head is filled with the sight of it. He knows he won't be able to get Grace's face out of his mind. It brings back too many memories of what he saw twenty-two years ago, and there is too much of a link between that and the events of last night.

The thought of talking to the husband and the child sits hard in his chest. The little girl is only eight and it's unbearable to think she will soon find out she has lost her mother.

It is not his case but he has offered to speak to them because he has gotten to know Grace Goodwin over the last couple of weeks, and he feels like he owes it to her to tell her family. They have talked to each other openly. They became friends of sorts as she listened to him and he shared with her the sordid details of his divorce and she with him the imminent demise of her marriage. Somehow that she was going through it makes her death seem sadder, he thinks, though he cannot begin to express why.

Maybe it is nothing more than the randomness of life. That it keeps spinning through its highs and lows until it suddenly stops at any one given point.

Once he has had the conversation with the family, Marcus will speak to his chief. He might not be in charge of finding out what happened to Grace, but he wants to look at a cold case. He is no longer sure that Heather Kerr was alone the night she died and he needs to speak to Anna Robinson.

29

Wednesday, 1 January

Anna

It is not the New Year any of us expected. Planned family lunches have been canceled. None of us has slept, though not because of the usual celebrations that would have had us drinking and dancing into the early hours of New Year's Day.

All eight adults are gathered around our kitchen table, Eric having joined us as soon as he was told the news. All our children are upstairs, thrilled at the prospect of watching a movie together so early in the day.

One by one the others start to say they need to go home and try to catch up on some sleep. Or what sleep we can get when our heads are still spinning with thoughts of Grace and the words we exchanged with the detectives at the scene. Words that we have gone over and over between us.

Soon it is just me at the table. Ben has gone upstairs to see Ethan, and the two of them are building a Lego fire station. I don't know how he can do it but I am glad for him, making a pretense of normality for our son, while I continue to replay what I told the DCI hours earlier—wondering whether or not I said the right thing.

"Grace was so close to the edge," I told him. "I remember someone trying to grab her back."

"Who was that?" he asked me.

"I think it was my friend, Nancy, but it was dark and all such a blur. None of us were near her when she fell."

"When you say you weren't near her, how far away were you?"

"Well, we were still close," I told him, "but we weren't touching her, she just . . ."

"Just what, Mrs. Robinson?"

"She just slipped. She just fell. I don't know, the ground must have given way. But suddenly she wasn't there."

The DCI nodded. He must have known there'd be a team checking shortly, if they weren't already up there. Forensics studying our footprints, the ground, how much our story stacked up. It had been too late for that to happen when it was Heather who had fallen off the edge of the cliff because no one had known she was gone for hours, and even then no one knew to be looking at the cliffs.

This is a very different story, and I have to keep reminding myself that whatever they might find, I didn't push Grace. As much as I might have wanted to at one point last night, I hadn't done it. I am not to blame. I have told the police the truth.

And yet I feel so guilty.

I hang my head as tears cascade down my cheeks. Is it because I got what I wished for? I wanted Grace out of my life, and now she is. But I didn't want her dead. My shoulders heave as I start to sob. I never wanted her dead.

The doorbell rings. For a moment I hesitate, but when I don't hear Ben's footsteps, I make my way to the front door. I can tell by the stance of the person standing on the other side of it—by the way they are holding themselves straight, stepped back from the door—that it is a formal visitor. As soon as I open the door I recognize Marcus Hargreaves.

"Mrs. Robinson?" he asks me. His eyes are searching my face, possibly for some sign of recognition.

I nod.

"I'm DS Hargreaves. I'm sorry to be bothering you this morning, so soon after what happened last night."

"It's fine." I open the door wider, expecting he wants to come in.

He steps inside. "I'm sorry about your friend. It must have been a horrible thing to witness."

"It was. It—" I don't finish because I don't know what to say.

"I'm not on the case," he adds as he follows me through to the kitchen. I offer him a coffee, which he declines.

"I'm not here because of Grace."

"Oh?" I gesture to one of the dining chairs and we both sit down.

"I don't know whether you remember me, but I was investigating the case of your friend, over twenty year ago, Heather Kerr?"

"I do remember you," I say.

"I don't think I'd have recognized you," he goes on. "I did Grace, eventually. I met her when she came to report you missing."

"That was a misunderstanding," I tell him. "I wasn't missing. I just needed some time . . ."

Hargreaves nods but he doesn't comment. "I've met up with Grace a few times recently."

"Yes. She told me." I hear the wobble in my voice. He must be able to hear it too. In the back of my mind I expected I would get a visit at some point after what Grace told me, but I didn't imagine it would be so soon.

"She talked to me a lot about things: what's been going on in her life lately; her divorce; moving back here; you."

I don't trust myself to speak and so I say nothing.

"She talked about your friendship when you were younger. It was interesting. It was a little . . . You were very close," he says, "by the sound of things?"

I do not like the anticipation of where he is going.

"She talked about Heather," Hargreaves tells me, biting the corner of his lip as he studies me. My hands are clenched together under the table, slippery with sweat. Upstairs a shriek of laughter comes from Ethan's room, and I think of him and Ben and how in just one moment everything can be shattered into tiny pieces.

"That's why I'm here," he is telling me, though his voice is beginning to blur into the haziness of the room. I am too hot all of a sudden, and desperate for a glass of water, but to get one I would need to move from the table and I am not sure my body could do that.

"I didn't . . ." My mouth is moving and words are coming out, but it feels as if I have no control over them. "I didn't do it."

But I wait for him to tell me that he believes I did. That from what Grace has told him he knows I was at the cliffs with Heather and I argued with her, and that for whatever reason I chose to keep this to myself and let the police search for a week. He will arrest me, charge me with murder or manslaughter perhaps, at the very least with obstructing an investigation.

A surge of nausea rises so quickly within me that if I wasn't so rigid with fear, I know I would be sick again.

But then he says, "No. I didn't think you did." He is looking at me questioningly.

I clamp my mouth shut.

"I just read between the lines, Anna. A lot of what Grace told me didn't make sense on the surface, but like I said, I met up with her a few times. I got the impression there was something she was trying to tell me in a roundabout way. She was ill; you know that, don't you?" He gently presses a finger against the side of his head. "And I think that something else was triggered in her in the last two weeks, which I'm thinking must be the divorce?"

Hargreaves pauses as if he is prompting me to add that there was something else, too, but right now I still cannot speak.

"I was hoping if she kept talking to me I'd eventually find out what happened. I think Grace was there the night that Heather died."

"She didn't say—" I break off quickly, my mind galloping to keep up with what he is saying.

"No. She didn't specifically say she was, but like I say, I definitely think it was where she was heading."

I attempt to swallow the lump lodged in my throat.

"I was worried about her, though. About her state of mind. I guess I was expecting something like this to happen. Deep down, you know?"

"Something like what?" I ask, my mouth painfully dry.

"Last night."

"How do you mean?"

"The way she was talking to me, she was so unhappy, so up and down. I blame myself for not stepping in more, that's what I'm thinking. I could I have stopped her . . ." He trails off, letting out a sigh as he looks away.

"You're saying you think she jumped?"

"Is it possible?" he asks.

"I . . . I don't know," I admit, as my mind flashes back to the night. "I mean, it's possible. It all happened so quickly; I thought she fell, but . . ."

Did she? I think. *Was it possible?*

"She loved you," he tells me. "I could see that much. I mean, she was a bit all over the place, but that came through as clear as day— what good friends you and she were—so I'm sorry." He leans across the table and reaches a hand towards me. "I'm sorry that you've lost such a good friend."

Epilogue

Two weeks later, we hold the funeral for Grace. Two weeks to the day, because they had to keep her body for a postmortem, investigate, and rule accidental death.

When the investigating officer called me with the news I burst into tears, possibly through sheer relief that there would be no more investigation, partly because I still felt so terribly guilty.

I look around at the crowd that is leaving the church. There were a surprising number of people in attendance, given that Grace knew so few of them. Some are parents from year four, and there are even a few women whom Grace and I went to school with so many years ago, who heard the news, as of course everyone has in Clearwater. A mix of faces from my past and present are there, and I turn my head and lean into Ben, who wraps an arm around me.

"I need to find Catherine," I say. "I don't know where she went."

"She's with Matilda." He nods across the path to where Grace's mum and daughter are sitting on a bench together.

"Oh God," I whisper, closing my eyes for a moment before opening them to look over at them. Tears start to spill at the sight of them together. In some ways I feel like I have learned more about Grace in the last two weeks than I ever knew in our two decades of friendship.

Conversations with Catherine, piecing together the reality of Grace's childhood, as we pored through pictures and remembered stories.

"All she wanted was attention and acceptance," I told Ben one evening. "She didn't get any from her dad, and she felt Catherine's focus was divided between her and me."

Catherine feels guilty for that, she has told me. "I should have reprimanded her for cutting up your dress," she said only last week on the phone. "I often look back and think I didn't give her the chance to know what was right or wrong. I just let her get away with things. She grew up with no boundaries. I let her down."

It was a funny thing, to feel sorry for Grace that she hadn't been punished for what she did, but it got me wondering if maybe Catherine was right. Grace was crying out for attention, but she was always being ignored.

"I should go over there," I say to Ben, but I don't move. His arm squeezes tighter around my shoulder.

Since New Year's Eve, Ben and I have spoken about everything that happened the night Heather died. He has listened to me dissect it over and over. While he will never be able to understand fully how I didn't do the right thing in telling the police, in giving them the leads they needed to possibly save her life, he has reached a level of acceptance that allows us to move forward.

"Maybe you just need to put it to rest now," he told me. "There is nothing you can do to change what happened. Twenty-two years have passed."

Yes, I will put it to rest for the sake of Ben and Ethan, and little Zadie, who we have just spent our first weekend with. I will put it to rest for them because I have to—but the memories will never leave me.

"Anna?"

I turn around to see Graham behind us. He looks handsome in his dark tailored suit, a thick black coat hanging open on top of it. But behind the clothing his eyes are empty, his face drawn and gaunt. I wonder how he has been looking after himself and Matilda over the last two weeks, whether Catherine's company has helped or made it harder for him.

"It was a lovely service, Graham." Ben holds out his hand for the man to shake.

"Thank you," he says, his brow furrowing as he glances at his daughter.

"You know we are always here if you need any help," Ben continues.

"I appreciate that," Graham says. "Actually Anna, do you mind if we . . . ?" He gestures to the path that leads towards the graveyard. I nod and release myself from Ben's grip, and we walk away out of earshot.

"How are you honestly doing?" I ask him.

Graham shrugs. "Oh, you know, holding up, beating myself up, wondering what I could have done differently . . . All those things," he says.

"I don't think you could have done anything differently," I tell him. "For what it's worth, I think you put more into your marriage than many would have done."

Graham raises his eyes as if there is a part of him that knows this, but it won't stop him from questioning himself anyway. "The detective, the one who says he knew Grace," Graham goes on, "Hargreaves?"

I nod. "Yes?"

"He said something odd to me the other day. He said he thought Grace seemed tormented the last time he saw her, on New Year's Eve."

I recall Marcus's words, how he wondered whether Grace might have jumped that night on the cliffs. "Graham, it was an accident," I say. "She slipped, she fell. It was nothing more than that."

Graham nods. "You honestly think that?"

"Yes," I say. "I honestly do."

The truth is, three things could have happened that night. She fell. She jumped. Or she was pushed. We will never know for certain, but after the detective left on New Year's Day, I thought about what he had suggested and realized I didn't believe for one minute Grace had jumped. That wasn't Grace. However complex she might have been, she was a fighter, and she was here to stay. "I'm never leaving Clearwater," she had told me that night.

I glance up at the swath of people making their way back towards their cars lining the long path out of the cemetery. She was right, I think. At least she got her way in the end.

She will never leave now.

Acknowledgments

Writing *The Whispers* in the middle of a pandemic has at times been challenging, given the addition of home schooling to my day, but at others a welcome break from the weird and scary news surrounding us.

I was lucky enough to be able to visit Portland in Dorset in the summer and this was thanks to Lorna Phipps. Before this trip I was struggling to find the fictional town of Clearwater's "place," but as soon as I stayed in Portland I was inspired to base Clearwater on this area.

As always there are many people who have helped me write this book, and not least the outstanding team who support me. My agent, Nelle Andrew, who continues to be a huge and important influence on my writing, and who I couldn't be without. And the team at RML: Alexandra Cliff, Rachel Mills, and Charlotte Bowerman.

My editor in the US, Jackie Cantor, who continues to be brilliantly insightful and is such a pleasure to work with. And everyone else in the Gallery team who work fantastically hard to get the books into stores and get the word out there, including: Jennifer Bergstrom, Aimee Bell, Jennifer Long, Eliza Hanson, Caroline Pallotta, Allison Green, Andrew Nguyen, Alexandre Su, Daniel Taverner, Michelle Marchese, Sally Marvin, Abby Zidle, Michelle Podberezniak, and Paul O'Halloran.

Acknowledgments

I am so excited for you to read this book. I have loved writing it. Readers and bloggers are integral to what I do and I am so grateful to all of you for choosing me, reviewing my books, recommending them, and writing to tell me what you think.

The Whispers is about friends—new and old, and it is the intricacies of these friendships that I have enjoyed exploring. I am lucky to have the best friends in my life, some who have been in it for as long as I can remember, others who I have met more recently. Thank you all for your love and support.

And of course, as always, to my family. My mum, who I am incredibly lucky to have around the corner, which has meant I have been able to see her throughout the year, even if it has been through a window!

My husband, John, thank you for your continued support and encouragement and all the laughs. Lockdown brought your job home and we are all so lucky to have you here.

Finally, my amazing children, Bethany and Joseph, who are my world. I am loving watching you grow into the wonderful people you are. Thank you for being so special and for allowing me the time to write around being your mum. Reach for the stars—you can do anything you put your minds to.